"You're in danger, Haley. Real ___ ___er. You could have d___ ___ Knowing tha___ ___ distraction I ___ ___ y job." He didn___ ___ ___it any clearer to her___

"I'll be in danger wherever I go. And I'm helping here. You have no idea, when you find the baby, what you're going to be facing. You might need me to care for him or her while you take care of the kidnapper. Or you might need my official position as Kelsey's executor and beneficiary, or as a blood relative, to legally get the baby out of danger."

All of which was true, but... "You can be on a flight back to Vegas to handle legalities within an hour," he told her.

Taking another step closer, she said, "I'm not going."

Paul didn't back up. Or back down. "If you don't, I quit."

"You won't quit, but if you don't agree to let me help, you're fired."

He didn't need her money. Didn't even want it.

"I can look for whoever I want," Paul said. "I don't need your permission."

Dear Reader,

Family's a tricky topic. My family is everything to me. I have a couple of close friends who have become family. And yet...family is hard, too. You have to take them, good or bad. Sometimes, you love them good or bad, whether you want to or not. And sometimes they're good, lovable people who just happen to drive you up the wall.

Then you get married and you've got two families! Now that's tricky. And, in my opinion, still the course to finding the greatest joy. I did some personal soul-searching as I wrote this book. As I looked at what family takes from us and what it gives to us, too. In the dark night, I wondered if it was all worth it. I stayed on the page. I lived with Haley and Paul, hurt with them and through them reaffirmed what I already knew. Family is everything to me. Biological and otherwise. I love to travel, to shop, to see new things, to spend nights in fancy hotels. But it's the people in my tribe who bring me the greatest joy in my life. I hope Paul and Haley help you find a piece of joy, too!

Tara Taylor

THE BOUNTY HUNTER'S BABY SEARCH

Tara Taylor Quinn

HARLEQUIN®
ROMANTIC SUSPENSE™

Recycling programs
for this product may
not exist in your area.

ISBN-13: 978-1-335-73836-3

The Bounty Hunter's Baby Search

Copyright © 2023 by TTQ Books LLC

For questions and comments about the quality of this book,
please contact us at CustomerService@Harlequin.com.

Harlequin Enterprises ULC
22 Adelaide St. West, 41st Floor
Toronto, Ontario M5H 4E3, Canada
www.Harlequin.com

Printed in U.S.A.

A *USA TODAY* bestselling author of over one hundred and five novels in twenty languages, **Tara Taylor Quinn** has sold more than seven million copies. Known for her intense emotional fiction, Ms. Quinn's novels have received critical acclaim in the UK and most recently from Harvard. She is the recipient of the Reader's Choice Award and has appeared often on local and national TV, including *CBS Sunday Morning*.

For TTQ offers, news and contests, visit www.tarataylorquinn.com!

Books by Tara Taylor Quinn

Harlequin Romantic Suspense

Sierra's Web

Tracking His Secret Child
The Bounty Hunter's Baby Search

The Coltons of Colorado

Colton Countdown

Where Secrets are Safe

Her Detective's Secret Intent
Shielded in the Shadows
Falling for His Suspect

The Coltons of New York

Protecting Colton's Baby

Visit the Author Profile page at Harlequin.com for more titles.

To Agnes Mary Penny Keller Gumser. My mom. You are so many things to so many people, but I'm the only woman in the world who got lucky enough to be your daughter. You gave so much of yourself to me by word, but mostly by example, and I hope my life brings you joy.

Chapter 1

Kelsey had a baby and it's in wrong hands. The typed, unsigned note shook in Haley Carmichael's trembling fingers as she quickly looked both ways, up and down her quiet neighborhood. Who'd left the note stuck to her front door? Glancing at the sheet of plain white paper, its edges ragged from being torn out of a notebook, she was momentarily blinded by the stab of pain brought on by her deceased sister's name. Haley quickly turned around and closed the door safely behind her.

And then, standing alone in the entryway, heart pounding, she read again. *Kelsey had a baby and it's in wrong hands.* She'd had it right the first time.

Kelsey had a *baby*?

Haley leaned back against the wall, sliding down to sit on the cool tile floor, shaky knees pulled up to her chest. She hadn't seen Kels in months, but they'd talked on the phone regularly. Her sweet, gorgeous, somewhat misguided, bit of a gold-digger sister had said she'd finally found the man of her dreams. Not only was he rich, but he was also smart and sensitive, he liked to watch old movies with her, to take long walks, to have romantic dinners by candlelight and to talk about current affairs, too. Mostly, he liked *her*. When she got upset, making a bigger deal out of most anything—as she had a definite tendency to do—the man was patient with her. Tender.

And he'd gotten Kelsey pregnant?

Because Kelsey hadn't wanted to jinx anything, she'd said she wasn't telling anyone who the guy was until she had a wedding ring next to the two-carat diamond he'd already placed on her finger.

But Kelsey would have told Haley if she'd known she was pregnant—

Right?

With a confirming nod, accompanied by a resurgence of the resilient strength gained from growing up with her sensitive sister and mother—drama queens, she'd unfortunately called the two of them at one point in her life—Haley stood up.

Glancing at the bizarre note again, she dropped it on the floor. She shouldn't be touching it. What if she'd messed up the fingerprints of whomever had left it on her door?

No way did Kelsey have a baby.

But why would someone leave such a note on the door of the older sister of a deceased woman?

Haley, who had the same naturally wavy blond hair, dark brown eyes and soft features of her mother and sister, had to put forth some effort to get anyone to notice her. Because, thankfully, she didn't overflow with effervescence as the other two Carmichael women did. Or *had done*—past tense—in Kelsey's case.

Haley didn't *exude*, her little sister had once told her. Jet-setting Kelsey had then followed the statement with her usual clueless generosity, gently and sweetly sharing easy tips to correct the lapse. Tips Haley had immediately relegated to her "never in your life" memory bank.

Kelsey, who hadn't had a mean bone in her body, had meant well. Her priorities—number one, always, to find a rich man to take care of her—were just vastly different from Haley's. She'd come by them naturally, though. Gloria Carmichael, their mother, had preached them as gospel all the days of their growing up.

And standing in her foyer frittering was just like something her mother and sister would have done.

Note in hand, still by her front door, heart still pounding, she pulled her phone out of the bag she'd dropped to the floor and hit Speed Dial for her mother.

Gloria had flown home for Kelsey's funeral, a small service with no casket due to the condition of Kelsey's remains after the fiery crash that had killed her, but had immediately returned to the home of a wealthy female friend of hers in Florida where Gloria was recovering from her most recent relationship break up.

AKA, looking for her next rich catch.

If Gloria could just find someone wealthy who didn't mind coming second to her love of money, she'd be a kind, respectful and faithful wife to him.

Unable, or unwilling, to deal with her mother's acute reactions to emotional situations, Haley stopped short of telling Gloria about the note, but she did establish that her mother had absolutely not spoken to Kelsey for a few months before her younger daughter's death.

For the first time in her life Kelsey had refused to let her mother come visit her and meet her fiancé. That unheard-of choice had created a rift between them that hadn't yet been repaired.

A rift that would never be fixed now. That fact had become the focal point of Kelsey's funeral and the gathering that had followed as Gloria had tearfully regaled every single attendee with the details of her severely broken heart.

The emotions were real. Haley didn't doubt for a second that Gloria was devastated by her youngest daughter's death. Or that the pain was more acute due to the rift.

And the drama…was hard to take.

And that was why Haley called the police without telling Gloria about the note. Or even letting on that she was stressed. She had to give all of her focus to the immediate situation, not be distracted from a possible endangered baby by her mother's reaction to it.

A day later, Gloria Carmichael was completely relegated to the back of Haley's mind.

"Now are you going to call him?" The question came from Jeanine Harbor, Haley's next-door neighbor and best friend from college days. Still in her nurse's uniform, Jeanine had stopped at Haley's when she'd turned onto their street to find a police car in Haley's drive— for the second day in a row.

Jeanine had arrived just as Detective Morrow had been telling Haley that there was no record of Kelsey Carmichael giving birth. Not in California, nor in Nevada, where she'd died in the car accident. Haley had been grateful for her friend's presence at her side as Morrow had also told her that they hadn't been able to lift any prints from the note that had been left on Haley's door the day before.

His last bad news was that the department's request to neighbors for surveillance video hadn't turned up anything unusual in the area, or any video of Haley's front yard, driveway or house.

"You need to call him, Haley." Jeanine's teddy bear emblazoned scrubs didn't soften the blow her words sent through Haley. In her own mauve scrubs, standing in the foyer alone with her friend, Haley still didn't respond to Jeanine.

Haley had been planning to run some errands on her way to work when the detective had called and asked to stop by. She'd really just wanted to make a quick trip to the drug store for new razor refills and head to her job as charge nurse of the emergency department. She was scheduled from three in the afternoon until three in the morning for the next two nights. And with it being a Friday in the beginning of June, beginning of summer break for kids when they were outside and active, they'd likely be busy.

Jeanine, who worked in the cardiac unit, had just come off two back-to-back twelves and needed to be home showering and heading to bed. Not standing just inside Haley's front door worrying about a random, untraceable note.

But it wasn't the note that was bothering either one of them.

It was the idea that a baby could really exist and possibly be in danger.

Someone had reached out to Haley for a reason.

The police had asked about any possible disgruntled patients from the hospital. Someone who might blame Haley for a painful diagnosis, or a lost life, but in her job, she didn't get to the point of diagnoses. And she hadn't lost a patient during her shift in months. Morrow found it more likely that someone from Kelsey's past, from the family's past, was pulling a cruel prank on her.

"I can't believe I'm pressing this," Jeanine spoke again. "Paul Wright is absolutely the last person I'd ever thought I'd suggest you seek out, but as much of an ass as the man is with relationships, he's the best people finder there is, and he'll get to the bottom of this."

Haley nodded, feeling the seriousness of the situation escalating with her friend's suggestion. Since Haley's horribly painful marriage and divorce from Paul, Jeanine had been playing watchdog to make certain that Paul—compelling and mesmerizing to her as he was—never got another chance at Haley.

While Jeanine's efforts had been sweet, Haley had known from the moment the marriage ended that Paul would never be bothering her again. He'd been as eager to put distance between them as she had.

Still, to hear Jeanine reiterating aloud, multiple times, what Haley had been thinking to herself—that she had to call Paul—severely increased the lump of dread filling her midsection. She could physically feel the muscles in her chest cavity tightening.

Could the whole thing be a prank?

More of the drama the Carmichael women were known for? Just one more reason for Paul to look at her with distaste? Already the tumult of intense emotions flowed through her.

With the life of her deceased little sister's possible baby in the balance, could she risk not reaching out?

"I have to call him," she said aloud, a shard of physical pain striking through her. She'd promised herself the day she'd signed the divorce papers that she never had to open that door again.

But she was older. Wiser. The eight years they'd been apart had been good to her, building within her a sense of her own identity, a confidence and strength that she was proud of. She could handle his disdain without a blink.

So why, most particularly in the midst of dealing with the alarm she felt over the note, did her friend's compassionate nod feel like a nail in her emotional coffin?

The photo wasn't even grainy. Not in the least bit. No, the dark-haired beauty was shown in such clear detail he could see the two small freckles just to the left of those soft, kissable lips. His memory filled in the woman's mouth, covered by the surfer dude's lips in the photo.

Paul's memory had no way to fill in the guy's fingers that were missing down the back of his ex-girlfriend's bikini bottoms. His brain was too busy focusing on the photo's time stamp. The previous September. Months before he and Sarah had split up.

He'd known she was cheating on him. Could have easily produced the proof himself. Blindfolded and asleep.

Instead, he'd waited until after they'd broken up and then had given the assignment to a junior skip tracer trying to break into the business. When you were looking for someone, or something, who didn't intend to be found, you had to be able to come up with inventive ways to find things. To think outside the box.

Or, in Sarah's case, just ask Surfer Dude for a glance at the SD cards from the surveillance camera of the guy's private beach.

Paul had known. Hadn't wanted the confirmation.

And then, weeks after she'd moved out, he had sent a PI after the information. Fitting that the email had arrived from the guy he'd hired in time for Friday night's solitary dinner.

Go figure. The woman hadn't loved him. Sarah had loved the mystery of his profession. She'd loved that he could work magic and seemingly produce things that no one else could. She'd loved the elegance of his beach house, the housekeeper who kept it running smoothly and the Jaguar he drove.

He didn't kid himself about that.

Just as he was honest with himself, and had been with her, about the fact that he hadn't loved her, either.

Not like he'd wanted to or had hoped he would.

For only the second time in his life, he'd been ready for a life partner. Unlike the first time, when the woman had blindsided him, the choice to get monogamously serious with Sarah had been driven by where he was in his life, rather than feelings for the woman in question.

There was no reason for him to glance at any of the other photos. He moved the first to the bottom of the stack in his hand, eyed the second. Another outfit. Different day. He knew that based on the cloud formation even before checking out the time stamp. December.

Christmastime. A black-tie affair on the beach, apparently. One attended only by the surfer dude and Sarah...

The ringing of his phone had him reaching in his pocket, but wasn't enough to distract him from the photo.

The brief glance at the phone's caller ID screen changed that circumstance in a heartbeat.

Haley Carmichael was calling him?

The irony of a call coming in from his ex-wife during the exact moments he was coming face-to-face with his most recent ex's infidelity might have amused him in other circumstances.

Irony could come with some humor. A call from Haley would not. Of that he was certain.

He answered on the second ring. "Paul Wright." As though he didn't know the woman he'd once believed to be the love of his life was on the line.

He needed the distance the formality put between them. And really, she was a stranger. They didn't know each other at all anymore.

"It's Haley."

Probably too late to acknowledge that he knew that. The only reason she was in his contacts was because he'd needed to know that he'd never be caught unaware answering a call that could be her.

There'd always been that possibility.

He'd told himself it would never happen.

Had felt better being prepared just in case.

And he'd still answered.

That hadn't been in the plan.

Which was why he sat there saying nothing. Focused on remaining calm. He was over her.

She would not bring her maelstrom back into his world.

He'd rather live without love than get sucked into that tornado a second time.

"I'm sorry to bother you, Paul." Her voice sounded thick. Like her mouth was dry. Or she'd been crying.

He still said nothing.

"I've been to the police. They've done what they can, but it didn't help..."

The police?

She was in trouble?

He sat up straighter.

"Jeanine agreed that I should call you."

The comment might have come off as manipulative, except that he knew how much Jeanine Harbor had grown to hate him. Haley had to be in real trouble if Jeanine had told her to call.

Haley's troubles weren't his problem anymore.

"You still there?"

Sort of. But he didn't want to be.

And heard the beep signaling the dropped call before he'd had the chance to hang up.

Chapter 2

Ten minutes into agitated pacing, ten minutes after she'd hung up on her ex-husband's silence, Haley jerked as her phone rang. Almost dropped the thing she still held in her hand.

She should have gone in to work instead of calling off.

Yeah, she had so much paid time off accumulated that the powers that be had been after her for some time to use a bit of it, but work was what cured her.

Always.

Caring for others, particularly for children who didn't feel well, made her her best self.

Thinking maybe her friend had woken up and was checking on her, she lifted the phone. And almost dropped it again when she saw the number.

Her most recently called.

"Hello?" There might have been a bit of petulance

in her tone. She couldn't tell. Didn't much care. He'd been rude.

She didn't blame him.

And she had bigger fish to fry.

"I apologize."

He didn't say what for. She didn't ask. "Accepted."

"Why did you need to speak with me?"

It had been eight years since they'd spoken. And not even a *how are you*?

"I need your professional help."

"I assumed as much. Tell me what's going on."

I assumed as much. After he'd had a few minutes to recover from the shock and had actually put his brain in gear.

Again, she wasn't going to blame him. He was who he was, and didn't often venture into emotional territory. Rather, he avoided it at a lot of cost. It had always been like that with them, and a major reason why they hadn't worked as a couple.

"My sister, Kelsey, died." As though she had more than one. There'd only been the one. And she doubted Paul would ever forget her name.

Or the fact that Haley's dedication to her dramatic sister had been a terminal sore spot between them.

He'd be sitting there thinking that nothing had changed.

Didn't matter what he thought.

As long as he helped her.

"Did you say Kelsey's dead?" His tone had softened, so much so that she had to strain to hear him.

"Yes." She couldn't dwell on that part. Not at the moment. The arrangements had been made, the funeral was over, she was back to work and the rest of the grief process would happen whether she was ready for it or not.

"When?"

"A few weeks ago."

A few weeks was an unbearably long time in the life of a misplaced newborn. Who knew if the child, if it existed, would even still be alive?

But would someone have left a note just the day before if it wasn't?

"I'm so sorry, Haley. Seriously. I was an ass, as usual, and…" His tone. It went straight for the heart of her. *Paul.*

"No. It's okay. You had no idea. And that's not why I called." She paused and then ran on with, "Well, it is, in part, but her death isn't what this is about."

She didn't want his sympathy. Couldn't allow any emotions between them. It had to be strictly business. And so she rushed on, telling him about the note on her door, what it said and what the police had said, ending with, "I want to hire you, Paul. I need you to do what you do and find that baby."

"If there is one."

"Right. And if not, then hopefully you'll find who left the note and why…" He was an elite brand of bounty hunter, investigator and money collector all rolled into one. A skip tracer. Someone who specialized in finding the impossible to find. "Are you executor and beneficiary of her estate? Do you have the means to fax me permission to access her credit report and bank and credit card statements?"

The sound of his voice spread through her with a familiarity she hadn't expected. "Yes."

He was good. So good he'd been hired by a nation-

ally renowned firm of experts. And she was shaking at
the knees. "I was planning to call Sierra's Web to hire
you, but thought I should give you a heads-up first, before you see the job order come through." She needed
to get things back under control. Her control.

"You don't need to hire me. Of course, I'll help."

Sirens went off inside her.

"No, really, I do need to make this official. Either
we go through Sierra's Web, or..."

What?

She'd let the baby remain in the wrong hands?

If there were any.

Not even knowing how those hands were wrong.
Were they abusive? Or just not the right ones?

The line hung with silence. He didn't ask her, "Or
what?" and she didn't back down.

"You're right, and, again, I apologize. But you don't
need to call the firm," he told her. "I'll report the job
and make it official."

The air, and every ounce of strength she'd mustered
to deal with him, left her body. Sinking down to her
couch, Haley stared at the tightly woven wool throw
covering the tile under her coffee table. "Thank you."

She'd known he'd come through for her.

Now every part of her body ached—though some
of that could be due to the sleepless night she'd spent,
worrying about her possible niece or nephew, crying
for Kelsey and...needing Paul.

Only to help her find answers.

She promised herself she would only need his professional skills. The rest...dealing with whatever she
found...that would be solely on her.

Separate and apart from him.

There would be no drama entering his life through her.

She was going through his firm of experts to hire his services and it would all be just business.

Paul put in a call to his buddy Hudson Warner, one of the six Sierra's Web founding partners. He let Hudson know that he had a new job—even if he didn't mention that their new client was his ex-wife—and then went to work.

If all went well, he could be unemployed again by morning, and able to take the yacht out for some fishing and R & R. He'd been planning the time off since April, had already put if off twice, thought maybe he'd head down to Catalina where he knew some people and actually had a bag packed this time. A rich guy like him never had to work hard to find people to relax with him.

He'd only ever found one person who'd fight with him.

And as much as he'd loved Haley, he'd hated the fighting. The emotional vulnerability.

The rest...never knowing if someone was with him because of him, or because he came with inherited family money...he'd come to terms with all that. Accepted it as the shadow side of a good life.

And he had a good life.

Not following in his father's globe-trotting playboy lifestyle, but actually using his mind, his talent, to contribute to society. While enjoying the peace provided by comfortable living.

He didn't need Haley coming back into the picture and messing him up again.

Which logically led to the conclusion that he had to get rid of her as quickly as possible. By using his mind, his talents, to find out what in the hell Kelsey had gotten herself into for one last time.

Hands suspended over the keyboard at the mammoth cherry desk in office, he felt a pang. Wasn't sure what it was at first, but was suddenly consumed by a long-ago memory. One he hadn't accessed in…ever.

His wedding reception. While Haley had been cutting in so her mother and his father, who'd just met, didn't make fools of themselves drooling all over each other on the dance floor, Kelsey had wrapped her arms loosely around his middle and pulled him into motion before he had a chance to say no. Their little swaying to music hadn't lasted but a few seconds. Just long enough for Kelsey to lean in and tell him that he better never hurt her big sister because Haley was different and truly special. For the only time in the four years he'd known her, Kelsey's tone had been deadly serious.

And then she'd actually pushed him away, flitting off to try to snag any one of the rich friends he'd invited to the party.

Just as her mother had snagged his father…

And as Haley had lassoed him? At least, a little bit? Subconsciously? He couldn't blame her for gravitating toward money, having grown up as she had, moving in and out of fancy mansions as her mother moved in and out of relationships and marriages when limits were put on the spending or finances took a nosedive. Kelsey and Haley had learned in the cradle that the way to provide security and a good life was to snag a rich partner…

An hour after he'd opened his search, Paul's mood, his momentum and his plans for a cruise took a major downward turn. He'd unearthed over a hundred pages of Kelsey information during that time—down to the exclusive lingerie shop she purchased from frequently—all dating prior to a year before her death. And in that last year…nothing. The kind of nothing that took a lot of money, greased hands and powerful people to produce.

The kind that always, always, always spelled trouble.

And greatly increased the possibility that there could be a baby in wrong hands. Or, at the very least, that someone was luring Haley into danger.

He skimmed through the pages a second time, his gut hard as a rock inside, instinct pushing him to act sooner rather than later.

And the way to do that was to get someone who knew Kelsey, who'd been in contact with her, to look over what he had and see if anything jumped out as more meaningful than something else. If anything was different than Kelsey's norm he'd have a more immediate starting place.

Even just a restaurant visit to a place known for food she didn't like.

He could find the information himself. Eventually.

A possible baby in danger didn't give him eventually to work with.

He needed Haley.

In his office.

As soon as possible.

The drive from Santa Barbara to Mission Viejo was an exercise in self-discipline. Controlling her thoughts had been a habit ingrained from the time she was old enough to understand that her mother's reasoning didn't always make sense. She'd been four at the time. And noticing that her mother's take on the breakup of her marriage to newborn Kelsey's father—her retelling of circumstances—wasn't actually as it'd happened. Dale hadn't slapped her. He'd swung his hand in a slapping motion in front of his own nose. As though swatting her away.

She had no memory of the rest of what went on there. Just remembered so clearly that slap versus hand swat. It hadn't been easy for a little girl being uprooted from the home she loved to also realize that her mother wasn't completely right.

And it wasn't easy driving herself into the tragedy of her own past, either.

So she focused on the conversation she'd had with the Emergency Department director, saying only that, with her sister's death, she needed some time off. Kathy couldn't have been nicer. Or more supportive.

That kindness was welcome. And brought with it a wave of calm that got her half a mile farther along the three-hour drive on the busy Friday night California freeway.

She moved from there to another reassessment of the bag she'd packed. Paul had said something about perhaps traveling to Vegas yet that night or early in the morning, which told her that he was already onto something. And she was going to go with him. She'd made up her mind about that.

Vegas. A place they'd been together once before— to celebrate their first anniversary. They'd both found the place too frenetic and ended up driving across the desert to a secluded beach Paul had known about. He'd had someone meet them there with his yacht. A friend who'd then driven their car back to Santa Barbara while she and Paul had spent an idyllic three days all alone in the world...

No.

She whipped her thoughts back to the bag she'd packed. Had she remembered deodorant? Her makeup bag was easy. She'd pulled it out of the drawer in her bathroom and thrown it in.

Maybe he'd found where Kelsey had been living. Maybe she'd be able to bring home her sister's things.

Kelsey's wardrobe choices had been very different from hers. The clothes Haley had just packed could attest to that. Shorts, shirts and underwear, with a pair of jeans just in case. Kelsey would have sun dresses, heeled sandals, a black low cut cocktail dress, and never, ever jeans.

Haley had thrown in three days' worth of changes. Paul had only asked her to look over the report he'd put together, to see if anything jumped out at her, but if he had an actual lead she was going to fight tooth and nail to go with him.

She'd packed her toothbrush. Oh. Had she remembered toothpaste? She was pretty sure she had. She could always pick some up if necessary.

And…

In less than an hour, she'd be seeing Paul for the first time since their divorce.

It had been eight years. Four times as long as their two-year union.

When it came to marriage, she'd apparently been far more like her mother and sister than she'd ever known. Two years was also the exact length of Gloria's relationship with Haley's father—who'd paid child support but had publicly claimed she wasn't his daughter—and also the amount of time Gloria's marriage to Dale, Kelsey's father, had lasted.

Yeah, so, she wasn't marrying again. That's how Haley took care of that similarity. While she adored her mother and sister, she was not going to be like them. Multiple men, relationships…and for Gloria, multiple marriages, too.

Not that she was all that eager to take after her irresponsible, philandering father, either. The man had fooled around with Gloria and then denied his own flesh and blood in order to keep his marriage—and his comfortable lifestyle—intact. The money had largely been his wife's.

Yet…he was still married to the same woman.

That said something.

She wasn't sure what…but it was something.

All the years of her growing up she'd promised herself that she'd only marry once. That the marriage would last until death did them part.

She'd been so certain of herself, that she'd have risked her life on the longevity of the vows she and Paul had taken.

But even so, she'd begun doubting them the night of their wedding when she'd overheard his groomsmen, his loyal-to-the-death entourage, giving them six months max. And less than that before Paul started fooling around on the side. More than just that overheard conversation had fed the doubts. Her mother and Kelsey, while encouraging the wedding in full force, had also warned her, several times, about getting so deeply committed emotionally to the man. They'd worried about her being heartbroken. Had constantly tried to school her on holding back a part of herself so she'd have something left if the marriage ended. Had called her out on instances where she was getting too far in with Paul.

Added to that was his self-confessed penchant for relationships that went nowhere—for both participants. He'd been shocked, he'd said, at the depth of his need to be with Haley, and so had asked her to marry him. And she, idiot that she was, had fallen hard for his confession.

Fallen for the idea that someone could want her around so badly, the need had completely changed him. She'd changed him...

Long Beach. She'd made it four exits without thinking about Paul and there she was again, getting sucked back in by the garbage stored in her brain...

Distracted by the ringing coming in over the car's audio system, she was relieved to see Jeanine's name show up on the in-dash touch screen.

She pushed the button on her steering wheel to connect the call as though jabbing for a lifeline.

"Hey, what's up?" If she pretended that she was fine, would it become so?

"Oh, my God, Haley...there was just someone at your house!" Jeanine's normally placid tone was now anything but. Which had Haley quickly taking the exit so she could stop the car.

"Are you okay?" Heart pounding, she asked the question first on her mind.

"Yeah. I'm fine. I was actually just heading out for some ice cream when I saw him sitting there, all hunched half hidden in the bushes at the side of your front step..."

Jeanine didn't sound fine. Her friend was clearly agitated. Which fed the panic Haley was trying to hold at bay. "Him?"

"Yeah, he was wearing a dark gray hoodie, so I couldn't really tell, but when he saw me he jumped up and ran around the side of the house and I followed him…"

"Oh, God, J, really? You chased a stranger in the dark?" Her voice, filled with fear-driven condemnation, rose several decibels. "You could have been killed!"

In spite of all of her efforts, life was spiraling out of control and she didn't know how to stop it. "Stop watching my house. Right now," she said, feeling helpless. Weak.

Ineffective.

And scared out of her wits.

"I'm fine, Haley."

"Are you inside now? With the doors locked?"

"Yes, of course. And I called the police. Morrow was here in less than two minutes, but he was asking as much about you as anything. His angle is clearly that someone's pranking you. No one's been hurt, and there's been no crime. It's not illegal to visit someone's home, or wait to see them, unless there's notice not to do so…"

Obviously, something Morrow had said.

Closing her eyes, Haley shut out the gas station parking lot where she'd stopped, the bright lights and people coming and going. She had to think.

To take back control of the situation before…

What?

Before a baby was hurt?

It could already be hurt.

Or before she made a fool of herself, chasing a nonexistent child? Someone could very well be pranking her. Because of Kelsey.

It wouldn't be the first time, or even the tenth, that she'd been disrespected because of her relationship to her family. Guilty by association and all. Her mother and Kelsey's lives always had seemed to be careening out of control. Even in good times.

"Did you get a look at the guy?" she asked, her head buried in the hand at her forehead, eyes still shut tight. Focus came from inside.

She knew how to do this. How to deal with the off-shoots of loving her mom and little sister.

"Somewhat," Jeanine said, sounding no less worried at all. "I described him to Morrow, but he didn't take any of it down."

Hearing the tension in Jeanine's voice, she suddenly heard herself, as a teenager, asking for help and being blown off because of a person's familiarity with her family history. High school principal. Guidance Counselor. Neighbors. Friends. You could fool people for a while, but eventually folks started to catch on to the fact that if you dealt with one of the beautiful Carmichael women, drama would follow. And facts would be skewed to make them appear as victims. Everyone knew about them. And while she'd been different, her reasonableness had been so overshadowed, so…quiet… no one seemed to hear her above the constant noise from her mother and sister.

So why had she stayed in one of the towns where she'd grown up?

"I'm sorry," she said now, knowing exactly how Jeanine felt, how powerless and foolish you could be made to feel when you were trying to get someone to take you seriously and they couldn't even seem to hear what you were saying.

"Sorry for what?" Jeanine asked, her tone more normal. Matter-of-fact. "Morrow's an ass. It's you I'm concerned about, Hale. This guy, he was youngish, maybe

Kelsey's age. And kind of elfin looking. It was dark and with the hoodie I didn't get a look at his face, but he stopped long enough to give me a message for you," Jeanine's words started to run into each other again in their haste to get out. "I didn't tell Morrow that part, Haley. I probably should have, but I wanted to talk to you, first, because it…the message wasn't criminal in nature. The kid's scared and risking his life to help you is how I took it."

And yet Jeanine had called the police. As she should have done.

Haley's heart sank to a place where dread could pour in.

"What did he say?"

"He said to tell you that, I quote, 'I might have led them here.' He's afraid that, because of him, you might be in danger."

"Led who there?"

"I have no clue, and I know I should have told Morrow. I just thought that decision was yours, as the message was for you. And…he said one more thing, Haley. He said to tell you that he loved Kelsey."

Oh, God.

Whether there was a baby or not, something was wrong. Enough so that a young man was running scared to the one person Kelsey had always run to for help. The one person Kelsey had counted on to get her out of the messes she inadvertently landed in.

And then something else horrible occurred to her.

Maybe her mind was getting caught up in the drama. Maybe she was wrong.

But what if…

What if Kelsey's death hadn't been an accident?

The ropes were tightening around her. She could feel them closing in and couldn't do a thing to slow their restriction.

So, she put her car in gear and sped toward the one person she knew who could help. The man who brought out the absolute worst in her. The only person who'd ever imploded her life.

Her ex-husband, Paul Wright.

Chapter 3

By the time he saw Haley's headlights turn in down at the gate to his property, Paul had stopped pretending to work, and was standing at the window of his casita, watching for her.

It wasn't his job to keep her safe. Or his place to worry about her. No, her text message, letting him know that Jeanine had had a run-in with a guy at her house, had spurred the energy-driven activity he'd been engaged in, waiting for her. It would have been that way with any case.

At least he'd keep telling himself that.

The hooded visitor on her stoop just validated what he'd already suspected. Kelsey had somehow, once again, brought trouble literally to Haley's doorstep, snagging Haley by the love Haley felt for her.

And while Paul's job was not about keeping Haley

safe, he was charging himself with finding the danger that seemed to be seeking her out. Didn't mean there were any vestiges left of the love he'd once felt for her.

It only meant he was a decent guy.

One who had something to find and didn't have time to waste spinning his wheels in the wrong directions. He needed Haley's input. Or to know that she didn't have any. If all of Kelsey's activities seemed completely normal to her older sister, including Kelsey's disappearance over the past year, then that would be a start in itself.

If Kelsey had a habit of disappearing, there'd be some pattern. Something that drove the absences…

The headlights were almost upon him. Haley hadn't wasted any time getting up his long drive. Nor had she slowed as she'd driven right past the front door of his house, using the circular drive out front to continue on to the casita just as he'd directed when'd he'd called earlier requesting her presence.

A call that had taken all of sixty seconds. He'd stated his point. She'd agreed, accepted directions and had disconnected.

Could they really get through this…seeing each other again…working together…without the past biting them in the ass?

He'd like it if they could.

And was pissed as hell as his penis sprang into life the second she slid one long leg out the driver's door of her newish model middle-of-the-line four-door sedan.

Had to be muscle memory. Habit. His subconscious playing with him because he'd known he was going to be seeing her and had refused to think about Haley personally, or dwell on their past.

Let loose, a thought presented immediately. His ex-wife was one gorgeous woman. Without even trying. That long blond hair—the natural body and curls… didn't matter that she kept it all swept back tightly in a ponytail, or in some kind of twist bun thing at that moment…he knew how those silky strands came to life when she let them free…

Just as he knew, in intimate detail, how those long legs felt wrapped around a man's neck…

He was at the door before she got there. Pulled it open while she was still walking up. Noted the way the black shorts hugged her pelvis, jerked his gaze upward, and smacked it into the mouthwatering breasts loosely outlined by the white shirt she was wearing.

Really? It wasn't like she was the only beautiful woman in the world.

After eight years he was still that attracted to her?

With his body's confirmation trying to take control of his brain, he stood his ground. Took in the area around them, illuminated by the security lights he kept on at all times, making certain that no one had followed her. That there were no unfamiliar shadows lurking on the edges of the estate.

By the time she'd approached, his penis was shrinking again. The distraction had worked.

Good to know. He could face reality. Deal with the feelings logically, rather than being held hostage by them.

"Haley." The crack in his voice was because his throat was dry. He stood back, gave her plenty of room to enter the large main room of the casita. And grabbed a bottle of water out of the refrigerator on the wall behind the door as she took in the place. The oversize leather couches set perpendicular to each other around the large wool rug in fall colors, put there to soften the porcelain tile floor. The entertainment center with large screen TV, but no home theater system. The small table with a couple of chairs to the back of the small kitchenette.

He liked it. Wanted her to like it, too.

The old Haley would have loved it. And she'd never have agreed to live in the mansion he'd bought a couple of years after their divorce. Part of the reason he'd bought it. It occurred to him, too late, that he should have had the meeting there.

Meeting.

"Here's the file," he said, moving quickly to his desk to retrieve the report he'd amassed on Kelsey in the short time he'd had. "I need you to look through it. Tell me anything you see that surprises you. And similarly, if there's nothing that seems amiss, I need to know that, too."

She turned from her position facing the kitchen and the short hall beyond that led to a full bath and small-ish bedroom. Studied his face for a few intense seconds before meeting his gaze.

"Hi, Paul."

Nodding his reply he reached the file out a little farther—far enough that she could retrieve it if she leaned in with arm outstretched.

"You're looking good."

He'd run his fingers through his thick blond hair when he'd seen her car pull onto the property. But the khakis and polo shirt had been on him since he'd showered early that morning. They'd been meant as traveling clothes. Boat shoes included. Same went for his lack of a shave.

"Your hair's longer," she said next.

She'd always wanted him to grow it out a bit. Maybe that was why he had. Because she'd been right about some things. He could acknowledge that.

"Time's of the essence." And unless she wanted to watch his penis lengthen and harden right there in front of her, they needed to get on with the business for which she'd come.

"I know." She took the file. Looked all professional and emergency-department-like as she took a brief look at the pages with a focused frown. She could have been looking at a stranger's medical chart for all the calmness she presented. Barely breaking her concentration, she moved toward the little round table for two at the far end of the room.

He turned on more light for her.

"You want some water?" He sure as hell wasn't going to offer her anything stronger, though he'd love a shot of something with some numbing power at the moment.

Haley didn't even look up as she shook her head, declining his offer. And there he stood, master of his universe, owner of the estate, unsure what to do with himself.

Because one slender blonde had entered his domain. His ex-wife.

She'd been there less than five minutes and already he was getting caught up in the messiness of the emotions she always brought with her.

Caught up in the overwhelming swirl of emotions seeing Paul again had brought on, Haley could hardly focus on the words on the page, let alone make sense of any of them. The way he stood there, watching her, made her want to jump up and confront him.

Or leave.

Confront him for helping her?

Run out and lose the assistance she so desperately needed?

Maybe he'd leave. They'd once promised each other that they'd never turn their backs or walk out on the other.

But they weren't married anymore. And she was here to focus on her sister.

Tattoo. The word jumped out at her. Tattoo? What would Kelsey be doing paying for a tattoo?

"This charge here…at a tattoo parlor…do they do things other than tattoos?"

"Some do, some don't. Why?" Paul approached and the air got thinner.

But the way he sat down opposite her, fully focused on the sheet in her hand and what she had to tell him… pulled her right into the same place with him. On the case at hand. "Kelsey was deathly afraid of needles. She made me go with her last time she was in town and cut her foot and had to get a tetanus shot. And she also had a thing about tattoos. What one man might like another might not…"

She stopped, thinking of how that sounded, and then remembered that she was with Paul.

His nod was…nice. Being understood when it came to her family…that didn't happen a lot. Jeanine and Paul were the only two who had ever…

"I'll start there," he said, making a note of the line information on the list and handing the sheet back to her. He left her then, crossing the room to the massive desk on a shag-type carpeting that had been installed over that half of the room. Two minutes later he was on the phone with the parlor. Apparently, it was open past eight on Friday nights. It was in Vegas. Made sense.

And, partially because it was under new ownership, the parlor manager had nothing to give him.

She went back to her perusal, feeling a different kind of pain as she immersed herself fully in the task at hand. Grief hit her hard. Harder than it had yet.

Seeing evidence of her sister's life, feeling the choices Kelsey had made, noticing how many times she'd been to her favorite lingerie shop, made her loss seem that much more acute.

And then… "Wait," she said aloud, looking up to find Paul engrossed with his computer screen. In that split second, her heart ripped open and he was hers again. For the split second it took her heart to fuse shut. He was a skip tracer she'd hired. But for that second…the intensity he brought to his work…she'd been flung into the past. She'd loved that about him. He'd been just as focused on his studies, had carried straight As through his dual criminology and business majors, a tough feat even though with the money in his trust fund, he never had to actually hold a job.

"What?" His glance completely impersonal, he looked over at her.

"This…cigar club. I have no idea what it is…a bar maybe? Her credit card was used there several times, but Kelsey gets sick to her stomach at cigar smoke. Seriously, she can't tolerate it. She says…said…it's because her dad smoked them, and while I never really bought into that explanation, as other things about her dad didn't make her throw up…cigars really did. They triggered her gag reflex."

As before, Paul came over, jotted down particulars about the line items she pointed out and then headed back over to his desk.

"This makes no sense." Ten minutes later, Haley was shaking her head again, getting up, that time, to head over to Paul, dropping down into one of the two leather armchairs in front of his desk. "These charges are all at The Gladiator." She named one of the most expensive newer high-rise hotel properties on the Strip. "No way Kelsey would go there," she said, perusing the list of charges, the amounts. The dates. Her sister would have had to have been staying there for days…

Paul frowned, took the sheet, but barely glanced at it before he glanced over at her. "She would if she was dating someone who was a regular. I actually thought those charges fit…that the type of guys Kelsey was attracted to would fit right in at The Gladiator."

Haley shook her head again, swifter. With more force.

"She dated Thomas Gladstone, the son of The Gladiator's highest investor," she said. "Thomas raped her. She was already sleeping with him. But I guess he liked it rough." She shook her head again, thinking about the doctor's office visit she'd made with her sister, in doubt herself at the time about Kelsey's story. Until there'd been medical evidence. She'd begged Kelsey, along with the doctor, to press charges, but her sister wouldn't do it. She'd seemed truly frightened. "I'm telling you—I know my sister. I get that she had her shortcomings, and even allow the fact that she put herself in precarious situations if she thought it would help some rich guy hook up with her on a permanent basis, but not this. Kelsey was really shaken up by this one. Didn't date for over six months." Her sister hadn't gone that long without a date since she was thirteen years old.

"How long ago was that?"

"Three years ago." A hundred wouldn't have made a difference. Not even if the guy was dead and gone. For the first time in her life Kelsey had felt powerless. It had been a tough lesson for her sister to learn.

Unfortunately, while it had kept her out of The Gladiator, and made her a bit more cautious and choosier, the incident hadn't changed Kelsey's overall lifestyle.

Frowning again, Paul seemed intent on the page she'd handed him. Then asked for the full report, which she gave him, waiting silently while he thumbed through pages as though committing them to memory. He wasn't a speed-reader, but he was close to it.

When Paul looked up, he seemed to have come to some kind of decision. His expression resolute, he said, "I've found my starting place."

That was it? "Mind sharing it with me?"

"All of the inconsistencies you've pointed out have one thing in common. The charges were all on the same credit card."

She'd been reading payees, dates and amounts. Hadn't paid any attention to numbers.

But… "I'm still working through last year," she told him, having taken the report he gave her from page one, figuring there was a reason he wanted her to start there. "Shouldn't I see if there's anything more recent before you go any deeper?"

"Last year is the most recent we've got." His gaze softened as he looked at her. "I would have told you sooner, but I needed you to have an unbiased, and as unemotional as possible, look at what I had. If you'd known we've got nothing recent, that would have been on your mind…"

It was a cheap shot at the way she'd gotten so emotional around him. But he'd had his share of letting his emotions get away with him, too. And they'd taken care of both of their shortcomings by divorcing.

"It would be on anyone's mind, Haley," he said, his tone as soft as his gaze had been. "I didn't want you distracted, thinking about, looking for reasons for, or thinking we're wasting our time on last year's stuff, when it's a big deal that there's nothing more recent."

She'd hired him because he was an expert at what he did. And what he said made sense. She still didn't like that he'd withheld information, but her feelings were irrelevant at the moment.

"You're telling me that there was nothing on her credit report to show any credit card history for the past year?"

"That's what I'm telling you."

"What about bank account withdrawals?" Haley had money she'd amassed through her father and various partners and a couple of ex-husbands over the years. Pay off money. Alimony in one case. It wasn't enough to support her life, and she only used it when absolutely necessary.

"There were none."

"That indicates that she was with someone who was taking care of her, financially at least."

"Or that she was unable to access any of her own funds."

Heart pounding, she stared at him. "As in, she was being held captive?"

He just looked at her.

"For months?"

The compassion that flowed from his gaze might have been the same for any client he had sitting in front of him getting hard news. It didn't feel like that to her. It felt personal.

"That's why I needed you to have a clear mind to look at the records we do have." She let his warmth pass over her. Let it touch her. She couldn't let it in, though.

"I'm hoping that these inconsistencies might help us find who was holding her. If, indeed anyone was."

"She didn't just wreck a car. She was killed. Because whoever was holding her wanted the baby she was carrying...it has to be Thomas Gladstone, doesn't it? He somehow got to Kelsey, raped her again, she got pregnant, and he's been holding her captive until she had the baby and then he killed her..."

It made horrifying sense as it all came crashing through her.

"If that was the case, why wouldn't Thomas have just killed her as soon as he knew she was pregnant, to get rid of the evidence?"

"Because he couldn't bring himself to destroy his own flesh and blood," she said. Then added, "I don't know, but the rest of it makes sense."

He nodded. "He's at the top of my list at the moment," Paul conceded.

"Which means that, if we go looking, for Kelsey, for Thomas, and most importantly for the baby, we might be walking into danger, too."

Sitting forward, Paul shook his head. Then stood. "Wait a minute. *We?*"

Haley rose, too. All of the fight she'd had in her in

the past coming right back to the fore. She could hold her own with most people by just walking away, but not Paul. If she didn't stand up to him, he'd crush the heart out of her. "I'm coming with you, Paul. Think about it. I'm probably already on this guy's radar. Either Thomas or whoever is behind this. I'm certainly not safe just staying home."

"No, but you could take a vacation. Go visit your mother."

He grimaced as he said the words, obviously knowing they were a mistake. So she let him stew in his own juice rather than adding more of her own to complicate the issue. Or to further raise his defenses.

It occurred to her, in the back of her mind, that maybe she really had grown up some where he was concerned. That would be nice.

"I can't be distracted by watching out for you, Haley. Surely you can understand that."

"No, but you could be helped by my input and insights," she said. "While I take care of myself as I'd do if you went without me. As I've done for most of my life."

She didn't refute the possibility that she could very well be in danger, if her intruder was correct in what he'd said.

It all could also be a hoax, but that didn't explain a year's worth of no credit card or banking activity on Kelsey's account.

"Kelsey's body was too burned in the crash to be identified, but I was told that they matched her DNA from tissue samples," she offered aloud. "People with money are able to get a lot of things done that shouldn't be done," she continued. "Do you think the coroner's office could have been bought off and Kelsey is really still alive?"

"Nothing points to that theory," he told her. "Why would anyone be alerting you if that was the case? For that matter, why fake her death at all if she was already quietly off the radar?"

Right. And then she really started to think. To be of use. "Something else doesn't make sense."

"What's that?"

"She called me, several times, over the past year."

"But you didn't see her."

"No."

"What about Gloria?" She gave him credit for naming her mother without any indication of the disregard he felt for her.

"They actually hadn't seen each other in a while, and hadn't spoken for the last few months, at least. Kelsey said that she'd finally met 'the one.' She didn't want to jinx things by introducing him to Mom and didn't want to muddy waters by bringing me into it yet, either. She said she was waiting until he put a wedding ring on her finger along with the two-carat diamond he'd already given her."

"She told you that."

"Yeah."

"Didn't you find it odd that she didn't want to see either of you? You and Gloria were Kelsey's rocks. She couldn't change eye shadow color without an okay from both of you."

The eye shadow thing. Kelsey had interrupted a romantic moment with a call and three texts and Paul had grown impatient, getting out of bed and putting on his pants, because Haley had answered them. They'd already made love. Had just been lying there listening to music. And what she'd known was that if she hadn't answered the texts, her sister would have just kept calling.

Besides, the texts had been quick and...

She should have ignored them. And the initial phone call, too. Chances that it had been an emergency had been slim. And if it had been, Kelsey would likely have left her a 911 voice mail.

Which might or might not have turned out to be an emergency...

Not a big deal when you lived alone. But when someone else had to put up with your needy mother and sister who didn't respect your boundaries—or even get that you should have some...

"How'd she sound when you talked to her?"

Paul was still on the case at hand. As she should have been. "Great!" She shook her head. Looked up at him, leaving the past in the ashes it had become. "That's just it, Paul, she sounded happier than I'd ever heard her. More, I don't know, peaceful somehow. Like she really was in love."

"So maybe he was keeping her so well she didn't need to use her own cards or accounts."

That didn't ring true. "No matter what, Kelsey always used her cards enough to keep her credit current," she said. It was one of the few things that Paul had admired about Haley's little sister. Commended her for, even. The one good thing she'd learned from mandatory visits at her father's place. The woman who watched over her most often had taught her about the value of credit. About how even poor people could get more out of life if they had good credit.

From the very first long-term relationship Kelsey had engaged in, she'd insisted, before she'd moved in, not that she have a ring, but that the man take out a credit card for her in her name, using her social security number so that all of his money that she spent would reflect on her credit.

"If she was as in love as you say, maybe she didn't need him to take out a credit card," Paul offered, but he didn't sound like he was really buying the idea. And Haley didn't, either.

"Didn't matter if he was the richest guy in the world and married her, she'd still want her credit. The guy could die. His family could sue for the money. They could win. No, Kelsey would never willingly let her credit go. That girl truly took her own self-worth from her credit report."

"Yet her last known address is over a year old." He named a high-rise luxury apartment complex not far from the Las Vegas Strip.

"Did she give up the place?"

"I don't have confirmation of that one way or another. Only that rent payments stopped a year ago."

"Someone else could have taken over the rent. But that doesn't make sense in terms of Kelsey's regular method of operation. She'd have let him pay, but the money would still have run through her bank account."

"So we're back to her being held captive. Needing to look first at Thomas Gladstone."

He'd said *we're*. Haley wasn't sure if Paul had heard the concession or not. But went with it. "Should we call the police?"

He shook his head. "Not yet. All we have so far is theory and questions. There's no crime to report."

Just as Morrow had said.

"And no record of a baby being born to Kelsey, either.

Not in Nevada or California at any rate," she repeated what the detective had told her that afternoon.

"I don't have time to wait for you to pack a bag."

"I brought one with me."

"Of course, you did." That glint in his eye…did it hold just a tad bit of admiration?

She used to fly high with the strength of his regard beneath her wings.

But, of course, when you flew with someone else's strength, the crash to the ground when they took it away broke you. After her divorce, after she'd put back together her shattered pieces, she'd made certain that she only ever flew under own power.

Paul went to his desk, stacking things and shoving them into a big leather satchel, adding a laptop last. "We'll take my SUV," he said, heading toward the door. Not waiting for her.

Not inviting her to leave with him.

Leaving it up to her whether she kept up with him or not.

She'd keep up. With him, she'd always keep up.

He'd asked for her input.

He was the one who'd called her. Telling her to come as soon as possible.

He was the one who'd introduced the drama element, rather than taking things methodically.

Because there could be an innocent baby's life at stake.

Just as Kelsey or Gloria could have had real emergencies every time they'd called during his marriage to Haley, telling her there was an emergency and they needed her help.

Just as his own father could have truly loved Gloria as he'd first said he did. Paul had known better. Edward Wright didn't love anyone but himself. Not really.

Sure, he was good to people. Generally kind. But he was also one of the most narcissistic people Paul had ever met. Ed was good to people because it suited his self-image to be so. Because having people need him, fawn all over him, shower him with thanks, aggrandized him. Not out of the dictates of his heart.

Once Paul had learned that lesson, understood the difference, accepted Ed for who he was, he'd had a much better, happier relationship with his only living parent.

No way was he letting Ed know that he was working for Haley. He did wonder, though, if his father knew that his one-time stepdaughter had died.

And if so, why Ed hadn't told Paul about Kelsey's death.

"I will… I promise… I'll let you know as soon as we get there…"

He'd been trying not to eavesdrop on Haley's phone conversation—a feat that was a little rough with her sitting in the passenger seat next to him. Yeah, the large SUV was luxurious, but highway lanes were only so wide, which limited how much space a manufacturer could leave between two bucket seats—no matter how much money one was willing to spend.

Clearly someone cared about Haley, where she was, her safety.

Someone who was not him.

And it was none of his business.

His jaw clenched anyway. As did his gut. He might not want to be married to Haley, or have her in his life, but she used to be his wife. He didn't like hearing her converse with whoever had taken his place.

It was more proof of how right their choice to split had been. The woman had a way of getting to him and stabbing him, like no other. During their two years together in college, he'd been in heaven. Maybe even for the first month of their marriage, too.

But then Ed and Gloria had shown up to tell them they'd gone to Vegas and married and there'd been no more joy, once his dad and her mom had married.

Not that Paul could remember. He'd seen the writing on the wall. His father didn't love Gloria. He'd move on. The divorce would be messy. He and Haley would be caught in the middle...

But Haley had already been pulling away from him by the time their parents had shown up. As though she didn't expect the marriage to last.

Or he'd imagined she had.

She'd received a signing bonus from the hospital and had opened a bank account in only her name to deposit it.

After he'd just added her to all of his personal accounts.

She'd said it was so that she could buy him things without him knowing. Maybe if he hadn't remembered Kelsey talking one time about always having an escape plan in any relationship, he'd have believed his wife.

Not likely, though. He'd been with Haley for a couple of years by that escape plan conversation. He knew Gloria and Kelsey. Was privy to their gold-digging tendencies. And knew how close Haley was to them.

Maybe he'd always had doubts about why she'd married him, or rather, about whether or not his money had also played into her love for him—maybe he'd asked her to marry him in spite of them.

Hard to tell when one was too busy enjoying life and avoiding difficult topics to be honest with oneself.

If he had to ask himself if Haley was with him, at least in part, for his money, he'd have to look at everyone else he enjoyed hanging out with, too.

Friends from high school.

The tennis coach who'd kept after him until he won his state championship and still drove down to Mission Viejo to play golf with him a few times a year.

The scores of women he'd dated.

Hudson and the rest of the people at Sierra's Web whom he respected so much.

Haley was off the phone, finally. And there they were…trapped in the relatively small interior of a vehicle, speeding down a highway, in the dark of the night. Alone. For hours.

"That was Jeanine."

Oh. Oh! Oh.

At one time in his life Jeanine Harbor had been like family to him. The time that he'd been with Haley. The two women had been together at an outdoor concert on the beach the night that Paul had met Haley.

He'd been with a guy he'd encountered on the tennis court…they'd played in a couple of doubles tournaments…and Jeanine had fallen as hard for Todd as Paul had for Haley.

They'd been like a television sitcom, the four of them. For a while at least.

Haley had been on the phone with her best friend. Haley and Jeanine were still best friends. And Jeanine was the one worried about Haley to the point of her promising to stay in touch.

Jeanine. Who'd once been like the sister he'd never had.

His heart grew lighter as he pushed a little harder on the gas, and then, noticing his speedometer climbing, let it back off again, and set cruise control.

"How's she doing?" he asked, his first easy question since Haley had stormed his fortress earlier that day.

"Good. She's working at the hospital now, too. In the cardiac department. We're on opposite shifts."

"You're still in ED?"

"Yeah."

Emergency medicine suited her. After a lifetime living with Kelsey and Gloria, she was an expert at bringing calm into stressful situations. Handling the details. Getting things done that needed doing in the midst of emotional turmoil.

Until it came to Paul and the turmoil was inside their home.

Still, he'd always been proud of her medical vocation. It took a special person to work with sick people day in and day out.

And there they were, ten minutes into a four-and-a-half-hour drive and they'd exhausted the non-landmine topics between them.

He was in for a long night.

Chapter 4

Haley was ready to jog to Las Vegas if it meant she didn't have to sit silently with nothing to see but miles of unending darkness covering the desert through which they were driving. As soon as she realized that Paul's vehicle was equipped with its own Wi-Fi, she suggested that she drive while he work.

The trip wasn't bad after he agreed to switch seats with her. It was actually kind of peaceful, driving out in the middle of nowhere with very little traffic, and Paul by her side, his features highlighted by the screen he was perusing. His fingers, swift and sure on the keyboard, gave her some moments, as they reminded her of things that took her back too far—to the lovely beach cottage Ed had bought them for their wedding present, and those fingers playing exquisite melodies up and down her body.

Paul had definitely been the best sex she'd ever had. By far.

"What?" His question broke into her reverie, seeming to take away the protection of darkness.

"What, what?" She sort of glanced his way, but mostly kept her gaze on the road ahead.

"You moaned. Are you in pain?"

"No. Just...hungry," she blurted. She was, kind of. She'd been in such a hurry to get to him she hadn't stopped for dinner.

"You should have said something." Unfastening his seat belt, Paul turned and reached to the seat behind them, pulling a sizable duffel over the back of the seat and onto his lap. "What sounds good? I've got cheese and crackers, peanut butter and crackers, peanut butter with pretzels, chips and salsa and beef jerky. It's with jalapeños, though, so you won't like it."

She almost laughed. With all of his refined tastes, he'd always been a sucker for junk food.

"Oh, and there's a couple of things of tuna and crackers left, too." He pulled a small rectangular box out of the bag that showed a small can of tuna and crackers on the front of it.

"I'll have the tuna," she said, and when he served it up, can open and dipping crackers within reach, she finished it all. "Got any more of the peanut butter pretzels?" she asked then, having seen him already down a bag of them. And a pack of cheese crackers sandwiched with peanut butter in the middle of them.

"I do." He handed them to her. Along with a much-needed bottle of water, which he uncapped and put in the cup holder for her. It was warm. But wet and so, wonderful, too.

"I'm impressed that you thought to pack all of this," she told him, munching more slowly on the pretzels. Kind of enjoying their little impromptu road trip in spite of all of the adverse circumstances.

"It's my go bag," he told her, tossing the duffel back over the seat and opening his laptop. "Just part of becoming a skip tracer. I sometimes spend twelve or more hours in one spot, waiting or watching, to find what I'm looking for. And when I'm following someone, I can't just ask them to hold on while I get something to eat."

Made perfect sense. She'd just never thought of wealthy and fun-loving Paul Wright without all of the luxuries he'd been born to at his beck and call.

Not that he'd ever flaunted his wealth with her. Or been at all irresponsible or lacking in work ethic. He'd just never seemed like the type to go without.

Not sure what to make of that—her early assumption, the correctness or error of it, changes in him that might have occurred between then and the moments she was sharing with him—she drove for the next hour while he worked, their silence only broken when he had a question for her, or made a comment about something he'd found.

Just outside Boulder City, the mountain town just before Vegas, he made a somewhat significant announcement.

"The luxury high-rise Kelsey was living in before she disappeared, her last known residence, was paid for by a shell company."

She didn't ask how he knew that.

"A company that doesn't exist?"

"A company that legally exists, but is mostly just a name and some bank accounts through which money is moved. Makes it possible for people to buy and sell things without record of them doing it themselves. Or for companies to move assets. In this case, it means that someone was paying Kelsey's rent, but not doing it out of his own accounts."

She wanted to be shocked. Or, at least, to not understand the significance of that. "The guy she was with didn't want someone to know he was with her."

"That's the most likely conclusion."

"Is that what you think?"

"I think I need to find out what else this company has paid for, and who owns it, before I form any more conclusions."

She knew he was right. Appreciated his professionalism.

And wanted him to agree with her at the same time. To tell her that they were getting closer to their answers, not just digging up dirt.

"Uh-oh." Haley's words weren't said in an alarming way, but they pulled Paul from the digging he'd been doing with a spike of dread.

"What?"

"What the heck?" she said then, a definite note of annoyance in her tone now as she looked in the rearview mirror. Before he could turn around, he noticed the red flashing lights reflecting off the inside of the Expedition.

"I wasn't speeding, Paul, I swear. I have no idea what…"

"Just pull over," he told her, trying not to let her see his tension. "Let's see what he wants." It wasn't going to be good. All of his instincts were telling him…it wasn't going to be good.

Especially given what he'd discovered while she'd been driving—but hadn't yet told her about.

He'd been trying to find out who'd hacked into his computer search more than an hour before, but something told him that the cops had something to do with it. "Just be yourself and answer his questions honestly," he said, and gritted his teeth as he waited, powerless to do anything but sit in the passenger seat and pay attention.

As Haley rolled down her window to the approaching officer, he thought, too late, that he should have gone with his instincts and made her switch seats with him. And be damned with how that would look.

If he'd put her in danger...

"License and registration, please."

Haley dug in her purse for her wallet and Paul grabbed the vehicle registration out of his glove box.

"I'll be right back," the heavily armed officer said.

"When he returns, if you see any sudden movement, duck," Paul told her. "And if I move, at all, except to answer a question if it's asked of me, you duck, got it? No arguing, no hesitating. You duck."

She nodded. "What's going on?" He could hear fear in her tone, but she appeared calm. In control.

The Haley who got things done in times of stress. He calmed a bit. "I'm not sure. Maybe nothing." He'd tell her about the computer hack. But not until the cop was gone.

Though it seemed interminable, the wait was only a couple of minutes, and the officer, as he reapproached, seemed to be more at ease. "Everything's in order," he said, handing back to Haley the documents he'd taken. "You two heading into Vegas for holiday?"

Haley hesitated. Paul decided just to sit still and see

what happened next. To study the officer. To listen. If the man reached for his waist, Paul would get to his first. "No," Haley answered after a brief pause. "My sister was living here and was killed in a car crash a few weeks ago. We're hoping to get into her apartment and collect whatever personal items might be left."

If the situation hadn't been so tense, Paul might have smiled. He was impressed.

And aware, too. The officer had ducked down twice to get looks at him. He'd have introduced himself but he'd told Haley to duck if he spoke without being spoken to.

"You Paul Wright?" the man finally asked. Haley had given him the vehicle registration. The man could have just run a check on him.

"Yes," he said then. "Owner of the vehicle and licensed officer," he told the man, without pulling out the credentials he always carried.

"You're a bounty hunter," the man said.

"A skip tracer, yes, but, as the lady said, right now we're heading into town for the weekend to clean out her sister's apartment."

"You two are friends, then?"

"Exes, actually," Paul told the officer, getting more and more certain that the man was looking for information. He just wasn't sure yet, what. Or why.

"Well good luck," the middle-aged cop said, tapping the top of the Expedition. "And sorry for the inconvenience. We had reports of a stolen vehicle in the area that matched this description."

"No problem, Officer," Haley told the man and as soon as he stepped away from the SUV, rolled up the window. And then, when the cop was heading toward his vehicle, said, "What was that?" She didn't sound pleased.

"Just put this thing in gear, pull out normally and head toward Vegas," he told her. "I'm not sure what that was. Maybe just a report of a stolen vehicle that looks like mine."

She pulled out, seemingly calm as could be. And said, "You don't think it was a stolen vehicle report."

There was no question in her delivery.

"I take very few things at face value when I'm working. That's my job. To look deeper."

"Paul…"

How could she know him that well? They'd been apart far longer than they'd ever been together.

"My computer was hacked about an hour ago. I've been trying to follow the IP address to find out who was looking at me, and why."

"You think it has something to do with the searches you did on Kelsey's accounts? Or the call to the tattoo parlor?"

"Could be either. Or neither." It was the nature of his work, keeping an open mind as he collected all evidence he could find. The puzzle pieces would fit together when he had enough of them. That was when he could identify and discard extraneous information.

Both hands on the steering wheel, she was clutching it so tightly her knuckles were white—while she continued to glance often in the rearview mirror.

"You want me to drive?"

"No. I want you to focus on figuring this out. Keeping the vehicle between the lines and on the right road, I can do."

Traffic was picking up as they got close to Vegas.

No way he was burying his head in files. But he liked the ability to focus on every single car, every movement around them.

"He turned off," she said, as he watched the police car exit. Didn't mean the guy hadn't talked to another car up ahead—police or not.

"We should take the next exit," he told her. "I was going to steer clear of the strip, but now I'm thinking that would be the best place to blend in, get a room in a busy casino and get some rest so we can start fresh first thing in the morning."

"One room," Haley said. "Or adjoining rooms with a door we can keep open between them. Until we know more, I'd feel better if we stick together."

She'd taken the thoughts right out of his head. Except that in his version he'd been trying to figure out how to get her to agree to the plan without argument.

If he didn't know better, he'd think he and Haley made a good team.

The smell of coffee woke Haley sometime after daybreak. Lying still, taking in the streaks of light coming from the closed blinds, she listened for sounds in the adjoining room. She heard none, and figured Paul must be in his shower. In the shorts and shirt she'd slept in—just seemed smart in case they had to leave in a hurry—she hastened past the opened door adjoining their two rooms toward her bathroom.

Glanced in his room...and their gazes collided. In black jeans and a short-sleeved shirt that hung loosely over the gun at his waist, he was standing in front of the cheap built-in desk bearing his open laptop, pouring himself a cup of coffee from the pot on top of the equally inexpensive built-in dresser.

"I'll just be a few minutes," she threw over her shoulder as she continued into the bathroom.

And made it back out in a little more than five, showered, in clean brown shorts and short-sleeved beige shirt, her hair up in a bun and her face already bearing a coat of the sun protection makeup she always wore.

Paul stood waiting for her, a grim look on his face.

"What?"

"A couple of things." He poured a cup of coffee, handed one to her. Picked up his from the desk.

Stalling.

She took a deep breath and waited. Storming him for immediate answers might feel good, but would serve no positive purpose.

The warm cup felt good against her cool hands. As in most Vegas hotels, the air-conditioning was set way low. She'd been too tired to notice the room's frigid temperature the night before.

And too eager to get fully dressed into bed and pretend to be asleep so that there'd be no further awkwardness between her and Paul.

He'd entered through his door, she through hers... they'd opened their adjoining doors as agreed upon, and said good-night.

It had been painful. At least for her.

"First, I called Hudson Warner, one of the Sierra's Web founding partners, and my direct contact with the firm. He's also one of the best IT guys in the nation. And he knows more people than I do, believe it or not."

He kind of grinned. She tried to return the gesture, to

lessen some of the tension suffocating her, but it didn't work. She could hardly breathe.

How could she possibly have a light moment in a hotel room with Paul, his unmade bed right in front of her face, and him bearing bad news.

For a second she allowed herself to think about his naked limbs with the curly dark hair, rumpling the sheets. As a distraction from the dread of what was coming, it worked. For giving her back her air, it was a total fail.

"Hud made a discreet inquiry on the officer who stopped us last night. The guy has run off-duty security for Gladstone functions a few times over the years."

"Next you're going to tell me that you found your hacker and it was Thomas Gladstone," she jumped in, unable to just be patient and wait for him to lay the news on her gently.

He shook his head. "No, I turned that job over to Hud. I'm sure he'll have an answer for us yet this morning. But what I do know is that the credit card used at the tattoo parlor, the cigar shop and The Gladiator was always paid by the same bank account. And that was registered to Thomas."

Careful not to spill her coffee, she set the cup on the counterlike top of the dresser and sank down to the end of the second, unused, bed in the room. "It makes no sense to me," she said, her stomach knotted to the point of pain. "There's no way Kelsey would have willingly gone near him again—let alone gotten involved with him. He offered her a payoff after the rape, to keep her mouth shut, but she refused to take it.

"She kept her mouth shut because she knew he'd just deny everything and that he'd be believed before she would. Even if it took money to get people to stand behind him. He had enough of it to make that happen."

"I only know what the facts are telling me. That he paid her credit card bill."

"Did he pay the others, too?"

He shook his head. "At least not that I've been able to trace. So far, everything I've seen has been paid out of bank accounts in her name, except that one card."

"She preferred to have her man deposit money in her account and pay the bills herself, but generally with each new relationship she'd open a new account. She was always paranoid about an ex having her account information."

Her throat thick with tears, she made herself stand up. "Gladstone raped her, and then he kidnapped her and, after his baby was born, had her killed."

"We don't know that, yet."

"And as soon as he knew you were looking at that account, he had us stopped. That's why the cop was asking why we were going to Vegas." Clarity came like a tornado, whipping through her and leaving her devastated.

And frightened.

The Gladstones had money in establishments all up and down the Strip. She'd only visited Sin City once before, but she'd learned a ton about the underbelly from Kelsey during her little sister's liaison with Thomas Gladstone.

"And this guy Jeanine saw, the one who left me the note, he was someone Kelsey knew, someone who loved her, and he knows where the baby is. We have to find this guy." It made sense. Sickening sense.

"If Kelsey was being held by Gladstone, and against

her will, why would she have stayed in touch with you and sound so happy?"

She didn't have the answer to that.

"It's possible that the reason she was keeping her new fiancé a secret was because it was Gladstone and she knew you wouldn't approve because of the way he'd treated her in the past. It's possible that Thomas somehow convinced her he'd changed, that he adored her and that he was going to marry her and they were going to live happily-ever-after."

Her stomach lurched. No way Kelsey would have fallen for that. No. Way. Her sister might have been somewhat shallow, but she was not stupid, or weak.

And yet, Haley had no explanation for her sister's phone calls over the past several months. The note of happiness in Kelsey's voice…there'd been no mistaking it. Haley had believed her sister had finally found the love of her life and was going to settle down, raise a family someday and be truly happy.

"We have to find the guy who left the note." She kept coming back to him. He'd started her on the journey and now he had to show her the way. "Maybe we should be in Santa Barbara, after all…"

Her voice trailed off as she caught Paul watching her with an odd expression on his face. She couldn't read him.

And didn't like that, either.

"What?"

"You hired me to do this job. You're here to help me identify oddities or similarities and likenesses where Kelsey's concerned. And to identify any possessions we might find, if you can. If you want this arrangement to change, let me know."

"Why would I want it to change?"

He waited, arms crossed, now, his coffee on the top of the dresser not far from hers.

"I'm not an equal party here," she half mumbled as she looked back over the last few minutes and saw herself standing there telling an expert how to do what he'd proven he could do better than most. If he weren't Paul, if he'd been any other expert, she'd have asked questions. And waited for direction.

"You're always equal, Haley."

"Just not in terms of this job. I apologize. I didn't mean to disrespect you or your abilities, Paul. I swear."

"I know that. I also know that if I'm going to do my best for you, I have to do things my way."

"I understand."

He nodded. She stood there, feeling somewhat superfluous and painfully idiotic. And then said, "So what's the plan?"

Chapter 5

Interviewing associates, friends, loved ones of someone he was trying to find was a common part of Paul's job. Having one beside him every step of the way was all new.

In some ways, having an associate help find the "skipper" could be a huge asset.

Knowing that Haley was close by in case of danger was one less distraction. One less thing to worry about.

But it was a huge distraction, too. Because of the risk imposed by the case.

And the hidden dangers that came with being around his ex-wife.

Haley had been back in his life for just over twenty-four hours and already the hours were filled with confusing circumstances. Nothing was clear-cut. Good and bad on both sides.

But always…bottom line…the chance that a baby

could be in danger topped everything. Kelsey wasn't his skipper. A perhaps nonexistent baby was.

Who'd ever heard of a skip tracer tracking down someone who might not even exist? It added an element to the job that made it seem nearly impossible. Because if there was no baby, it would be impossible to find it.

Cloudy waters. That came with high emotions.

Haley in a nutshell.

And still, there might be a baby in danger.

The only known associate of that child would have been the woman who bore the baby. Which meant that he had to start with Kelsey.

He was on the right track.

Had to make certain he stayed there. In spite of the huge distraction connected to his hotel room.

"Pack your stuff. We'll leave the room reservation, so we can use it if we choose, but take our things in case we go in another direction," he said. "First stop, after grabbing something to eat on the way, is Kelsey's last known address. I want to know when she moved out, *if* she moved out, maybe show her picture around, see if I can get anyone there to talk to me..."

"That's where I might be of help," Haley called from inside her room. He heard a zipper. "As her sister, I can probably get people to have some compassion for the fact that she's just passed, get them to open up where they otherwise might not and maybe learn some things."

She was right, of course.

And it was good to focus on the ways in which she was useful.

To the case.

Only to the case. Right?

When they arrived at Kelsey's apartment building,

Paul spoke to the representative on duty for the real estate company that managed the place and found that Kelsey had moved out during the last paid month of her rent, leaving an extra two weeks rent in lieu of notice of departure.

She'd left no forwarding address. Any mail that had come for her after she vacated had been returned to the post office.

And while Haley had been able to get several people in the building to talk to her about her sister, to offer condolences and share tidbits of their time with her, the only true information she managed to come away with was that Kelsey had lived there alone and that she'd put her things in storage when she'd first moved out. The woman next door, a young widow, had recommended the company and Kelsey had stopped later to say that she'd rented a climate controlled indoor unit, and to thank her.

Kelsey hadn't said why she'd needed a storage unit, or where she'd be staying in the meantime, and the woman hadn't thought it appropriate to pry.

She'd also added that Kelsey had hired a company to do the actual moving for her, but didn't remember which one.

As Haley climbed into the passenger side of the SUV in the building's basement parking garage, she said, "We have no idea if she made it to wherever she was planning to move," disappointment in her voice. "And no way to find out, since we have no idea where it was."

"We can check to see if she rented the storage space as she'd said she did. I didn't see an accounting for it on any of her credit cards, but if she rented a place, there will be accounting there."

And they had other avenues awaiting them as well. They'd be making a physical stop at the tattoo parlor, Paul had told her on the way to the apartment building. And then on to the cigar club. He had a plan.

Letting someone else take control didn't come easy to her. She'd been the problem solver, the doer, since childhood.

Still, if she wanted to find that baby—to know that her niece or nephew, if the baby really existed, was okay—then she had to sit back and trust Paul.

It might prove to be the second-hardest thing she'd ever done.

The first had been getting over him.

When they stopped at the storage company, the owner first refused to give Paul access to records without a warrant. When presented with the legal proof that Kelsey was dead and that Haley, Kelsey's closest living relative, executor, and beneficiary of her estate, wanted to take possession of any uncollected property in any unit with Kelsey's name on it, he admitted that she'd had a unit. That she'd paid cash for one month's rental. And that she'd emptied it within a month.

He only ever saw her there once—the day she'd rented the space. After that he'd seen a moving company come in and unload, couldn't remember which one exactly, something with the word *man* in it. Or *men*, and a few weeks later, she'd left a message that she'd moved out. He'd found the unit empty and swept clean.

He had no idea who'd helped her get her things out. And their surveillance video, which would also require a warrant to access, was erased every six months.

Another disappointment.

The cigar club turned out to be private, upscale

and discreet. Maybe it was a cover for high-limit card games. Maybe just a place for men to bring women they wanted to be with, but not be seen with. No one there was eager to look at a picture of Kelsey, and those who did, didn't recognize her.

Or wouldn't admit that they did.

When Paul asked for a comprehensive receipt, to know what Kelsey's money had been spent on, he didn't even get as far as being told he'd need a warrant, or providing proof of Haley's right to know if there were possessions of Kelsey's that belonged to her. He was told, quite succinctly, but with quiet and well-spoken words, that their computers were down.

In such a way that he was certain they'd be down anytime he went back asking.

If there was a crime, and he was an investigator, he could get a warrant for the computers, and maybe it would get to that point.

It wasn't there yet.

One thing was becoming clear to him, though. Even before Kelsey disappeared, she'd lived a somewhat secretive life—being seen, but not giving up any personal or pertinent information about herself.

The tattoo parlor offered a little more information, once Paul convinced the new owner that it was in his best interests to let Kelsey's beneficiary know what Kelsey's money had purchased.

"Those receipts are for a tattoo. Administered in three parts. A name. Elaina." The twentysomething, with as much body art covering him as clothes, read from the computer screen in front of him.

And then he let them know they'd need a warrant to

find out whose body had been the recipient of said art, as bodies were private entities.

Could have been Kelsey's.

Most likely hadn't been, as her body would no longer be protected under the same privacy laws.

At least not if law enforcement was investigating a crime.

Though he wasn't yet telling Haley, he was fairly certain there'd been a crime. At least one. Kelsey's murder.

But while his tentative theory was based only on supposition and instinct, he wasn't going to put it out there.

Most particularly not to the deceased's closest loved one.

Who also happened to have once been *Paul's* closest loved one.

Haley had just stepped outside the tattoo parlor ahead of Paul, onto a sidewalk with throngs of people, when she felt a jerk on her forearm, just below the elbow.

Thinking at first that she'd been jostled by the crowd, by someone maybe who'd had a little too much to drink and eager to get to the next slot machine and try to win a fortune, she stepped back toward the building, toward Paul, only to be held firmly in place alongside the base of a streetlamp. The pressure on her arm wasn't just a passerby, nor was it letting up.

As the intensity of the fingers holding her grew, bruising her skin, she froze, looking for Paul. Trying to warn him. Too shocked to be afraid, she stood there, feeling protected by the crowd, by the sheer number of witnesses, until she realized that with one backward thrust, she could be pushed into the open door of a car parked on the curb directly behind her.

Paul appeared before her eyes, on his way to her, just

as she opened her mouth to scream. And searing pain shot up to her shoulder as her arm took another jolt.

"See how easy this could've happened?" A male voice said through seemingly gritted teeth, from just behind her, his lips close to the back of her ear. She could smell him. Something heavy and evergreenish. Way too much of it. The tips of his shiny leather shoes seemed at odds on the dirty sidewalk. "Go home."

And then, with a lurch forward due to a shove from the hand clutching her arm, she was free. Paul reached her, his concerned gaze landing on her face briefly, before turning toward the expensive dark luxury sedan that had pulled out into traffic.

The crowd continued to push forward around them, anyone who'd been adjacent to her as she'd been held captive already up the street. Shaking, she focused on Paul's tall strong form, his white shirt and black jeans, the way his chest rose and fell with each breath he took. And she took a breath in unison. And then another.

She was fine.

Her arm had already quit hurting—as though her attacker had known just how to hold it to inflict the most pain without causing actual physical injury.

"No license plate. Damn!" Paul said, and then turned the intensity of his attention on her. "Let me see that," he gently lifted her arm, brushing his thumb lightly over the red area where another man's fingers had so recently been. "What did he say?"

With an arm around her back, he moved her quickly to his SUV, parked just around the corner from the building, watching their backs and their fronts as they went. She could see his head in constant movement, like a video camera taking in the scene.

"See how easy this could've happened." She repeated, slowly, also watching the area around them, wanting to know for sure that the unpleasant episode was truly over. That there wasn't another thug waiting to jump out and grab her.

"And then he told me to go home."

Paul walked her to the passenger door, unlocking it with his key fob as they drew close, pulled open the door and shut it behind her once she was safely inside. He was around the front of the vehicle and in beside her in seconds, starting the engine and backing out immediately.

"I'm not going home," she told him, having already made up her mind. Obviously they were onto something, getting closer to it, or there'd have been no reason to warn her away. "But I wouldn't mind making a stop at the police station."

Certain now that Thomas Gladstone had raped, abducted, and killed her sister—and fearing that the privileged fiend had her newborn niece or nephew, too—there was no way she could leave. She couldn't turn her back on her family. Not for anything.

And most certainly not when said family was a helpless innocent baby.

"I'm not ready to call the police, yet. Even for a look at a surveillance camera that may have captured what just happened." Paul's words sounded non-negotiable. He was angry. The way he got angry. Silently. With a strength building up inside him that would drive him to resolve the situation even if the other party needed time to decompress and regain calm before having conversation.

In a marriage the trait was counterproductive. But

on the hunt for a kidnapper with a baby…she was suddenly thankful for the slow burn that wouldn't stop.

"Until we know what kind of money and connections we're dealing with…until we know how far reaching this all is, I prefer to reach out to only those I know I can trust."

Still shaking from the encounter on the street, Haley started to feel just a tad bit safe again, sitting there with Paul. She waited for him to determine their next move. Taking deep breaths. Trying not to think about Kelsey, to imagine what horrible things she'd endured during her last months of life.

And her last moments.

Had she known she was being murdered? Had she known she was going to die? Or had it happened fast enough that she'd left life the way she came in? Unaware of what was happening to her.

She'd been driving the car, had been the only occupant, during the one car crash that had taken her away. Had she escaped her captor? Thought she was free?

Paul drove them outside the city and then pulled onto a narrow desert road, drove a mile or two and then pulled off into the hard dirt of the desert floor.

"I had to make sure we weren't being followed," was all he said as he pulled out his phone.

"Hud? Yeah, it's me…"

The familiar tone of voice… Paul talking to a close friend…could she really have just felt a pang of jealousy?

Yeah, emotions were running high—understandably so—but she was not going back there. Friendship with Paul Wright was not an option. They couldn't be friends. They hurt each other too much.

They'd made that decision the night of their second anniversary. The night they'd decided together to divorce.

She caught bits and pieces of the conversation. Paul reported in with a fairly thorough listing of what had transpired since he'd last spoken to his associate. Listened. Made arrangements to drop his car off where it would remain parked in someone's extra garage, just in case someone was tracking the license plate. And to borrow another, older model SUV.

"So, you agree, leaving the police out of it for now is probably best?"

What? Paul was asking for an opinion of his decision?

That was new.

He listened some more. Haley could hear the rumble of a male voice, but couldn't make out any words. They sounded serious, though not fraught with emotion.

Exactly the type of conversation Paul needed. The kind she'd never seemed able to have with him.

And the stab of jealousy segued into envy.

Chapter 6

Paul needed to find his calm. To get out of himself and into his work world. Focusing on becoming the best skip tracer he could be was what had saved him after his divorce. His job gave his life a meaning he'd been unable to find anywhere else.

And then there came Haley again.

Seeing that man holding Haley's arm…he'd forgotten he was working. That he had a job to do. He'd plowed through the throng of people on the sidewalk to get to her side, period.

And had found her just fine when he got there.

He'd lost his head.

That was why they'd split. Not because he'd been unfaithful, or because she'd married him for his money. But because they were too volatile together. Couldn't think straight.

The only way for them to be their best selves, or even to function well, was for them to be apart.

He'd left. She'd been thankful.

The divorce had been one of the quickest in history. Completely amicable. He'd opened a bank account for her, deposited her settlement.

And had buried himself in finding the impossible. Become great at it.

"I'm sorry you had to leave your car behind." Haley spoke for the first time since they'd pulled away from Hudson's associate's house in a nondescript brown SUV. But Paul was still in his own head.

He'd left. She'd been thankful.

Now she wouldn't go home.

And he couldn't leave her. Not until the job was done.

He needed his entire focus in his work world to do that. And if that meant bringing Haley into it with him, then that's what he had to do.

Just work. Only work.

"Hud and Win, the firm's lead financial expert, traced the shell corporation that paid for Kelsey's apartment," he said, to that end.

It was business. Not personal. Whether or not she was emotionally okay after her near abduction couldn't be his concern. If she needed emotional assistance, she had Jeanine and her many colleagues—medical personnel in her life to whom she could turn.

She had Gloria.

And the rest of the life she'd built, quite successfully, without him.

For all he knew, she had a boyfriend. Though not a live-in one. When she'd first called, she'd said that the note had been left on her door while she'd been at work and that no one else lived in the home.

A home his settlement money had purchased for her?

"And?" Head slightly bent, she was giving him a quizzical look.

And...work world, buddy.

"So far, the trail has led to other shell corporations, not all within the country, and that's where the problem comes in. We have no way of tracing companies in the Cayman Islands, but they did find a home in Las Vegas, on Calypso, that was paid for by the same corporation as paid Kelsey's rent. No one can trace it to Gladstone, yet. Or anyone, except other companies. We're heading to that home now."

She nodded. Her beautiful features introspective as she stared out the front windshield. He had to hand it to her...if she was afraid, she was hiding the fear well.

"Could be a corporate house," she said, then. "You know, one of those places used for entertaining and to house out-of-town business associates."

The assumption was a good one.

He didn't bother saying so.

No point in risking a fall back to personal by making her feel good.

The home was beautiful, in an upscale neighborhood with lots that were at least a couple of acres a piece. Two story, white with black shutters—a stick-built home with siding, not stucco, in the desert. An anomaly in and of itself. And the yard was all grass—another anomaly in the desert. The underground irrigation required to keep it so green had to come with an astronomical water bill.

And yet…it appeared that the home was abandoned. While they couldn't get past the ten-foot-tall wrought iron gate, Haley noted the unmowed lawn out loud, first.

"Yeah, definitely looks like no one's been here for at least a month. Probably more like two."

Leaning forward, heart pumping, Haley asked, "That wreath on the front door…is that two angels hovering over roses?"

The wreath was huge. Taking out his phone, Paul took a picture, then enlarged it on his screen.

"That's what it looks like," he said, showing her the screen. With two fingers, she widened the photo more, moved the image around the screen so she could see more of it. And hoped that Paul didn't notice that her fingers were trembling.

"When we were little, one of Kelsey's caregivers at her father's place told her that there were always angels watching over because she was a little angel. And if she ever started to doubt, all she had to do was smell a rose to know that they were there. She always used to say that someday, when she had her own home, she was going to have an angel wreath on the door…"

She broke off, throat frozen as she teared up, and then, when she could, said, "About six months ago, in one of our phone calls, she told me she got her wreath. It was one of the things that convinced me she'd really found a man with whom she was truly happy. I didn't think of it until right now, but…"

Heart racing, she leaned forward, as though something in the air would confirm her suspicion. "This is where she was living," she said. "It has to be."

She had no proof, but intuition told her she was right.

The same shell company that had paid her rent had purchased the house. It all made sense.

Including the ten-foot-tall wrought iron keeping her and Paul out.

"This is where she was being held," she said.

His silence beside her didn't bother her at first. She was too filled up with her discovery. She was looking at her sister's wreath. They were getting closer.

Had the baby lived in the home, too? At least for the first few days?

Had Kelsey had at least those first hours with her baby?

And then Paul's lack of response resonated.

"What?" she asked him.

"How many captors do you know who buy wreaths to please their prisoners?"

Okay, there was a slight flaw in her theory. But...

"Maybe he was playing her, Paul, did you think of that? Maybe he'd convinced her that he loved her, that they were going to be together, and played along with her fantasy. Until the baby was born..."

It was possible.

"Not likely. He'd have had to let her come and go to get her to believe that. She'd have had a car...even I know Kelsey wouldn't be stranded without her own wheels."

He was right about that.

"Maybe the pregnancy had her bedridden."

"And what, he put the wreath there to appease her, took a picture of it to show her that it was there, and then left it there?"

"It could happen." She'd spent her entire life watching people deceive each other. It was the world in which she'd grown up.

Giving a rich man what he wanted so he'd give you everything your heart desired.

As long as your heart just desired monetary things.

Problem with that was, inevitably, there came a time, usually with the passage of time, that what you had to give, the man no longer wanted.

Paul didn't argue with her.

Just put the vehicle in gear and drove slowly down the road.

He needed time on his computer. Hudson was doing what he could, but had another case that he was working on. Same with Winchester. But Paul's hunches with innocuous, seemingly small things sometimes took him to his prey.

As a precaution, he checked out of the Strip hotel with a phone call and took them to a freestanding highrise casino just outside town. There were no adjoining rooms, which meant they'd be sharing the large space with two queen beds, but it had a separate living area. It gave them at least some privacy.

Treating Haley like any other work associate, he left her to figure out what she wanted to do, and set to work at his laptop on the desk in the sitting room section. He had questions…like why would one corporation pay for just an apartment and a house and seemingly nothing else? And, why move from the apartment to the house?

Unless one didn't want one's activities to be seen.

There was some merit to the conclusions Haley had drawn at the house they'd visited. But there were inconsistencies, too. First and foremost, he had to know who was behind the shell corporation. He couldn't legally access Thomas Gladstone's financial information, but there were a lot of public records that would allow him to get closer to the man's activities. Phone number databases, criminal background checks, utility bills, public tax information. And Kelsey's credit card application, her department store loyalty cards and air travel records for either of them.

There were also some avenues he could follow directly from Kelsey's accounts. Her other credit cards, as well as the one tied to the corporation. He'd already run her through most of his other resources.

Two hours later, he had a ton of information, and didn't feel any closer to finding the answers he sought. As though she could sense his mental break, Haley appeared with a cup of coffee and a plate in hand bearing a sandwich, chips and a pickle.

"I ordered lunch and am assuming you still like beef with beets, lettuce and mayo," she said, setting the plate beside him.

So, she remembered. It was an odd sandwich combination. As she'd told him laughingly many times over their years together.

No weirder, in his opinion, than her microwaved tuna, onion, cheese and mayo, served over tortilla chips, he'd always shot back.

She'd taken a seat on the couch, where she'd been on and off while he'd been working—mostly off—and was munching on a sandwich of her own.

Tuna and lettuce by the look of it.

Maybe she'd grown up in her tastes.

No reason to entertain any nostalgia over the mayo and cheese and onion with chips.

"When you get a chance to check your email, I had

some video footage sent over to you," she said, as though asking how his sandwich tasted. The way she only looked at her own late lunch as she spoke made him curious.

"What video footage?"

"From a position of being Kelsey's grief-stricken sister, needing answers, I called an attorney whose child I had in the ED, who called the Las Vegas Police Department and requested traffic cam footage for the time and area of Kelsey's accident. I know it's already been thoroughly gone over, and that nothing was found, I just thought maybe you…"

He nodded. Smiled. Took a man-sized bite of sandwich.

And suddenly felt glad that she was there.

The sun was still shining in their tenth-floor windows at seven that evening. Feeling like she'd been in the room for days, instead of hours, Haley looked up from the pages she'd been combing when Paul suddenly stood up.

Other than one trip to the bathroom, he hadn't left his seat since he'd taken up residence. He'd given her the fifty-page list of credit card charges, assigning her the task of comparing card numbers to types of charges and locations of establishments, and the spreadsheet she'd been compiling was almost done.

She had observations to share—including a text conversation with Jeanine reporting that there'd been no more activity at home—but had planned to wait until her task was completed since she didn't want to interrupt his concentration.

"There's no clear designation for Kelsey's choices of which cards to use when," she told him. Her little sister had had a total of six VISA credit cards. There was record of all of them having been paid for out of her bank accounts, other than one. The one used at The Gladiator. "Other than that one card, she seemed to trade off, not in any particular fashion, and not for any particular purchases. She'd used different cards in the same stores and restaurants, even getting her hair done."

The only conspicuous thing was that one card. "And there were no other charges that stood out as being something Kelsey wouldn't do," she added.

He stood there, watching her, making her mouth a little dry, so she continued, because talking was easier than letting him get to her. "The other thing of note, she used her other cards at the same time she used the one with the oddities. Often even on the same days."

"Always in Vegas?"

"Going by her credit card usage, she was always in Vegas on the days that both cards hit."

"And sometimes charges hit a day or two after the expenditure was made," he said.

She had no idea how anything she was doing was going to help nail Gladstone, or find proof of the existence of a baby, let alone find the baby. She'd begun to wonder if he'd just been keeping her busy so she didn't make any other phone calls or in any way stick her nose into his search.

She hated to even entertain such a catty thought.

Yes, she was tired. Tense. Grieving more than she'd realized. And, most particularly after her earlier near kidnapping-turned-warning, afraid.

Paul still seemed to bring her emotions out in all the wrong ways. He made her do and think things she would not normally think or do.

"I need to go out for a while," he said, his tone too

easygoing, as he passed her and headed toward the duffel he'd left on the floor not far from the door—telling her to use the luggage rack for her little bag.

"Where?"

"Just going to do some surveillance."

Something that could be dangerous, she translated. His back to her, he was hunched down over his pack, passing over some loosely folded articles until he pulled out a dark T-shirt.

And her heart lurched. No way she wanted to sit alone trapped in a hotel room with no transportation and nowhere to walk to but the desert, while he was out there facing God knew what on her behalf.

She stood up, headed toward her bag which was about halfway to his. Looked for her own dark clothes. Jeans and a black pullover shirt that she normally wore with her white shorts. "Two sets of eyes are better than one. Can cover more ground in more direction."

"You aren't trained if things get dicey, nor are you armed."

At least he hadn't denied the danger. Since he'd carted her around everywhere else, and then the last place had turned dangerous for a second there, his motivation had been fairly obvious.

A white button-down shirt and pair of black pants came out of the duffel next, with a white T-shirt. The black shirt was shoved back in.

He was going fancy?

And it hit her. He was going to confront Thomas Gladstone. No way she was missing that. If she had to hire a cab and follow him. She hadn't come that far to lose the chance to confront her sister's killer and find out what he'd done with the baby...

With a strong retort on her lips, she heard herself a split second before the words were uttered and took a mental step back.

An emotional step back so that her mind could work best. She had to a find a way to be a legitimate asset to the operation.

"At least if I know where you're going, I'll know where to start looking if you don't make it back."

Upright, he turned, clothes in hand, facing her. And then said, "You're not going to like what I have to say."

She shrugged. With their history, nothing more needed to be said on that one.

"I don't think Thomas Gladstone was involved in Kelsey's death."

Heart sinking, she stood her ground. But, damn. He was right. She didn't like what he was thinking. At all.

But she'd hired him. Could fire him just as easily. After she heard him out. He was an expert—and he'd earned that reputation the hard way.

By proving himself.

"Why?"

Dropping his clothes to the bed, he reached for the ironing board hanging in the closet, set it up, plugged in the iron, set it upright on the board and turned to her.

He held up one finger. "First, I've been through the traffic cam video and there's no sign, whatsoever, of any kind of foul play. Kelsey's driving the vehicle that was registered to her at the time of her death." Something they'd already known. "One camera caught her face and she didn't appear to be in distress. There's no sign of her being followed. And when the crash occurred there weren't even any other vehicles by her."

She'd asked. It was still hard to hear. Licking her lips and then pursing them, she held her tongue.

"This doesn't tell me for certain that there wasn't foul play, but it would appear that she wasn't under duress in terms of being held captive. I don't know that. But my process requires me to factor in every piece."

Her tension eased slightly as her faith in him returned.

"Second," he flashed up two fingers, "I've just been through the criminal database—with legal access granted me by my licensing—looking for known associates of Thomas Gladstone and searching for the man I saw accosting you this afternoon—and came up with faces, but none that even slightly resembled the guy I'm looking for."

"Did you find him, though? In the database apart from Gladstone?"

He shook his head. And held up three fingers. "Third, I've completed the check on Gladstone and there's absolutely nothing in his report that links him in any way to anything to do with Kelsey, other than that one credit card. I've got data from as recently as last week, and there's nothing that indicates any hidden life, no unusual disappearances, no changes in his patterns and absolutely nothing that ties him to anything to do with babies or children."

She opened her mouth to protest. Of course there wasn't! If he was hiding a pregnant woman and killing her after she had the child, wouldn't he be careful not to seem as though he was an expectant father?

On the other hand...the man had managed to hide so well that he'd convinced Paul he probably hadn't taken

Kelsey. From what her little sister had told her about the Gladstone heir, he wasn't *that* good.

He wasn't dumb. But he just wasn't that smart, either.

"What about the officer who stopped us last night? The one who does Gladstone's private security."

"He's handled a few security jobs for him. I admit there's at least coincidence there."

There was nothing left for her to do, but nod. And say, "So…where are you going?"

"To an entertainment club Gladstone frequents every Saturday night that he's in Vegas. It's upscale, discreet, with a cover charge that insures that only the most wealthy will enter…"

"You're still looking at him."

"She had a credit card paid for by one of his private bank accounts. And she used it to frequent places she doesn't normally go. That's suspicious. It's not enough, however, without any other corroborating evidence, to get me to go at him. Not in any official capacity."

Aha. Haley bit back a grin. She was up to speed. "You're posing as yourself, a wealthy man, one of the California Wrights, with a plan to try to get close enough to Thomas Gladstone to have a conversation with him."

Licking his finger, he tapped it quickly to the plate of the iron. Haley heard the slight singe and watched as Paul proceeded to iron his shirt. This was new. He'd always sent his laundry out when they'd been married. Even in college, he'd had his clothes laundered. "I'm hoping to at least get close enough to his party to over-hear conversation, if nothing else."

The plan was good. But it could be better. "You'd look less conspicuous if you had a date. And less suspicious if it looked like you and that date only had eyes for each other."

Part of her couldn't believe what she was suggesting. The other part knew her idea was not only solid, but pretty damn good.

"I'm not just a pretty face," she blurted, then winced. She'd said the same thing to him when he'd accused her, that last horrendous anniversary celebration, of marrying him for his money. She'd not only been devastated, but insulted as well. As though she'd ever use her physical attributes to lure anyone. For anything.

And yet, there she was, suggesting Paul take her along to his undercover work as a physical distraction.

"There's something suspicious about Gladstone," Paul said, sliding his shirt off the board and grabbing the pants. "As you pointed out, I didn't find the thug from this morning in any database, so while we can't connect him to Gladstone, that doesn't mean they aren't associated. Whoever came at you this morning wasn't playing around. And he wasn't an amateur. If they'd wanted to do more than warn you, you'd be gone.

"I can't do my job, focus fully on the room, the man, if I'm also worried about watching out for you."

"Then let *me* watch out for me, Paul. You aren't my husband. You aren't responsible for me in any way. And, frankly, at this point, if there's really a baby out there, I'd rather die trying to find it than to let it be in danger. Be harmed. Or worse."

She knew that they could already be too late. It had been almost two days since the note had been left on her door, and twenty-four hours since the man was back at her home, telling Jeanine to warn Haley. Anything could have happened since that time. And they both knew it.

Paul finished ironing. He took his clothes in the bathroom and shut the door. She heard the shower start.

She didn't have anything sexy or black to wear. But the shops on the first floor of the hotel would. Grabbing her bag and a key to the room, she slipped out the door.

Chapter 7

When Paul emerged from the bathroom, fully dressed, combed and shaved, Haley wasn't there.

What in the hell had Haley done? Had someone come for her? Had she fallen in a trap? It took him a full thirty seconds to pull out his phone and dial her number.

And then saw her cell on the table by the couch where she'd been working, just as it started to buzz a call. She'd put it on silent while they'd been investigating.

With his brain heading into full gear, overgear, he went for the phone, as though the left-behind article could give him a clue to what had happened to her.

Had she been in touch with someone else, besides her attorney and the Las Vegas police, without telling him? Made some kind of arrangement to gather information?

Oh God, had she fallen prey to someone who was out

to get her because the visitor to her home had led some-one to her as he'd feared?

Why in the hell had he agreed to bring her to Vegas with him?

And to think, he'd come out of the bathroom ready to tell her that her plan to accompany him that evening was not only solid, but that he'd decided to accept her offer. His options would be greater with Haley as a cover.

He didn't like it. Couldn't come to terms with her in any kind of danger, but for all he knew, she'd be in more danger at home in California where the unknown man had first found her.

At least with her right by his side, he had a chance to protect her...

Her phone was password protected. Before he could even finish his first guess, he heard a key swipe at the door, and quickly put the phone back where he'd found it—reaching for the gun he'd just strapped to his ankle...

It spoke to his training, and the seriousness of his choice to be the best at what he did, that he had the re-volver in hand and pointing toward the door by the time it opened.

He almost dropped the thing when Haley walked in. Alone.

And completely...done up.

Stunned, he stared, felt his arm fall to his side, the revolver hanging there against his thigh, while he took in the remarkable beauty of the woman who used to be his wife.

He'd seen her fully made up before, of course, a couple of times. Their wedding day, certainly. But the woman with perfect, more mature curves, standing there in a skintight black dress that ended a few inches above her knees...the high heels...

His gaze slinging back up, it stumbled onto those bright red lips, the flawless skin, eyes that seemed to have grown twice as large with lining or whatever she'd done to them.

And the hair, blond with soft curls and falling everywhere...

He swallowed.

"Were you just pointing a gun at me?"

No mistaking the tone in that voice. Or the voice in general.

Nor did the sound, or the words, ease the constriction that continued to pound uncomfortably beneath his fly.

"I didn't know where you'd gone. If you were okay," he said, suspecting that he sounded as out of control, as defensive, as he felt.

"I didn't have dress clothes. I went downstairs to get some, and then, figuring you'd still be in the bathroom, popped into a bathroom stall downstairs to get dressed so I'd be ready to go when you were..."

Made perfect sense. Rational. Professional.

Made him look like a fool.

Why hadn't she left a note to tell him?

So instead, he was left standing there, fearing for her safety. Pulling a gun on whatever bad guy had been coming back to, what, get him? Take him along so he could watch her being held captive? Or worse...

Shaking his head, Paul took a much-needed breather as he bent to replace his gun in the ankle holster he wore pretty much every day of his life.

By the time he'd straightened, he had himself back in check. Firmly, he hoped.

Either way, he was going to do the job for which he'd been hired. He was going to find Kelsey's supposed fiancé, find out if there'd been a pregnancy, and if so, find the baby.

And then he was going to walk away from Haley Carmichael for a second time and never look back.

Or die trying.

Paul meant business. He'd always been serious about his studies, about making a difference in the world, about being different from his fun-loving, jet-setting playboy father.

But the way he'd held that gun…as though it was an extension of his hand, something he was master of and wouldn't hesitate to use…that was new to her.

And attention getting.

As she rode silently beside him in the gathering dusk that was turning the mountains pink in the distance, she was quite put out to admit to herself that the gun thing kind of attracted her.

Not having it pointed at her…but him…being so… strong and in control of it.

And as it had turned out, he'd already decided she should accompany him. And, once he'd put his gun away, had calmly told her so, collecting keys and reminding her to pick up the phone she'd left on the table on their way out the door.

Which further baffled her. Where was the man who always wanted to fight with her? The one who was so passionate he couldn't always find his zen around her?

That man had driven her nuts.

Hadn't he?

When he hadn't been taking her to heaven. Or making her laugh so hard she peed her pants.

Or saying something so moving he brought tears to her eyes.

And the night she'd found out he'd been unfaithful to her...he'd broken her.

She couldn't forget that.

He'd denied it, of course. Repeatedly. Adamantly.

Had even offered to call the woman to confirm that he hadn't been with her.

But who wouldn't deny it? And how much of a stretch would it have been for a woman to lie about such a thing to protect the man she'd just been with? Or to protect herself? Or her future with him?

She knew the woman side of things. Had watched it happen with both Gloria and Kelsey.

But sitting there with Paul, seeing what he'd become, what he'd made of his life—exactly what he'd said he was going to do—she wondered, not for the first time, if she'd been wrong about his infidelity.

Not that it mattered in the long run.

He'd thought she married him for his money. She thought he'd been unfaithful.

The sad truth had been that they hadn't trusted each other.

That was what had ended their marriage.

That and the fact that they brought drama into a home they'd promised each other would be drama-free.

They'd both grown up with emotional chaos in their homes. Neither of them had been willing to face a lifetime of it.

And they hadn't seemed to be able to stop from getting riled up around each other.

So, yeah, the new Paul could turn her on. But he couldn't play games with her.

She couldn't go back, and neither could he.

No matter how his eyes had widened as she'd walked in the hotel door. Or how his mouth had hung open.

No matter how deep the pool of desire grew to be inside her.

A fact of which she reminded herself as she walked with him into the softly lit club an hour later, posing as his date.

Now this was business. He'd gone over an exit strategy with her on the way in, first giving her a spare key to the SUV that he'd left parked just a few feet down from the club. He'd made sure she had 911 dialed on her phone, only requiring one finger push to send the call. She needed to keep her back to the wall and trust no one. And if she needed to, she had a can of pepper spray he'd supplied her with. She'd use it and ask questions later.

While Haley knew she should be afraid, she wasn't. Not consciously, anyway.

More, she was determined to make Paul proud of her.

And most importantly, to find her sister's captor and make him pay.

And still, as the doorman let them in the vestibule, a renewed surge of want hit her down below as Paul offered her his arm—just as he had on their wedding day.

When she saw the large amount of cash he had to turn over as a cover, she leaned in and whispered, "I'll reimburse that. Just add it to your expense report," partially to remind herself that they were working. They were not there as a couple. Or even as a couple of friends.

He didn't answer, and she was too distracted by her entire body's state of fissure as he slid his arm around her, resting his warm hand at her hip. Letting herself lean into him was more of a natural reaction than a response chosen to keep up their act, and she put herself on high alert. She didn't *just* need to worry about whoever might have killed her sister, stolen a baby, and been after Haley, too. At that moment, it seemed as though Haley's biggest threat came from within. It was like putting on the fancy clothes, the makeup and changing her hairstyle had transformed her into someone she was not.

Someone she could not only not afford to be, but someone she didn't even want to be.

Paul took his time guiding them toward the bar where he ordered them each a shot of whiskey and a glass of soda, and, handing her one of each, took the other two to a nearby table along the wall.

Pulling his chair close to hers, he leaned, his lips right and her ear, and said, "I'm going to lean over the table to adjust that chair." He nodded toward the empty seat next to her. "When I do, act like you're pouring the shots into the soda, but dump them in the centerpiece instead."

He half stood then, his arm covering the distance between his body and the table, as he reached with his left hand to push the vacant seat away from Haley.

By the time he sat back down, the shot glasses were empty.

And Haley, with a silent apology to their plant, couldn't help admiring the man her ex-husband had grown to be.

Paul had seen no sign of Gladstone. No sign of anything covert or underhanded. Just wealthy people drinking, eating fancy appetizers and visiting. The small stage at one end of the lush room was dark and empty. Canned classical music provided background for conversations and occasional bursts of laughter.

Mostly, he wasn't sure what people did there on a Saturday night. He could see the venue for business meetings. High-dollar deals finalized over only the best alcohol.

But a place a young wealthy man would go every Saturday night?

Unless it was to have some kind of private liaison…

Haley lifted her glass, glanced his way with a smile as she took a sip. She was playacting. His mind fully grasped the concept. But his body, already hard as rock, didn't.

But no way was he going to let anything get in the way of his trace, finding the answers he sought and ensuring that neither Haley, or any baby that might exist through Kelsey, was in danger.

Nothing.

And that focus paid dividends. After noting the fourth man walking alone down a hall to the right of the rest room alcove in the far back of the venue, Paul leaned over to excuse himself, enduring one more flowery whiff of hair and woman. Reminding Haley of her exit strategy in case he didn't return, he walked calmly off to the bathroom.

He wasn't letting her out of his sight for more than a second or two at a time. But he had to know where those men were going and why.

If his hunch was correct, if there was a high stakes card game being held at the club on Saturday nights, he'd know why Gladstone was there.

And have another puzzle piece to throw on the table with the rest of them.

Almost to his destination, Paul took a quick glance back at Haley and saw another man, walking alone toward him. Not him personally, just the place where he was heading. Bending down, he untied his shoe, worked slowly on retying it, making certain that he was done just after the other man passed him and then headed on seemingly toward the restroom.

Bingo.

His timing perfect, he got a good glimpse inside the room. Didn't make out much. No Thomas Gladstone.

But he saw the tables. The players. Male and female. Old and young. Serious expressions. And he saw the large piles of chips in front of them.

Gambling was legal in Nevada.

And some Vegas games were reserved only for the most serious players. The ones with thousands to bet on one hand.

He had no idea yet what a Gladstone heir's potential gambling problem might have to do with Kelsey Carmichael, or any offspring she might have had, but he was one piece closer to finding out.

Turning, eager to let Haley know what he'd seen, his gaze sought hers…only to meet a muted gray wall. And empty chairs with half-filled soda glasses at the table he'd left.

Blood turning cold, he made a quick visual search of the room, aware of his gun, of the innocent people filling tables and milling at the bar…

And there she was. Standing off from one edge of the bar, with a man cornered in front of her. Her prey would have to make a scene to escape the wall-and-table prison she'd managed to trap him in by stepping in front of him at just the right time.

To anyone else, it would have looked like two friends catching up. Or interested parties saying hello.

But not to Paul.

The man seemed amused, if you didn't take in the glint Paul caught shining from his eyes.

He recognized the man, of course, from the pictures he'd been perusing on and off all day.

Thomas Gladstone.

Chapter 8

With only one thought in mind, to get to Haley and keep her safe, Paul sped in their direction. He slowed when he got close and slid an arm around her back, almost weak with relief, as he had her where he could protect her once again.

He'd need to face those feelings. But not until their business at the club was done.

Thomas, a young man who, even cornered, wore his privilege with a nauseating stance, a half smirk…and that glint…didn't even seem to notice Paul until he was standing there holding Haley. The younger guy would be comical looking, something straight from a movie set, if he hadn't been taking on Haley.

"Look, man," Thomas addressed Paul without so much as an introduction between them. "She came on to me. I was just here minding my own business, getting a drink, and she approached me."

"But you like her type, don't you?" Paul asked, with a little, confident cock of his head. As long as the other man didn't have bodyguards hiding out at the tables behind them, he could take the punk with one hand, keeping Haley safely tucked with the other.

Haley knew his type, of course. And knew, done up like she was, she was it. She'd used the information. An admirable choice in his work world.

Paul wasn't feeling admiration toward her at the moment. He was mad that she'd walked into danger alone.

"Seriously," Gladstone said, backing up a half step and glancing over Paul's shoulder. Signaling his goons for help?

Did a guy bring his goons along to a high stakes poker game his father might not know about?

The question bore some weight. As did the puzzle piece that was seeming to settle.

"You eager to get to your game?" Paul asked, as though he knew far more than the little he'd actually seen.

"What game?" Thomas drew his head back, shrugged as though he had no idea what Paul was talking about.

"The one that's going on through that door back there," Paul said, motioning to the other side of the room. "That's why you're here every Saturday night, isn't it?"

Haley might have cornered their suspect physically, but Paul knew how to put people in corners that generally produced results.

"I don't know what you're talking about." Thomas's tone changed, held a note of steel as he put his drink on the empty table beside him and rocked back on his heels. "So, if you're here, working for my old man, you're going to have to just go right back to him and report that you got squat. Would I be hooking up with a pretty lady if I had other plans?"

"So, you admit you hit on her?" Paul put on the pressure, finding the job a little too easy to be as enjoyable as he'd have liked.

"He approached me," Haley said, staring straight at Gladstone. "I came up to the bar to get another shot, and he offered to pay for it."

Paul took a step forward.

"Look, man, whatever he's paying you, I'll double."

"I'm not on your father's payroll."

Even as overconfident as Thomas Gladstone was, he hadn't been able to hide his surprise at that one.

Because while the guy thought he was pretty smart, Paul was quickly figuring out he really wasn't.

Paul wasn't ready to show his hand, mostly because there were too many cards he didn't yet have, but with Haley having forced the issue, he knew he had no other choice.

"I'm here to find out why Kelsey Carmichael's credit card was used in places she would never go. But where you would."

Everything stilled for a second. Even the air seemed to stop moving. Paul was that focused. And Thomas was that shocked.

And when the world started turning again, Gladstone was clearly agitated.

Paul could read questions in his expression. The younger man didn't ask them. He glanced at Haley again, and then at Paul. If he suspected that Haley was Kelsey's sister, he didn't say. Might not even have known that she had one.

Didn't much matter at the moment.

Finding the truth, and rescuing the baby if there was one, were the only things on Paul's table.

"That...um...was over a year ago."

"I know."

"Why does it matter now?"

Paul took another half step forward. "Now that she's dead, you mean?"

"No..." Backing up, Gladstone shook his head. Back and forth. Repeatedly. "No way, man. If you think I had anything to do with that...or her...no way, man. I haven't seen Kelsey since she told my old man I mistreated her and walked out. She ruined my life. No way I'd go near her again."

Paul *almost* believed the guy. Could go either way.

"So why did you use her credit card?" Haley piped up, anger clearly burning through her at Thomas's crude dismissal of Kelsey. Gladstone glanced at her and then right back at Paul.

"You heard she was dead, right?" Paul kept up the pressure.

"Yeah, I heard. Saw it on the news. The crash, the way the car caught fire...it was on all the stations." Blubbering was generally a sign of telling the truth.

Not always.

"So answer the lady. Why were you using Kelsey's credit card?"

"What does it matter? It was way before any of that."

"It matters to her," Paul said, keeping his gaze fully locked on Gladstone while he side-nodded to Haley who was still held to him hip to hip.

His mind was racing. Thomas hadn't hired the cop to stop them the night before.

The realization bothered him almost as much as turning around to see Haley talking to Gladstone had done.

"Do you know who I am, man? One crook of my finger and I can have you taken down and taken in..."

"I know exactly who you are. I know that you have a gambling problem and that if your father knew about it, you might be singing up an octave by morning." He didn't have proof. But he knew. A few more puzzle pieces were falling into place.

"After Kelsey went to my father... I swear, man," Gladstone's chin dropped a couple of notches along with his tone. "I swear, I thought we were acting out a movie we'd seen. This couple, they decided to spice up their sex life pretending rough sex, but Kelsey, she went and told my dad I'd hurt her. What the hell! I..."

"The credit card," Paul butted in as he felt Haley stiffen beside him.

"Ever since Kelsey...the old man has had me on such a tight leash I'm choking," Thomas said, in a tone more defeated than anything else. "He has someone go over every single one of my credit cards every month, checking where I am and what I'm doing. He didn't know about the card Kelsey took out that I paid for. I'd insisted, since I was footing the bill, that I have a card to the account, too, and I used it sometimes."

"The cigar club...another high stakes game is hosted there..." Haley said from beside him, sounding numb.

And Paul was thankful. For her sake. Numbness would get her through.

"Whatever," Thomas said.

"What do you do now for money?" Paul asked, just in case the answer mattered to him for some reason.

"I've got a couple of girls…they took out cards… I pay them, the card bills and the girls…"

"Where do you get the money?"

"Playing cards. The old man might think I'm a loser, but I'm actually good at cards."

He could afford to be, having all of the Daddy-approved expenses covered for him.

"Why'd you stop using Kelsey's card?"

"I got a letter from some lawyer dude in Pahrump, warning me to cease and desist. I cut up the card. I mean, what the hell…she didn't want me using it, why not just close the account? It wasn't like I was sticking her with the bill. I was helping her build her credit which is why she wanted the damn thing to begin with."

Funny how people could justify their own wrong actions by making it seem like they were helping others.

"What's this lawyer's name?"

"I don't know…" Thomas glanced at Paul and then said, "I swear, man, I don't remember. Gilbert something. Or Gebhardt. Something with a *G*. What I do remember was the stationery. The envelope was brown. Not tan, or off-white, but light brown. Who has light brown stationary?"

With one finger applying pressure to Haley's hip to let her know they should go, Paul said, "Just one more question."

"What?"

"You have any idea who Kelsey was seeing?"

"I didn't even know she was still in Vegas, man. I swear to God."

Paul nodded, intending to leave the other man standing there, feeling uncomfortable and unsure whether or not Paul would report what he'd learned to his father.

That left Paul in the position of power if they ran into each other again over the next day or two. He took a step away and prayed that, for once, Haley would take his lead and walk with him without argument.

And breathed a quiet sigh of relief when she did.

"You did good in there."

Buckling her seat belt, Kelsey froze midaction, and stared at Paul. During the quick and watchful trek from the club to their vehicle, she'd been gearing up for the ire she knew he'd be showering on her as soon as they were in a safe space.

She'd failed to follow orders—approaching Gladstone alone.

And on their current project, he was the boss. A position they'd agreed upon. He started the SUV, seemingly oblivious of her perusal.

"I've been preparing for a fight," she told him, talking to the man she'd known, more than to the man he'd become. She knew the other one better. Knew where she stood with him.

And how to resist him.

Saying nothing, he pulled out into traffic and made a couple of quick turns. Driving them in circles, she knew, to make sure they weren't being followed. After only a couple of days with him, she was already learning the basics of tracing those who didn't want to be found.

"I can't believe you aren't mad." It used to infuriate him when she wouldn't just accept what he was telling her, but needed to find out things for herself. Sometimes by learning them the hard way.

"I admit to a few peevish seconds there," he said, switching lanes and turning right at a red light.

Rather than remaining still, waiting for it to turn green, she figured. Intrigued by the levels to which he took his job, by his focus and attention to detail, she had to remind herself that much of the time, the man drove her up the wall.

He'd always driven her to emotional highs and lows that put her in her mother and sister's world.

Now, it was just her mother's world.

"If you were in my employ, you'd be fired," he added, after another quick turn. "You got lucky in there, read the situation and helped the operation, but it could just as easily have gone the other way. Insubordination when lives are at stake is unacceptable." He flashed her a grin that took her breath. It took her back to the days when he'd made her life so bright she could hardly believe it was real. That life could be that…full. That she could be that happy. "There, that make you feel better?" he asked, turning his attention back to his driving.

No, she didn't feel better.

She felt…bereft.

Confused.

And glad to be sitting beside him.

Paul was hit anew with the reality of Haley's beauty, her body's sensuality, as they walked through the casino on the way to their room. Why that one woman, above all others, had the ability to lure him in, he had no idea.

There was no logical explanation.

Which pissed him off even as it fascinated him.

Reaching for every internal defense he had in his arsenal, he said, "I've got some work to do. I'll put on my headphones, in case you want to watch television, and will be on the computer so won't need much light.

I'd recommend that you get as much sleep as you can. We'll be leaving first thing in the morning."

"Where are we going?"

"Pahrump." About an hour away from Vegas.

"To seek out that lawyer that Gladstone mentioned."

"I plan to seek him out tonight. Figure out exactly who he is. Tomorrow, I plan to speak with him."

"On a Sunday?"

"You want to wait until Monday?"

"Absolutely not. I just don't know how…"

Another couple approached, a group of three women right behind them, and he was saved from saying any more as the seven of them rode the elevator up together, and the three women got off at their floor.

As they entered the room, Paul stood there fighting disappointment as she immediately, and wordlessly, grabbed her bag and went into the bathroom, locking the door.

Exactly as he'd have wanted her to do had she sought his opinion on the matter. He had no good reason to feel let down.

Shaking his head at the traitorous enemy lurking inside him, Paul dismissed the small chink in his armor and, changing quickly into sweatpants and a T-shirt, was already at the desk with the lamp on the dimmest setting, headphones on and typing on his laptop when he heard the bathroom door open.

Nothing was playing from the headphones. He'd yet to turn on the music he generally used to help him focus for work.

And he sure needed to focus.

In shorts and the T-shirt he'd seen on her the morning before, she shouldn't have been as breathtaking as she'd been moments before, turning heads walking through the casino. She'd gotten rid of the makeup, too.

His body paid more attention to her, not less.

Bracing himself for whatever was to come, he started typing. Deleted. Concentrated enough to get the words down that he needed on the page, to continue the search he'd just barely started…and heard covers rustle.

With the el shape of the room, he could only see the bottom of the bed. He saw the covers move, and then a foot-shaped lump appear toward the bottom of the bed.

No lights came on.

The television stayed silent.

And Paul somehow managed to get himself back from the near abyss into which he'd almost fallen, and get to work.

Chapter 9

Haley hadn't expected to sleep well, or much, but she lay down, listening to Paul type around the corner, feeling snug and secure. The next thing she knew, her phone, which she'd plugged in by her bed, read five in the morning.

And the shower was running.

Sitting straight up, holding the covers to her in spite of the perfectly respectable shirt she had on, she glanced over to the bed separated from hers by a nightstand. She saw the thrown-back covers, the wrinkled sheets and balled up pillow and knew that Paul had slept there.

In a bed right next to her.

He still balled up his pillow when he slept.

Looking at the evidence, she smiled. Then she jumped out of bed, pulled her blankets up, as though to take away the evidence of her having been sleeping next to her ex-husband, and rummaged in her bag for the clean clothes she'd need for the day.

The second he'd exited the bathroom, she'd enter, and they could vacate the room before anything exploded on her.

Wherever they stayed that night, she was getting a separate room. Adjoining or not.

Or she'd sleep in the SUV.

Or…maybe…they'd find the baby and she'd be holding it tonight.

A baby.

Could it really be possible that her sister had had a baby? That a part of Kelsey, a tiny human, was alive and breathing?

Uttering up a massive prayer that the baby existed and would be okay, she packed up her things and was ready and waiting when Paul opened the bathroom door.

"There's a fresh cup of coffee there for you," she said, sipping from her own cup as she waited for him to pass and then, bag over her shoulder, ducked quickly inside the steam-filled room.

He'd wiped a circle clear of fog in the middle of the mirror.

Maybe to admire himself.

But she knew it was for shaving.

Paul may have grown up wealthy and privileged, but he'd never been vain.

Or all that taken with his greatness.

She shook her head as if to rid herself of the memories. Thinking about him constantly—the man she'd known, the man he'd become—was not good for her.

For them.

They needed to focus. Their goal was to find that precious little baby who could be waiting for them.

She'd showered the night before, to rid herself of all vestiges of the part she'd played in the club, so took just a few minutes to wash and brush, put on her foundation with sunscreen, dress in the blue shorts, blue-and-white-striped tank top, slip on the white flip-flops and be ready.

Paul was waiting at the door, his duffel on his shoulder.

"You found something," she said, in lieu of good morning, or asking how he'd slept.

Both nonwork thoughts. Both forbidden.

"I found the lawyer. Marcus Grainger. From what I can tell, he only has a few clients. I've scoured public records and there's very little. A couple of small things—a DUI he defended. A small claims court suit. All wealthy clients."

They were out the door and heading down the hall as, heart doing double time, she asked, "You think he's Kelsey's guy? That she had an affair with him?" A new beau, in protective mode, wouldn't hesitate to intimidate a former abusive partner...

"He's in his sixties."

She nodded. Age wouldn't have mattered to her sister. As long as she respected the guy, enjoyed being with him. *And* if he was loaded and willing to marry her.

"He's also gay."

Probably not Kels's Prince Charming, then.

"Either she hired him herself, or he represents someone who hired him on her behalf, is my guess," Paul was saying as they waited for the elevator.

"Either way, they're protected by lawyer/client privilege."

"Unless the executor and heir to her estate can convince him to share. With the help of someone who might be able to convince him that there could be a crime involved. And a life at stake."

He was looking at the elevator door, and up at the lights above it, indicating that the car, while moving downward, was still three floors above them.

But she heard his message loud and clear.

And while it was businesslike in nature, the olive branch he'd just offered her most definitely was not.

Paul was treating her as an equal, fully including her, trusting her, which was nice.

He was also telling her he needed her.

And that made her weak in the knees.

Pahrump, a small town west of Las Vegas not far from the California/Nevada border, had a history all its own. Phone lines didn't arrive until the 1960s, along with its first paved road. The town—and access to Vegas—grew, but it was still a unique entity with a very distinct personality.

Including wineries and the successful and legal brothel ranches that boasted, at any one time, as many as twenty prostitutes taking clients.

Paul had done his homework on the place. And he hoped to God that he didn't have to tell Haley that her sister had switched from using her looks to gain a rich husband, to selling her body to support herself.

If Kelsey was employed by one of the brothels, and had gotten pregnant, the baby very well could be in danger. Especially if the father was someone who had money and didn't want it known that he'd paid for sex.

Or if he didn't want his wife and family to know that he had an illegitimate child.

He also wasn't looking forward to Haley figuring out that if the baby had disappeared and was "in wrong hands," there was a chance it had been sold. Human trafficking, especially of babies, was a far more prominent business than a lot of people knew. He'd traced a trafficker once and knew much more than he wanted to on that subject.

Paul let all the pieces he had regarding Kelsey Carmichael roll around in his mind.

With one currently on constant repeat.

Marcus Grainger's largest, most publicized client was Sister's Ranch, a luxurious brothel just outside town. Almost every case that had come up, and most internet mentions, of the prominent attorney were linked in one way or another to the sex ranch.

He didn't plan to tell Haley that unless he had to.

She'd react emotionally.

He didn't blame her. He just couldn't do the job she'd hired him to do if he was focused on how Haley was feeling.

He'd found a blog on Grainger's own website that talked about the man's penchant for a round of golf after church on Sunday mornings—there'd been a point to the story, Paul just hadn't bothered to remember it—and that's where he was headed. To the golf course.

As he told Haley when she asked how he planned to get to the attorney on a Sunday morning.

He knew how to play. She didn't. Neither of them was dressed for a round. "We're going to be there long before he is," he told her. "I'm hoping to catch him in the parking lot, preferably alone, and ask for just a minute of his time. Usually showing my credentials is all it takes to at least get that. In this case, I expect him to comply, if for no other reason, than to make certain that I don't have something on a client that he's going to want a heads-up on."

When she met his gaze, those big brown eyes of hers speaking their own language to him amidst soft features lined with worry, he wanted to tell her about the brothel. To let her know where they were most likely headed, but as a tracer, he knew he couldn't.

"What do you think our chances are that there's really a baby?"

Her question took him by surprise. "I have no idea." It was his professional opinion. He just didn't know yet. It was a piece of information sitting on the "table" in the form of knowing about the note that had been left on Haley's door. The possibility was figuring into every other piece of information he had. But...

"Just your opinion, Paul, not a professional assessment. Do you think there's a baby?"

Considering what he knew about Sister's Ranch? "I think there's a good chance that there is."

She nodded, and sat beside him silently as they waited in the parking lot for the lawyer to show up to play golf.

I'm sorry—I can't help you. The lawyer's words played themselves over and over in Haley's brain as she walked beside Paul back to the SUV.

"You believe he didn't know Kelsey?"

"I think it's possible."

"You believe she wasn't his client?"

"I do."

"He said that he wasn't aware that Kelsey was pregnant." Her spirits were way down again. Up. Down. A roller coaster of emotion and worry. And of hope. When, in the past couple of days, had she begun to imagine Kelsey's child in her life?

When had she not?

From the second she'd comprehended the note on her door, her heart had opened to the possibility.

She was just hoping to save a baby from danger.

She was hoping to hold her sister's baby. If the baby lived with the father, and the father was good, then fine. But she wanted a part in that child's life.

She wanted the child in her life.

"Just because he wasn't aware doesn't mean she wasn't pregnant." Paul's words, while potentially encouraging—as long as you didn't consider that if the baby existed it could be in danger—weren't offered in a way that sounded upbeat.

Something had been off about him since they'd arrived in Pahrump. And maybe before that. He'd been in his head since he'd come out of the shower that morning.

"He didn't deny sending the cease-and-desist letter to Thomas on Kelsey's behalf," she said, trying to make sense of what she knew. To get up to his speed.

"He probably assumed I either have, or have seen, the letter." Unlocking the SUV, he waited while she walked to her side of the vehicle and got in before getting in himself.

"So, now what? We head back to Vegas?" Every time they had a lead, every time she started to feel like the nightmare could soon be over. They reached another dead end.

"Now we start looking at Grainger's clients, to see if there are any connections to Kelsey."

A new door opened wide, shining golden light from within. And it dawned on her. "You already know who they are."

"It's my job," he said, seemingly fully focused on the road he'd just pulled onto.

"And you have a plan to get them to talk to you? On a Sunday?"

"I do. One of them, at least. His largest one."

Okay, there was definitely something going on. He wasn't looking her way at all. And Pahrump wasn't big enough, the road they were on wasn't that wide or populated enough, to need the amount of focus he was giving it.

And they seemed to be headed out of town.

"Paul?"

"Grainger's client is Sister's Ranch, Haley. We're headed there. If I had any hope at all that you'd agree to wait for me elsewhere, I'd tell you I'm going alone, but there's not much hope of that, is there?"

His gaze, when it finally met hers, was resigned. And steely, too.

"Sister's Ranch?" She was slow on the uptake. But she knew. She'd read the signs coming into town. "You think Kelsey was working as a prostitute."

That's what he'd been doing while she'd slept securely and trustingly beside him. He'd been letting pieces of information convince him that her sister had gone from rape in a bad relationship to a much harder life of sex work.

"So some things haven't changed," she said, anger boiling inside her without even warming up first. "You never liked Kels. Or thought she'd amount to anything. What was it you called her? A user?" She knew that was exactly what he'd called her little sister on more than one occasion. And her mother, too.

"To the contrary, I was always certain that Kelsey would get what she wanted," he answered calmly, as though he'd been preparing all morning for her reaction. Truth was, he probably had been. While she'd been riding blissfully along after a good night's sleep, telling herself that Paul would save the day. He'd been working and she'd been noticing the incredible beauty of the sunrise over the mountain and feeling thankful that she'd called him.

"She always did," he added. "And yes, I called her a user a time or two. Out of frustration from watching how she called and expected you to jump and tend to her every time she lost an eyelash."

His words did nothing to dissipate her ire. Quite the opposite.

But given their circumstances, she didn't voice the defensive response that was on the tip of her tongue. What did it matter what he thought? He was no longer a part of her life.

She just needed him to find out what happened to Kelsey and to find a baby—if there even was one.

"And I struggled with the fact that no matter what we were doing, if she called, you answered. You know how it feels to come second to a little sister who was known for making mountains out of molehills?"

His words stopped the thoughts raging through her for a second. "You never came second, Paul. That was part of the problem with us, as a matter of fact. I couldn't find a way to tone down my need to put you first all the time. If I'd done what I most wanted to do, I'd have married you and never answered the phone again as long as I lived. But that's not me. I'm a fixer. And I'm loyal to the ones I love."

His silence could have been an expression of acceptance. Maybe even of understanding. She didn't think so.

And had to say, "You know how much Kelsey's drama drove me up the wall. But at the same time, I knew that she couldn't help it. And in her world, what was drama to us was real life crisis to her. I also knew that I was the one person who could talk her down. When she called me, no matter what she said she wanted, what she was really asking for was for me to help her calm down. To think logically and look at the situation rationally."

So maybe she was overselling it a bit. It wasn't like her sister was incapable of being rational. Or that she'd needed a shrink or medication or something. Kels and Gloria...they just tended to overreact to things.

And Haley tended to bring things down to a manageable level. Manageable to her.

"In truth, I probably tended to them more for me than anyone else," she added. "They didn't know any better than to live on their emotional waves. It's me who needed them to find the calm."

He'd turned onto a long one-lane road outside town and her stomach got queasy.

"The ranch is up ahead, on a dirt road to the right. It's secluded to preserve client's privacy."

Every nerve at attention, every muscle stiff, Haley stared straight ahead. Kelsey had sounded so happy living the story she'd told Haley. The engagement. The man who loved her, just as she was. The man she loved. She wanted her sister to have found real love. To have known what it felt like to be truly adored.

Not to have been pleasure for men who felt like they had to hide what they were doing.

It wasn't about the work. It was about…being truly adored.

As Haley had once been by Paul.

Before they'd found out how bad they were for each other.

Of course, there was always the possibility that Kels had had both. The work…and the relationship.

No matter what, though, it wouldn't have been an easy life. Not when there was always the possibility of a client getting rough…

No way Kelsey could have handled that well.

No way Kelsey would have put herself in that position. Not after Gladstone.

Paul turned right. The road was dirt. But smooth. As though freshly plowed.

"You hired me to do a job."

"I know."

"This is how I do it. I don't get to pick and choose which information to follow up on. Whatever happened already happened. I can't change that by what answers I do or don't seek."

"I know."

"And if I form judgments before the truth is fully revealed, I risk skewing the investigation and don't ever get to that truth."

"I know."

Slowing the vehicle, he turned to her, met and held her gaze. He didn't say anything.

He didn't need to.

"I understand, Paul," she said softly. "And thank you for being sensitive to the fact that this would be hard for me. And for trusting me enough to bring me along anyway. Though…it would have been nice if you'd been honest from the beginning," she added. "You knew when we started out this morning that we'd be coming here."

"Unless Grainger gave me a reason not to do so, yes."

He didn't fully trust her.

She didn't blame him for that. She didn't fully trust him, either.

And that was why they were no longer married.

Chapter 10

Paul hadn't been second choie. After marrying him, Haley would have been happy to never answer the phone again. Had fought with herself not to answer it.

Didn't change who she was.

Or the other things that had ripped them apart.

Still it was good to know.

Halfway up to the estate, he hit pavement. It led to an expansive parking lot that was more than half full.

Having never visited a brothel before, he was surprised to see so many cars in there. Limousines with drivers standing outside them talking. Expensive sedans locked up tight, he was sure.

The plan to walk in, show his credentials and ask if anyone there had ever seen the woman in the picture of Kelsey he'd intended to show didn't seem like the best idea.

The place was a resort, with valet parking, no less, he noticed as he saw a gentleman exit and hand over a ticket at a booth.

Pulling into a spot in the lot facing the entrance to the resort, he took stock. He'd known there were cabins, places where a man could stay for the weekend, or longer, with however many women he'd paid for. There were restaurants, bars, a dance club and the place offered twenty-four-hour room service.

He just hadn't expected a brothel to look so...normal. Like the five-star resort it was.

If Kelsey had gone into sex work, she'd definitely picked a place that suited her chosen lifestyle.

A place that made it seem more believable that she'd done so.

Haley's silence pinged against him a bit, but he had to factor her out for the moment, while he listened fully to his work brain and figured out the best way to proceed.

A car pulled up in the receiving drive. A couple got out, turned the keys over to a valet driver and proceeded inside.

A few minutes later, an elegantly dressed older woman came out the main door carrying a cup of coffee and wandered into a magnificent garden to take a seat at one of the cement tables there.

Everywhere he looked spoke of safety. Discreet activity, but worry-free.

And he had his plan.

"I'd like to go in alone," he said, still watching the entrance. "I plan to show Kelsey's picture and request her services. It's the cleanest way to..."

"Tip no one off and have a good chance of finding

out if she worked here." He didn't recognize the tone in her voice, but after studying her for a full minute, he took it at face value.

Sort of. "You have something you're going to be doing in the meantime?" he asked, remembering having turned to find her with Thomas Gladstone the night before.

"I plan to walk over to that garden and have a seat until I see you come back outside." She looked him straight in the eye.

He held her gaze a long time. Saw no flicker, no change.

Nodding, he unclasped his seat belt.

"Paul?"

"Yeah?" He glanced her way one more time.

"Be careful."

"Always."

Her eyes filled with a warmth he hadn't seen in... seemingly forever. At least months before their marriage had ended. "And...thank you," she said.

With a curt nod he left the vehicle before he did something stupid like lean over and kiss her goodbye.

As she watched him walk away, walk into a place where the sole purpose was for beautiful women to have sex with men, Haley didn't even want to get out of the car.

She wanted Paul to climb back in and drive them away.

Away from temptation.

She wanted them on the road heading elsewhere. Fast.

He was bound to have had women over the years.

Plenty of them. Could even have one waiting in Mission Viejo for him. Although she hadn't been aware of him talking to anyone on a personal level since she'd shown up at his casita and other than bathroom breaks, they'd been pretty much together nonstop for almost two days.

Not her business who he did or didn't call.

And not smart to think about his love life. Not when the thought bothered her.

It shouldn't. They'd been divorced far longer than they'd been together. He wasn't her husband. Or anything to her but the man helping her find answers about her dead sister.

The fact that the thought of Paul with another woman bothered her probably posed a problem. One bigger than she had the resources to worry about at the moment.

No way Kelsey, after her rape, would have gone into sex work. Prior to that…maybe. If she couldn't find a rich enough man to support her. But after Thomas Gladstone? No way.

Haley would bet her life on that.

Glancing toward the entrance Paul disappeared into, she just wanted to see him exiting. Heading toward her.

When she realized that she was staring at the door with an intensity beyond what the matter called for, she forced herself to take in the grounds. The lone woman in the garden was gone, but Haley tried to focus on the space, to find beauty in the opulent blossoms and flowering shrubs that were dotted with cement statues of naked cherubs, cement tables, cement benches along walkways. To remind herself that the world was filled with beauty…

There. By that bench. A dark gray hoodie. It was there and gone. But she'd seen it. She knew she had.

Staring at the bench, moving her gaze slowly, she studied the right half of the garden. And a minute later, saw it again. The hoodie. On a body that wasn't curvy, and wasn't muscled or bulky, either.

When the body turned, she got a distinct impression that it was male. A hint of whisker on the chin. But definitely a slight build.

Could it be the man who'd left the note?

Thoughts flew through her brain. Jeanine's description. Someone who'd known Kelsey recently, knew she'd had a baby. Had loved her.

What if Paul was right and Kelsey worked at Sister's Ranch? Maybe the elfin man in the hoodie did, too? Was in the garden taking a break?

Or somehow realized who Paul was, had overheard him in conversation inside, knew that Haley was on the premises?

Had he come out hoping to see her? To get a message to her?

Haley flew out of the SUV so fast she stumbled when her feet hit the ground. She had to find him. This man who'd loved Kelsey. She needed him to see her, to be aware she was there. To tell her what he knew.

When she got into the garden, though, he was nowhere to be found. She hadn't been quick enough. She'd lost him.

She refused to accept defeat, however, and made a second, slower pass along the winding sidewalk of the completely deserted garden, paying close attention to all of the seating alcoves, most particularly those half secluded by bushes. And ended up at a skinny sidewalk that segued away from the garden and ended at a small building that appeared to be for servicing the garden.

Mostly surrounded by tall flowering shrubs, the building was clearly not intended for resort guests. Assuming it contained irrigation fixtures and controls, and probably storage for weeding and planting supplies, she studied it for any sign that someone was back there, inside, for any hint of a door moving.

Was elfin man a gardener at Sister's Ranch? Had Kelsey come out to the garden? Was that how they'd met?

She couldn't let herself fail. Not when she was so close.

Turning back to the garden, she'd only taken a step when her head was jerked backward by a grip on her hair. "Make a sound and you're dead." A hand filled her open mouth, stifling her scream before it got out. As she jerked, trying to pull free, the hand twisted in her hair yanked again. Hard. Hurting her neck. Squeezing her eyes shut tightly against the sting of pain, she felt herself being dragged, knew she was in serious trouble.

And felt fear in a way she never had before.

Heart pounding to the point of taking away her air, she went limp.

If Kelsey Carmichael had ever stepped foot anywhere near Sister's Ranch, no one was talking about it. Posing as a client looking for her had netted him nothing but head shakes and offers of other beautiful blonde women who were available that morning. When he'd pulled out his credentials, he'd made it all the way to the manager on duty, but still was told that not only had Kelsey Carmichael never worked there, but also that the woman, Angela Vance, didn't recognize her at all. Not even as someone who'd been in for an interview.

Angela checked her interview logs over the past two years, and implemented a search of her email program for Kelsey's name, and nothing came up. Paul stood there and watched.

It didn't mean Kelsey hadn't been there, but if she had been, it either hadn't been under her own name or the place had been wiped clean of any trace of her.

He was more apt to believe she hadn't been there.

Just a hunch, based on the openness of the people he spoke with. Reactions had appeared normal, not rehearsed.

Not solid proof. But a puzzle piece worthy of being on the table.

The good news was, Haley would be happier knowing that her sister most probably had not worked as Sister's Ranch. His step lightened as he headed down the marble hall toward the heavy revolving door that would take him back to his sometimes infuriating ex-wife.

Admitting to himself that it wasn't her who bothered him so much as it was his own reactions to her, he noticed not even halfway across the parking lot that she wasn't in the vehicle. Switching direction, he headed to the garden.

Eager to speak with her, he did a quick visual once-over as soon as the garden was in view.

Drawing closer, Paul scrutinized the area a little more closely. He didn't see anyone or notice any movement. Heart thudding, telling himself not to jump to conclusions, he entered the garden seeking Haley and nothing else. A minute or two later, he stood by the big cherub statue, and swore aloud.She'd promised she'd stay put. If not in the car, then the garden.

Had looked him in the eye and given him her word. She'd be in the vehicle, or the garden. Period.

Where in the hell was she?

He circled the garden again, checking every crevice, behind every shrub, finding nothing.

Frustration and anger warred inside him as he made the last turn at the back corner of the garden and...

The glint caught his eye.

Fear-laced adrenaline pushing him, he grabbed up the flip-flop, and spun around. Once. Twice.

She wouldn't walk out of her flip-flop and leave it there.

Could she have been chasing someone?

God, let her have been chasing someone.

The only other alternative, that she'd been taken against her will, was too god-awful to consider and still focus enough to find her.

He never should have left her alone. Yeah, his business in the brothel had been better conducted with him by himself, but he should never have left Haley.

If anything...

Who would she have been chasing?

Could she have seen her sister? Was Kelsey still alive as Haley had once suggested?

Shaking his head, he pushed forward down the small sidewalk leaning to the shed, found nothing out of place, no sign of Haley, or anyone else, and turned back. Running at full force, his phone already at his ear, he raced to the SUV. Checked her side for any evidence she might have left there for him, and his heart sank.

She'd left her phone. Haley never would have gone for a walk, without her phone. Sick with worry, feeling helpless for the first time in many years, he completed his call to the Pahrump Police Department, basically hearing that they'd do what they could, but an adult who could have just made a bathroom run or similar wasn't a high priority. Disconnecting, he set off at a run.

Whoever had lured Haley, or taken her, had no idea what he was up against. Paul wasn't an expert because he'd bought his way into the position. He was one of the best skip tracers in the world because he found people who'd been invisible for decades.

He would find Haley.

He just hoped to God he wasn't too late.

The searing pain in her neck had dissipated. Haley processed the dull ache as one of several discomforts attacking her as she continued to be pulled backward, with hard jerks. She still hadn't seen her captor. He'd stopped not far from the garden, pushing the barrel of a gun to her ribs as he looped some kind of plastic tie around her hands and tightened it, then applying a smelly, rough cloth around her eyes, tying it so tightly it cut into the skin at her temple. He'd pulled her backward again, then, rather than pushing her forward.

To keep her from more readily figuring out where she was going? The direction at least?

To keep her further helpless and off guard?

She knew one thing.

She was not going to die as her sister had, having it appear as an accident, with no evidence left behind to find a killer. She'd kicked off her second flip-flop during one of the jerks, hoping that her kidnapper was facing forward. When he'd failed to stop, or react in any way, she took the move as successful.

And took heart.

She might be less muscled and smaller boned, but she was mentally and physically strong. She was smart.

Paul would be counting on her to keep it together and get herself out of the mess she'd run into.

He'd give her hell for that too, likely kick her off the case.

She'd deal with him later.

First, she had to save herself. There was no telling how long Paul would be inside the building. And her disappearance might just trigger his ire as he assumed that she was off on her own sleuth pursuits again.

Easier to think of him angry, than worried.

Anger was an emotion she could use. The only emotion that was likely to do her any good at the moment.

Her heels raw from being dragged over dirt and rocks when her feet couldn't keep up the backward pace, she longed for softness. Cotton.

Sunrays warmed her face; smells around her changed from humanity—parking lot gas, cooking food—to open air. She'd been trekking barefoot, starting and stopping, for at least half an hour. Figured herself someplace out in the desert. Some of the sharp stings to the bottom of her feet were probably cactus needles. And prayed there were no rattlesnakes or scorpions in their direct path.

Or maybe that there were and they'd attack the man holding a gun to her ribs while he dragged her as though she was an inanimate object.

He never spoke.

And neither did she. She wouldn't give him the satisfaction of hearing her pain.

Her foot hit a bigger rock, with a pointed tip, and she felt the skin on her heel tear. As though that rip went up through her entire body, she filled with terror. And then anger.

Anger at the man who thought he could treat her as he was.

Anger at whoever had hurt her baby sister.

And livid anger on behalf of any baby that might be in wrong hands.

For a second she wondered if maybe help would come. Thought of elfin man, who she'd been seeking in the garden, stumbled and choked as the grip around her neck tightened.

She had to get free. To overtake a person who was easily half a foot taller than she was. And twice as bulky.

Thirsty, hot, desperate, starting to feel a little delirious, the nurse in her told her she was suffering from shock, not exposure, while she just kept trying to find ways to turn fear into anger.

Her captor stopped again just then, while she was refilling her well of venom, and she had no conscious thought. No plan. No sight. But her butt had been bumping against his thigh forever. And that made her mad.

Swinging around suddenly, she freed her right kidney from the barrel of the gun, brought her heel up to where she thought his groin would be and landed a blow with all of the force she had in her.

The gun went off.

Chapter 11

House Security was combing the grounds, cabins and rooms in the resort as well, having jumped immediately when Paul ran in reporting that his partner was missing.

His partner—no insinuation intended, just easier in the moment than taking time to explain his complicated relationship with Haley. Within five minutes uniformed men and women were dispatched to their search areas, with Paul invited to join in. He chose to set out on his own, looking for he knew not what, but trusting he'd know if he found it.

On foot—because if Haley had been taken by car, she was already too far away for him to catch up to her and he'd have more of a chance finding a clue at the abduction spot—he'd just started up the dirt part of the road into the ranch when he heard the gunshot.

And he knew.

As security crew who were closest ran toward the small pine orchard bordering one side of the ranch, he ran back for the SUV and headed across the desert, slightly ahead of the off-road vehicles filled with security guards who were also heading toward the pines.

One shot.

Chances of survival were better if there was only one hole to repair. As long as no vital organs were hit.

God, if he'd lost her…

A world without Haley in it…

He missed a dip in the hard ground, bottomed out and sprang up out of the seat, hitting his head on the roof of the vehicle.

Because, once again, he was losing his mind.

Over Haley.

Haley. She had to be okay.

The shot might not have had anything to do with her disappearance.

Pulling up just behind the first security guard who'd made it to the scene—a young man in his twenties who'd been almost on the grove when the shot had been fired—Paul was out of his vehicle in time to hear the guy say, "I found the gun! No one's here."

Paul skidded to a halt beside him, seeing the gun on the ground, the desert landscape giving up no other clues. Rocks were scattered, but that was normal. Nothing soft enough there for footprints.

Most importantly to Paul, he saw no blood. And didn't hang around for scuttlebutt. Back at the SUV, he opened his door, hand reaching with the key to the ignition before he'd even taken a step up—and nearly dropped it as he saw the woman huddled on the passenger floor, looking up at him with a mixture of fear, anger…and pride in her eyes.

"I kicked him in the balls," she said. And then her chin started to tremble.

Inside the car in seconds, he instantly backed around to head out of the desert, and away from Sister's Ranch. Paul reached for Haley, took the hand she reached out to him, but when she would have scooted up the seat, shook his head.

Him. She'd kicked him in the balls.

The bastard better have had his pants on at the time… Haley's shorts were intact, her shirt, too.

"Are you okay?"

"Fine. Except my feet which sting like hell. And I'm probably going to have a stiff neck." She licked her lips and he handed her a bottle of water. She sipped, swallowed and sipped again. Not greedily. Just steadily.

But the bottle was shaking in her hand.

"We should get you to the ER, just in case."

"I'm an ER nurse, Paul. I know I'm fine. Other than being scared out of my wits, having to walk barefoot in the desert with my hands tied and blindfolded, , having my hair pulled and an arm clutched around my neck, nothing happened. I didn't fall. No bones are broken."

"The gunshot…" He could still hear the sound reverberating…

"It went off as he went down when I kicked him. I scraped by head against the ground to get the blindfold off and ran back toward the parking lot before he had a chance to pick the gun back up, and I have no idea what he did after that. For all I know, he's still back there, cursing me…"

"We found the gun. No one was there."

"He was wearing gloves."

So there'd be no fingerprints. And chances were, no valid registration of the weapon, either.

"Did you get a good look at him?" At least. Please.

"Not a glimpse. He had me blindfolded before we were even out of the garden. But I did see a guy that looked like Jeanine's description of elfin guy. Hoodie and all. That's why I was in the garden."

There were smudges around her eyes and her temples were red. The blindfold explained that.

He noticed chafing on her wrists, and anger boiled. He tempered it with a deep breath.

He'd get the guy. One step at a time.

After putting a call in to Sister's Ranch Security to let them know he had his partner and was heading in to the Pahrump police to make a statement, he called the police with an update and let them know he was bringing Haley in.

He'd wanted off the property before anyone attempted to convince him not to get the police involved. He didn't know that they would. He just knew he wasn't taking any chances.

By then he'd hit pavement.

"And your wrists?" he asked, reaching a hand over to help her up onto the seat. No way a guy who'd just had his gonads sent up inside him would have been able to run a mile and half to the road in the time that Paul had driven it.

"I cut the plastic tie on the edge of the wheel well before I climbed back in the car. Thank you for leaving it unlocked, by the way…"

"You saw me drive up?"

"Yeah. But no way I was going to expose myself to

you or anyone and make a fuss while the guy was still on the loose. I didn't want my discovery to give him a chance to get away."

Which he apparently had done anyway.

Still, smart move on her part. She'd kept her head about her.

And he couldn't help but admire the hell out of that.

Haley didn't argue with Paul's suggestion that they get the hell out of Pahrump. As soon as they were finished at the police station—with a promise from them to scour every inch of the crime scene—they were on the highway back to Vegas.

While it seemed as though days had passed, it was just a little past noon. And they had a baby to find.

All Haley could think about was finishing their quest.

The thought of a baby possibly waiting at the end of this, a little body she could hold, a life that could be joined to hers forever, even through occasional visits, kept her drive on high.

And maybe, just maybe, she wasn't ready to say goodbye to Paul just yet.

She would. There was no doubt in her mind about that. But after the look in his eyes when he'd first seen her in the SUV, the unabridged flash of emotion, she knew they had things to clear up between them before they parted for the rest of their lives.

Feelings that needed to be hashed out, or, perhaps, the second time around, talked out, and put to rest. They'd both been so eager to be out of the marriage that they'd signed on lines, no one fighting for anything, and run in opposite directions. Her to a more modest home in Santa Barbara. And him to various places, until he'd ended up in Mission Viejo.

And, maybe, they both had scars that needed to be healed before they could move on to healthy relationships with other partners.

For the moment, she wanted to get to Vegas to check into a different hotel, one that wasn't sitting all alone out in the desert, with adjoining rooms, and take a shower before they got on with the day's business.

"How sure are you that you saw the guy with the dark gray hoodie, or just saw someone in shadow that made him look shrouded in gray?" They weren't five minutes out of Pahrump before Paul's questions started.

She was surprised it had taken him five seconds out of the police station where he'd seemed to commit to memory every word of the report she'd given there.

"About seventy percent," she told him. "At first, I thought I was seeing things, but I caught a second glimpse. He had a head covering of some kind. Who wears a hoodie in June? It has to be the same guy, right?"

"He could have been bald. And in the shadows, with the bright sun affecting your vision, it could have looked like he had a hoodie on."

She could see the logic in what he was saying. And still felt like there was a good chance she'd seen the dark gray hoodie.

"It's partially important because who you thought was the gray hoodie guy could have been your abductor."

"That guy wasn't out to warn me to be careful, fearing that he'd brought danger upon me."

"I'm not suggesting it was the same person, only

that the man you saw today could have been the one who abducted you."

Now that made more sense. It wasn't like the garden had been overrun with people. She'd thought herself the only one there—in pursuit of the shadowy gray, elfin man.

"The guy who took me, he was bigger than the man I saw," she said slowly, thinking about it. She shivered, weathering a huge shard of fear as it surged through her. Wanted to duck again.

And didn't.

She wasn't going to let the bad guys win. She had Paul on her side and he was the best there was. They were going to find out what was going on and get justice for Kelsey.

And for any child she might have had.

"It's possible he took you for sexual purposes." Paul's tone was softer, but no less tough, as he put the statement out there. He glanced her way. She felt his warmth.

And had to brace herself against an onslaught of emotion.

She could have been raped. She hadn't been.

She wasn't going to borrow tragedy. But she knew what he was telling her.

The abduction might not have had anything to do with Kelsey's situation.

It could have been as simple, and as ugly, as *wrong time, wrong place*. Particularly considering she'd been a woman alone at a brothel. There would always be those who thought they should have for free what others paid for. In the sex world and in all other business worlds, too.

Paul had told her on the way to the police station that

he'd found no evidence at all to support a theory that Kelsey had ever been at Sister's Ranch.

"I'm just glad to know that Kelsey wasn't working there," she said aloud, to solidify the direction her thoughts were taking.

"We don't know that for sure." His tone sounded warning. She knew he was doing his job—the job she needed him to do—but wished he'd quit thinking the worst of her sister.

The two facts didn't sit well together. If he only thought rosy positive thoughts of Kelsey, he wasn't likely to find her, either.

"People don't just disappear, as Kelsey did over the past year, when their lives are above reproach," he continued in a tone different than any that he'd used in the past two days. He wasn't sparing her feelings. "They disappear because they don't want to be seen for some reason. Usually criminal reasons."

She nodded. She believed him.

And she still hated that he hadn't ever been able to love her family —in spite of Kelsey's and Gloria's sometimes difficult behaviors.

But then, she hadn't ever warmed up to his father all that much, either.

Just two of the many strikes against them.

The missing puzzle pieces had to be in the shell companies. As soon as they were settled into a suite in Vegas, Paul focused on the financials. One shell company led to another which ended in the Cayman Islands. Following the second, not for money, as Winchester had, but to see what the business was moving around in terms of goods, or properties, maybe he'd land on an area of business—either physical or interest-wise. Like textiles. Or IT equipment. Maybe they managed cleaning services. He'd seen a cleaning service charge to the company that had paid Kelsey's rent and mortgage. He'd already followed up on that. After he'd made a few phone calls, he'd discovered that they had been hired to clean the home before the new owner moved in, but never actually met the owner. A key to the vacant home had been left in an envelope for them under the doormat.

But the other shell companies that also seemed to empty into the Cayman Islands account…he had no legal way into their records, but he could investigate their names, as he had the first one, then run a search and see if anything came up.

He wouldn't find the owner, but with many of their other leads dead for the moment, he'd be happy just to know where to possibly start looking. He wasn't done with Thomas Gladstone, either. The guy had capitulated too easily.

Which was believable if his father really had put him on a tight leash. Something that would be easy enough for Paul to find out with a single phone call to the old man. But not until he was sure he wouldn't be sending evidence further underground.

For all he knew, the Gladstones were in deep—and not separately, but together.

Maybe Kelsey had gone from son to father and the baby had been Thomas's half sibling… Lord knew, Kelsey Carmichael had Daddy issues. Had come by them quite honestly. Her old man had been a piece of work…

Had Kelsey's father even attended her funeral?

He could just imagine how that would have gone over with Gloria present...

"Paul!"

Phone to her ear, Haley burst through the door between their two rooms. "Turn on the TV," she said, grabbing the remote and turning it on herself. She'd showered, put on a pair of jeans and a white short-sleeved top, in spite of the 103-degree temperature outside, and was wearing the soft cotton socks they'd purchased, along with the antibiotic cream and bandages from shops downstairs.

The lone flip flop he'd carried from the garden had been thrown in the trash when the Pahrump police had determined that it wasn't evidence as no one but Haley had touched it during the crime and they knew where she'd been. As soon as she was ready, they were supposed to be going to another shop in the hall of shops between their resort and the next one, to pick up a few more things for both of them to wear. And then on to wherever he was taking them next.

She'd been swinging one knee impatiently as she stood there on one foot, with the other barely touching the floor by the toes, as she worked the remote.

"There," she said. "I've got it." Apparently meant for her caller as he had no idea what she had. Or why.

Based on the tense expression she was wearing, he wanted to know, though, and stood up, fully focused on the television screen as a commercial played.

"Jeanine just 911'd me. Said that she was watching the news, saw a preview of an upcoming story..." she said to Paul and then, into the phone, "J? I'm putting you on speaker phone."

She pushed the button. Jeanine didn't greet him. Did

he say hello to his ex-wife's best friend? They'd been close once upon a time. In the end, she'd hated him.

At least it had felt that way.

"Hey, Jeanine." The words pushed out of him.

"Hi, Paul."

That was it. No small talk.

But it was enough.

"A top story tonight with a sad ending... Noah Willoughby, heir to his deceased father's fashion label empire, a business currently being run by his mother, was found dead in his apartment overnight..."

"That's him!" Jeanine's voice came loudly over the phone. Filled with tension. Fear. "As soon as I saw his picture flash up as the coming-up-next story, I knew it was him. I swear to you, that's the guy I saw, the one who said he was afraid he'd led them to Haley..."

"Twenty-one-year-old Noah graduated from University of Las Vegas last month and was set to head up the production division of his father's label called Charles! next month. Noah's been working for the Charles corporation since his sixteenth birthday, starting out on the production line. His father, Charles Willoughby, also a racecar driver, died on the track when Noah was a freshman in high school. Noah was at the track with him and witnessed the crash..."

Paul's brain picked off words, key information, as though he were snatching them out of the air, bringing them to his mental table.

Associations he'd seek out. He didn't focus on the young face splashed on the screen, but he noted, quite clearly, that if it was Noah who'd traveled to California to warn Haley, and then he'd ended up dead, the chances of her being in very serious danger had escalated.

And that there could very likely be a baby.

Just as he acknowledged that the news was only going to broadcast the good stuff about the kid. He had to get to the real life, find out who and what Noah had been involved with outside his father's business.

And find out if Charles! had ever used the services of a lawyer named Grainger in Pahrump, and what connections, if any, there were between Thomas Gladstone and Noah Willoughby.

It was also possible that Jeanine was wrong.

"I thought you didn't get a good look at his face," he said now.

"I didn't think I did. Not that I could describe for the police. But when I saw him, I recognized him immediately. It's his eyes. I can't describe them, but I recognize them. And the forehead and bridge of his nose. They remind me of that guy who played Peter Pan. That's probably why he seemed elfin to me. It's him."

She was talking quickly, more like expressing aloud her internal free thinking, but the Jeanine Paul knew had been anything but a drama queen. She'd taken everything in stride. Too much probably.

Which was what had drawn her and Haley together.

"While cause of death won't be known until after an autopsy, a person at the scene, speaking with anonymity, said that it looked like he'd overdosed…"

Paul's internal sirens started ringing and, spinning around, he got to work.

He had a baby to find.

An abductor to find.

A potential killer to find.

And an ex-wife to protect.

Chapter 12

Her neck was stiff. Her feet stung, but with the salve she'd put on them, coupled with the cotton socks that had kept them moist, but breathable, for an hour, they were surprisingly walkable. With no deep cuts or punctures, she'd gotten lucky. It helped that the flip-flops she'd bought had thick yoga mat bottoms on them. She'd paid more than she ordinarily would for a pair of sandals, but Haley didn't even blink about that part. Picking them up in black, and white, too.

Money meant nothing to her at the moment, as evidenced by the new black cotton shorts she was wearing with a white tank that hung loosely down to her waistband. There were a couple of other outfits in the shopping bag she'd left in her room. They'd come back only long enough for her to change; no way was she taking time to remove more tags and put clothes away in her suitcase.

She'd have gone out in her jeans and the heels she'd bought the night before, just to get going sooner, but Paul had suggested that it would be better if she blended in more with the Strip's thousands of tourists. Wearing jeans in temperatures over a hundred could make her an easy spot. And she couldn't run in the heels.

That last comment had been sobering. Reminding her that they were facing impossibly high stakes. Taking on the moneyed world of Vegas to find something that someone didn't want found.

Paul had used his own moneyed influence to have a new car waiting for them when they got downstairs. He'd purchased it, another SUV, so it had temporary tags that wouldn't be traceable to anyone until at least sometime the next day, maybe longer, depending on how quickly the paperwork and DMV registration happened. The new vehicle was midnight blue.

He was donating the black one to a home for boys in Vegas, taking the suggestion from the dealership owner who delivered the new vehicle to the hotel.

The list of people the Charles! corporation was associated with, or had ever had a run-in with, or been to a party with, was seemingly nonending. The chances of Thomas Gladstone and Noah having come into contact was highly likely.

Paul had explained that he was zeroing in on Noah Willoughby himself, first. Before they'd left the hotel room the last time, he'd been on the phone and had told Haley that he'd used his own access to friends in high places, which vetted a call to the local coroner who admitted that Noah's cause of death was definitely an overdose. And it didn't look like an accidental one.

Added to the amount of drugs in his system, and a

suspicious-looking injection site, was the fact that while the kid had had a drug problem in high school, following his father's death, he'd been clean ever since.

"This first place we're going, Ambrosino's, why is it first?" They were running out of time and the only way to get the job done was to tamp down emotion and focus. A lesson she'd learned from Paul. In the past and during their current association as well.

After an hour on the internet, he'd emailed the list of their next stops to her, asking her to go over it and see if anything sounded familiar, or prompted a memory of something Kelsey might have said in one of their phone conversations.

With disappointment, bordering on despair, she'd recognized nothing, but had downloaded the list to her phone with a self-order to focus.

"A social media post showed a posthumous honoring of Charles Willoughby there this past year. A young man who'd been recipient of a scholarship from a program financed by Charles! was just hired by NASA, and that, among other ongoing accomplishments from the elder Willoughby's life, was highlighted..."

All of which was heartwarming, but what it had to do with Kelsey or...

"It makes sense that the Willoughbys would have chosen a favorite place, a place that had been frequented by the family enough to feel like home to them, to host such an evening."

"They'll likely know a lot about Noah," she translated, nodding.

"And family history. I'm hoping that someone there will be willing to speak with us and you might be better suited to make that happen."

"Taking the family angle." She nodded. "Me being Kelsey's sister, and her being recently deceased."

"I was thinking more that depending on how close Kelsey and Noah were, she might have been there before, and you, as her sister, are taking a nonthreatening look out of love, just to learn all you can about her life in Vegas, which makes them feel safe to be chatty..."

Truth. Without bringing in the drama.

Haley wasn't sure about the chances of either of them pulling that off, especially with the long line of dead ends they'd run into, the urgency pushing at her back and the butterflies in her stomach, but she liked the sound of it.

She liked working side by side with Paul, too.

Liked being with him without all of their crap getting in the way.

And was beginning to think that maybe, when the job was done, they could find a way to become friends.

Or, at the very least, to stay in contact with each other now and then.

Kelsey would like that.

Until the divorce, she'd been fond of Paul.

"Yeah, I know her...knew her. Noah... God rest his soul...told me she'd passed." The older woman with a white apron tied around her jolly-looking belly glanced up from the photo Haley had just shown her and motioned Paul and Haley toward a table off in a little alcove in the darkened room. A guest could easily get lost in time inside Ambrosino's. Going back years...with the photos of Rat Pack associates on the walls, red real-leather-padded booth benches and solid cherry tables.

And going back hours, too, as, even at three in the afternoon, it looked like nighttime.

Cozy nighttime. Family dinner nighttime. Friends getting together to laugh over good food and wine type of nighttime.

Paul followed Haley's lead and took the seat he'd been shown at the table. Haley's presence, her plea to the maître d' at the reception desk, had netted them the chance to speak to the head chef who'd been cooking for the Ambrosino family for over forty years. A feat which would have taken him longer than Haley to accomplish, if he'd been able to succeed there at all.

Sometimes credentials tore down walls, other times, they erected them.

"Did you know her well?" Haley asked Maria, leaning in toward the woman, her ponytail falling over her right shoulder—giving Paul an expected glimpse of her neck, and the bruise that was forming just beneath her left ear. Fury filled him, swift and sharp. Unlike any he'd felt before that morning when he'd known for certain that Haley had been abducted.

"…sweet and funny, and so good to our Noah…" With a moment of mental blankness, he returned to the conversation at hand, the important moment that was happening, and realized that he'd actually missed part of a critical interview.

Heat moved up his neck to his face, making it difficult for him to sit calmly, to sit at all. And he couldn't pretend that he wasn't in danger from a foe completely separate from the one they were seeking. He had to get the job done. To know Haley was safe.

And then he had to get out—of her space, of her

life—before she sucked him back under the spell that had nearly unhinged him the first time.

"I don't know how he met her—he just started showing up with her now and then, swearing that there was nothing between them, when I teased him, but I could tell he was sweet on her. Didn't matter to me that she was a bit older than he was. These days, who cares?" She threw up her hands, both palms to the ceiling. "He said they were friends, helping each other out some, and I know she definitely helped him, going with him to the first few Charles! black tie functions he had to attend as an official member of the board. I know 'cause they came back here afterward for ice cream. My boy all grown up, meeting his grown-up business responsibilities, and then sitting in his tux eating ice cream!" She chortled. And then sobered, her eyes, capped by wiry gray bangs, filled with tears. "I can't believe he's really gone," she said, shaking her head. Then, after pulling a handkerchief out of her pocket and wiping her face, said, "And don't listen to what they say about him. I saw the news. Ain't no way that boy took drugs and killed himself. He didn't even drink alcohol, not even for his twenty-first birthday, he was so afraid of kicking in an addiction. That's why they came here for ice cream…"

With a feeling that the woman was going to go on for hours—hours that could be critical to finding a baby alive—Paul said, "When was the last time you saw Kelsey?"

The chef frowned. "Kelsey?" she asked looking almost affronted. "Who's Kelsey?"

"She is," Haley held the picture back in front of

Maria. "You said you knew her." With a glance in his direction, Haley signaled distress.

"I do know her!" Maria tapped the photo gently. "But that's not Kelsey. The last time I saw that woman was about six months ago. But her name's Maya. Maya Ambrose. I know because we teased her that her name was so much like Ambrosino's!"

Click. Click. Click.

Pieces latching into place. Not to form a picture yet. But giving him a solid side of border—and a need to get back to his computer.

Maya Ambrose. Like Ambrosino's.

A fake name? Taken from a family place beloved by her lover?

Her lover. A man who'd risked his life to warn Haley—someone Kelsey would have told him about, as the younger sister had clearly depended on her older sister for every bit of strength she'd ever had—that Kelsey had had a baby that was in wrong hands.

Who better to know that than the man who'd fathered the child?

Who'd be more likely to risk his life, than the child's father?

Where Gladstone factored into it all—and a lawyer in Pahrump—he had no idea, but one thing was for certain.

The visit to Ambrosino's had been a game changer.

Flying high with hope, Haley wanted to hug Paul as they left Ambrosino's. She flung her arm through his, pulling it to her side as she always had in the past, without thinking about what she was doing.

As soon as his warmth pressed against her, she

dropped her arm, stepped away, but she couldn't undo what she'd done. Her side had felt him. Remembered him. Sent the message through the rest of her body. Which responded immediately. Strongly.

It missed him.

He didn't show any reaction to her blunder, but she didn't really look at him, either. Just started babbling about everything they'd just heard. Repeating herself more than once as she exclaimed over the breakthrough. The reason they hadn't been able to find records of Haley for the past year.

She'd been using an assumed identity.

"At least we know she was here," she said as Paul pulled out into traffic on his way to the next address on their list. A club that Noah had frequented, as found on the social media site of another young man who'd seen him there. Not someone he'd known, just someone with a quasi-celebrity sighting.

"But what I don't get is why they had to hide a baby. I mean, I know there's an age difference, but Kels was only twenty-eight. Seven years isn't scandalous even for a conservative family, if they are one. Especially not in Las Vegas."

"And that's one of the reasons we're continuing to look into Noah right now. If we knew why he might need to hide Kelsey's pregnancy, then we'd probably know who was behind this, which might lead us right to the child. If there is one. And Noah's the father."

So many ifs. Too many.

But they were closer. Getting answers. She had to keep her mind positive. Have hope. Believe they were going to find the answers they sought.

And hopefully ensure a child's future and safety.

"The fact that Maria hadn't seen her in six months… that fits a pregnancy timeline."

There was a baby. She just knew it.

At the moment, considering her near abduction and Noah's suspicious death, not to mention his warnings to Haley, the presence of a baby scared her more than anything. Because if there was one, it was looking more and more as though it was in "wrong hands." They had to find the little one before it was too late. If it wasn't already too late…

Stark cold stabbed her stomach, her heart, took her air, and she stared straight ahead. Caught in an emotional abyss…

"I'm going to hit these next two places because they're close by and could be pertinent if he took Kelsey there, and then I need a few minutes on my computer to look for Maya, see what kind of hits I get typing in her name with Noah's. There might be a much shorter trail to follow," Paul's words pulled her out of the vortex and her lungs filled with air. Sucking greedily she nodded. Grateful to have him in charge. She wanted to be strong.

Would be strong.

Had already been damned strong that morning.

And it was all getting to her, too.

As an ER nurse she was used to grueling long shifts on her feet, and had seen death. More of it than a lot of people. Deaths of children, even. But nothing in her life had prepared her for days on the road seeking, and running from, a killer.

"You're wondering why Kels changed her identity

aren't you?" she asked when the silence became more detrimental to her state of mind than conversation.

"Aren't you?" He didn't look her way, kept his attention where it needed to be, on the road, and around them, too. He was watching to see if they were being followed. The concentration, the constant checks in the mirror, the changing of lanes and sudden turns...they'd become so familiar she'd almost taken them for granted.

In just two days.

"I think if we know why she was hiding, or who she was hiding from, we'd be a lot closer to figuring out what went so horribly wrong."

"I'm guessing she was hiding from Gladstone."

She'd thought so. But, without proof, hadn't expected Paul to be forming conclusions. The fact that he had... scared her, too. Gladstone had given her the creeps the night before. Even when he'd been seemingly cowering. She wouldn't put it past him to have somehow orchestrated her abduction that morning.

"We lose all trace of Kelsey Carmichael about the time Gladstone quit using her credit card," Paul broke into her thoughts. "Which is when he claims to have been warned by an attorney from Pahrump to cease and desist. The timing's right," he said, as he pulled into the parking lot of an unremarkable building. Gray, not overly large, with no signage, it just kind of sat there.

"This is it," he told her, reaching for his door handle. "Since we have no idea what kind of club The Dream actually is, stick close to me. Let's do the couple thing, again. It worked well last night. And gives us a chance to stick close."

Nodding, Haley wet dry lips. Unbuckled her seat belt.

And focused on the only thing that made her feel good at the moment.

Sticking close to Paul.

The first thing they learned inside was that Noah Willoughby was gay. Paul hadn't seen that one coming. While Noah had been afraid to tell his mother, afraid she'd be disappointed that he wasn't going to give her the traditional family she'd always wanted, he'd been more worried about having to prove himself at the helm of Charles! Industries as a twenty-one-year-old, to add fighting his way in the diversity cycle at the same time.

His father had been in the fashion industry, but their investors were largely older men who'd been friends with Charles's father. Men of a different day who weren't as comfortable with the changing world.

Noah might not have found the courage to come out to his family, but he'd been firmly enmeshed in a lifestyle, and a family of friends, who'd supported his choices completely.

Maya among them.

"Not only was he not having a sexual relationship with Kels, he was in a three-year loving relationship with a man ten years his senior," Haley said, looking shell shocked, as they climbed back into the SUV just before five that Sunday afternoon.

It was 108 outside and she wasn't even sweating. How did she do that?

He felt like a sticky pig who'd rolled in the dirt.

And why would that matter? He'd looked and smelled a lot worse while on the hunt.

What was really bugging him, and shouldn't matter

as much as it did, was that he was disappointing Haley. Seemingly at every turn.

"This is how the job works, Hale," he said, subconsciously using his old nickname for her as he sought to raise her spirits, hearing it only as it came out of his mouth.

"If we knew everything, we'd know everything." As reassurance, his words sucked, but they were the truth of what he did every day of his life. The only way he succeeded was by finding out what he didn't know.

His truth.

If he knew everything, he'd know everything. Since he didn't, he didn't always get things right.

Like his life with her...

And the way he'd left.

"It's gratifying to hear that Kels was such a support to him," Haley said softly.

And his heart jumped sides on him. Aligning itself right there with hers.

"Her number one goal was to land a rich husband, but she also had a huge heart. It makes me feel good to know that she was there for Noah, not to gain herself a rich husband, but just to be a friend."

You had to admire a woman who could find a way up from the bottom of her barrel.

Haley had always been that way. Even in the emotional moments, she'd find the other side, find the good, or the better. How had he forgotten that part?

And yet... "Just because Noah wasn't having sex with her doesn't mean he wasn't supporting her," he had to remind his ex-wife. "I'm not trying to be mean, or unsupportive, or shed a bad light on Kelsey. Time's of an essence here, Haley, and we have to, *I* have to," he corrected, "look at what I know. It could be that Noah, in his attempt to hide his sexuality, had proposed to her, was maybe even planning to marry her. It's the type of thing I could see Kelsey agreeing to. Am I wrong?"

Her glare wasn't kind, and he was glad when she turned away. "No. You aren't wrong. I could see Kelsey agreeing to something like that." Her gaze swung back to him then, determined and fierce. "But that doesn't take away the fact that she was a good friend to him, giving him everything he needed, according to what we just heard. And…none of his friends in there mentioned that she was engaged. Don't you think they'd have said so if that was the case?"

Unless there was a reason to keep the fact hidden. "It could be that Noah was living a double life as well, and keeping the two more separate than his community in there knew. And that the shell company that paid for the house where we think Kels was living is somehow tied to Charles! or other Willoughby holdings."

"We're back to square one, though, on who fathered Kelsey's baby."

"I need to speak with Noah's mother. Obviously she knew Maya, since we know Maya went to company functions with Noah."

"She might not want to talk to us. Especially if she thinks that knowing Kelsey is what killed her son."

"And if Maya was as good a friend to Noah as we've heard, both in there," he pointed to the building they were still parked behind, "and at Ambrosino's, then it's possible she'd welcome a conversation. Either way, I have to try."

"It'll be best if I approach her…"

He agreed, but was disliking more and more having her on the front lines.

If something happened to Haley because he'd been distracted and missed something...

Then he'd never forgive himself. He'd already failed her once. Eight years before when he'd purposely been late for their anniversary dinner because, with the way they'd been fighting, the walls between them, he hadn't felt like there was much to celebrate. He'd refused to tell her where he'd been. He'd needed her to trust him. To show him that their love was real. Instead, she'd doubted him. Told him that maybe it was best that he leave.

At that point he'd been relieved to do so. He'd checked himself into a hotel and when she'd called later, asking if he was alone, he hadn't answered. Of course he'd been alone, sitting in his underwear watching television and feeling like a total loser. A failure.

Doubting Haley's motives for marrying him. How could they fight like they did, how could she argue with him so much, if she truly loved him?

He'd figured that if she wanted to think he was cheating, if blaming him made it easier for her to let go of him, then that was on her. There was no marriage to save without trust.

But he should have been honest with her. He should have stayed and tried to work on things. Instead, he'd booked. Bailed. He'd taken the easier way out.

And he'd carried the guilt around with him ever since.

She'd called him for help. She'd given him a chance to redeem himself.

One way or the other, he was going to have to get it right.

Chapter 13

They were shown into a large open-floor-plan living area at the Willoughby estate just before six on Sunday night. Paul had made a couple of calls, he didn't say to who and Haley didn't ask, and they'd been given fifteen minutes of the grieving woman's time. She'd yet to join them.

Shivering, Haley wished she'd chosen a seat beside Paul on the gray leather couch instead of the armchair perpendicular to it. With the way she'd been starting to rely on him, to think of him as a friend even, she'd needed to put some more distance between them.

Their time at the estate was brief, but it was bound to be emotional and that was something she was going to have to deal with, and contain, on her own.

Mrs. Willoughby, when she arrived, was well-dressed in a brown tweed suit, professional looking, made up, with her shoulder-length blond hair gracing shoulders held with pride. Or seeming so, anyway.

As Lenora Willoughby drew closer, choosing the armchair opposite Haley's, Haley had another impression of middle-aged woman entirely. The woman's eyes were well made up—but puffy. The lines on her face were camouflaged by expertly applied makeup, but they were still there. Still speaking their own truth.

She cried as she spoke about her son. About how she'd known he was gay, but had been waiting for him to be ready to come out with her—and the rest of society. She'd loved him. His sexual preference didn't change that at all, nor did it change how she saw him. "I thought I was being the most supportive by giving him space," she said. "The journey was his. I didn't want to make it more uncomfortable for him, pushing my way in if he wasn't ready…"

Tears flooding her eyes, Haley nodded, wishing she could take the woman in her arms and hug her. Parental pain was something very familiar to her. She dealt with every day at work. No mother or father wanted to see their child suffer—even if the suffering was just a blip in time.

Lenora's suffering was infinite. There'd be some healing, but the scar, the changed life, was permanent.

"He knew you loved him," she said. "And that love gave him the strength to not only admit to himself who he was, but to reach out for fulfillment, for love. Did you know he had a partner?" she asked. The story wasn't technically hers to tell, but comforting parents through the death of their child was something she knew how to do.

Long term, Lenora would hopefully get counseling.

"I suspected," she said. "Maya was always so respectful of him, physically. She didn't hang on him, or act in any way like they were lovers."

Haley's heart sank. She'd known Noah wasn't the baby's father, but a part of her heart had still hoped… that maybe.

"How well did you know my sister?" Haley asked, since Lenora had introduced the subject. Since Kelsey was the reason she was there.

"Not all that well, I'm sorry to say," the older woman said, her expression filled with a compassion that made Haley tear up again. In her universe, she was the compassion giver. Other than from Jeanine, it didn't often come back at her. "I know that she was good to my son, and that he was quite fond of her, but I only met her a few times. He never brought her here, but then he only came home a couple of times a week to have dinner with me."

Another thud to Haley's heart. When she'd first walked in she'd imagined that she was seeing a place Kelsey had visited.

"You don't know where she was living?"

"Yes, in a house on Calypso. I've never been there, but Noah mentioned it once, when we were talking about the neighborhood."

Heart thudding, Haley couldn't help a glance at Paul. The house they'd been by the day before, the one with the wreath, had been on Calypso. With a return gaze that held steady calm, he reminded her to remain so.

"Were you aware that she also went by another name?" Haley asked, afraid she was getting into deep waters, but also afraid to lose an opportunity to find out whatever Lenora might know.

The woman frowned, cocked her head. "Noooo. Why would she do that?"

"That's one of the things we'd like to know," Paul interjected, like a doctor soothing a jittery patient. "We didn't know either, until just recently."

Lenora studied him for a long moment. "Who exactly are you?" she asked. "Jonathon vouched for you when he relayed your message about a visit, but he never said exactly how he knows you."

Haley had no idea who Jonathon was.

"I'm a friend of Haley's and... Maya's," he said. And her brain computed that she was not to mention Kelsey's real name.

"Paul and I have been friends since college," she piped in.

"And Jonathon handled some work for my father once," Paul added.

The woman nodded, seemingly satisfied, turned back to Haley. "I had no idea, until Jonathon called, that your sister, Maya," she nodded toward Haley, "has... died...too." Her lower lip trembled and she unfolded a tissue she'd been holding bunched in her fist to dab at her eyes.

"In a car accident. Last month."

"Noah never mentioned that she'd died. I hadn't seen Maya in months. He'd quit bringing her around, so maybe they weren't as close anymore?" Lenora frowned again. "Though come to think of it, Noah didn't mention much of anything here lately. He'd been so busy with starting at the company, moving into his office, and...he'd been more and more tense... I figured it had to do with starting his new life under a falsehood, pretending to be straight. I'd actually hoped he was on the verge of talking to me about it so I could encourage him to be honest and proud and let himself be happy. It's what his father would have done. And what I wanted for him, too."

"Do you think he'd have had some pushback from the board?"

Her shrug seemed comfortable on her. "Probably. We sell high end men's clothes. Some would have said that Noah was set to be the new face of Charles! and that being so, the public's view of the brand could change. But Noah and I together owned sixty percent of the company so we'd have been able to deal with that. If people's perceptions changed, that's all for the better. Our line is changing, too. That's how fashion works."

"So…someone who might have known that Noah was gay, and who had stake in the company, could have had a problem with him coming out?" Paul's question was pointed.

Sitting up straighter, shoulders back, Lenora faced him. "What are you saying? You think someone hurt Noah? That his death wasn't accidental?" The change in Lenora was obvious. Even her tone was more like the president of a board than a grieving mother.

Paul glanced from Haley to the woman, seemed to make some kind of decision as he scooted more to the edge of the couch, facing Lenora.

"I'm a licensed law enforcement officer," he told her. "I work out of California as a skip tracer, and I'm Haley's ex-husband."

Wow. Just wow. When Haley realized her mouth was hanging open, she closed it. Met Lenora's gaze openly, and said, "Noah came to my home a few days ago. He left a note on my door that…led me to believe that my sister's death might not be an accident. He returned the next afternoon to say only that he might have lead them to me."

"Lead who to you?"

She shook her head. "We have no idea," she said. "At first, we weren't even sure his warnings were legitimate. The local police thought I was being pranked. But I couldn't take that chance and called Paul. We didn't even know who Noah was until today when we saw him on the news. My friend, who saw Noah at my house, recognized him."

"Noah was in California? On Friday?"

Haley nodded.

"I didn't even know he'd left town."

"Maybe he didn't want to bring any danger home to you."

The woman nodded, clearly distraught now, though holding up, too. "I was finding it hard to accept that he'd gone back to using drugs. Couldn't believe it actually. I know they were doing an autopsy, but was trying to brace myself for the confirmation."

"I can't tell you any differently," Paul said. "I'm not working on your son's case." His tone soft, he poured compassionate warmth over the woman and for a split second, Haley was jealous of her. "This was all reported to the police in Santa Barbara, and now here," Paul continued. "I have no proof of anything. It's possible that Noah was tripping when he went to see Haley, and was imagining whatever danger he perceived to be there."

"That's why Jonathon vouched for you, though. Because you think there's more going on."

He nodded.

So did Lenora.

If Gladstone was involved, and now the Willough-bys, someone in Pahrump, maybe Sister's Ranch, who else were they fighting?

Up against so much power and money, did they even have a chance?

Fighting panic again, Haley cried inside for her baby sister, for the child her sister might have carried.

And was fearing for its life.

"Who's Jonathon?" The question came at Paul before he'd even started his new blue SUV sitting in the circular drive in front of Lenora Willoughby's home. His mind spinning, he needed quiet time. Not questions.

And said, "Retired chief of police. I've never met him. Didn't speak to him. But someone I have worked with on the force took my call at face value, knew that Jonathon knew the Willoughbys and got us an interview. In exchange, if I find anything actionable pertaining to Noah Willoughby, I've agreed to turn it over to the police."

Something he would have done anyway.

"You've seemed to know your way around here well, and to know people. Did you live here for a while?"

An odd question coming from the woman with whom he'd expected to spend his entire life. But, considering their circumstances, a fair one. It just hit him uncomfortably. Haley seeming to know him so well, and not knowing him.

"Live, no. I've been here a fair amount."

The constant barrage of Haley feelings had to stop, though he didn't know how to make that happen. He had to find a way.

He had work to do.

A job that, if he failed, would haunt him for the rest of his life.

And so, as they returned to the luxurious Strip hotel he'd deemed safest for them to occupy for the night—one too filled with moneyed tourists for someone in the Vegas money business to risk having a murder in—he excused himself immediately to his room, explaining, quite legitimately, that he needed computer time.

Before long, he was fully engrossed in following trails and hours passed before he'd known they'd gone. Sometime around eleven he sent a text to Haley, letting her know to be ready to head out at seven in the morning, and through the small crack opening of the door adjoining their rooms, heard something drop. Another minute passed before his phone binged her affirmative response.

She was awake, even if he'd just woken her. He had to stop himself from pushing open her door, sharing the things he'd found.

His news would wait until morning, but if he went into her room, saw her in bed, there were other things that might not wait.

Like his body's need to find the sustenance that only hers could give…

He shook his head, stepped out of his pants and underwear and took himself into a cold shower.

When he returned to his room, his phone showed another text.

Sleep good.

The last thing they'd said to each other every single night of their marriage. Even the nights when they'd been raging mad.

Sleep good, he texted back.

Even though he knew he shouldn't have done so.

In new red shorts, a white button-up sleeveless blouse and her white flip-flops, Haley was ready and waiting when Paul knocked lightly on the door between their rooms the next morning. Her heart jumped when she saw him standing there looking so...utterly manly...in gray-white-and-black-plaid shorts, a gray shirt that, as always, covered the gun she knew was attached at his waist, and tennis shoes.

As liquid desire stroked through her, she broke eye contact and reached for her over-the-shoulder bag and suitcase. "I'm assuming we're taking everything with us as before?" she asked, and at his nod, followed him through his room and out the door.

She understood the process.

And consumed with worry for that baby.

Two people had been killed. She might have been a third...

And maybe that was why her body was overboard with desire for Paul's. Her psyche was fixated on the only emotion strong enough to distract her from fear. The explanation had flaws—one being that thinking of Paul naked scared her, too, because of the intensity of her wanting—but she went with the distraction theory.

She'd also started to comfort herself with the reminder that Kelsey might not have been pregnant at all. It was possible that there wasn't a baby in wrong hands, needing her to save its life.

Or any baby at all.

"I didn't get a list of visits," she finally said as they headed toward their vehicle in the multitiered covered parking garage, passing people pulling suitcases on their way into the casino as they left. He'd given her lists of where they were going every other time they'd headed out.

"I know." With a push of a button, Paul unlocked the SUV, threw both of their bags into the backseat—within reach, she knew—and waited for her to get in before he offered, "We'll grab some breakfast, first." He stopped, glanced in the rearview mirror, started the vehicle immediately and calmly pulled out.

"Are we being followed?" She didn't look in the mirror on the outside of her door, didn't want to make anything obvious.

"I'm not sure. Maybe."

Her tension flared, and yet anger did, too. "Who's behind all this?" she asked as much out of frustration as anything as he exited the parking garage with two other vehicles, one at least a rental with a couple inside because she'd noticed them, and the tags, as it exited before them. "Is it Gladstone?"

"Could be," he told her. "I'm sure he's involved somehow. And maybe someone connected to Willoughby. Someone wanted him silenced."

Her heart sank yet again as she realized that even after several hours of searching, he still didn't have answers. It wasn't fair to him that she be disappointed, but she was. Also not fair to him, but she'd wanted him to make miracles happen for her.

Not the kind of expectation she usually put on anyone.

Had she done that in the past, too? Expected so much more of him than a human being could produce?

Built fantasies and somehow believed they were true?

Was she her mother and sister, after all?

Haley's mind jumped and flitted as she remained silent, watching as Paul went through his turns and lane changes, either trying to lose a tail, or see if they had one. She wasn't interrupting. Alone the night before, she'd realized that having her around, distracting him, hadn't been fair to him, either. He was used to working alone.

Had become an expert by working alone...

She'd not only barged in with her request, with her desperate plea for him to take on her job, but she'd disrupted his process, too...

"I think I've lost him, for now, at least," he said. "But someone knew where we stayed last night. We won't be going back there."

He was expecting another night on the road. Chasing shadows?

"I'm sorry about the cheap food, but it's best at this point," he said as he pulled into a breakfast place with a drive-through window, stopping at the order speaker.

"You do what you need to do," she told him, ready to let him know that she'd get out of his way if it would make the going easier, wanting to believe she could, but gave him her breakfast order, instead. She liked bagels. And eggs. And they'd had fruit, too.

"I need to know that you're okay to hang tight for another tough day," he said after he'd placed their order and they were waiting in line to pay and collect their food. "Having you with me, Kelsey's grieving sister, her executor and beneficiary, and even occasional woman friend, has proven helpful and this day is going to be more of the same."

The way he said it, choosing his words with care,

watching her, sharpened her focus again. The hours alone the night before—they'd gotten to her.

But maybe because there'd been nothing constructive for her to do.

"Of course I'm okay. I'm always okay, Paul." He knew that, at least. She wasn't a woman who fell apart. At least not with anyone else around.

Sobbing in front of people—other than Jeanine—she couldn't do it. Just dried up.

Assessing her a moment longer, he nodded.

"Okay, I've found some things..."

And, as the line moved and he had to pay for their food, she knew. He'd been concerned about telling her. Which meant it was big. And probably not good.

Fine. She was ready. Having something real to focus on was better than listening to the doubts and suppositions floating around in her brain. The night of their second anniversary had taught her that much. By the time Paul had arrived home so late for the ruined anniversary dinner, she'd already been convinced he'd been with another woman before she'd asked him if he had.

As soon as she'd confirmed that he hadn't been in an accident, or detained by some kind of emergency, she'd gone straight for the other number one explanation on her mental list.

The other woman.

Paul handed a cardboard drink carrier to her, and then a bag, closing his window as he pulled away. Watching behind him.

"Is he back there?"

"Not that I can see."

"So what did you find?"

He reached for coffee. Taking his hint, she divvied

up the food, determined to show him she was up for the job, which included eating to keep her strength intact, took a bite and after a somewhat difficult swallow, took a coffee chaser and said, "Okay, now?"

Nodding, sandwich in hand as held the steering wheel, too, he kept his gaze toward the road in front of him as he said, "I found another shell company with dealings with the first one by searching Maya's name. Turns out Maya Ambrose has a credit score."

"With Kelsey's social security number?"

"Yes."

"So we're certain Kelsey assumed another identity. What we learned at the club yesterday was right. Maya Ambrose, Kelsey, was a good friend of Noah's." It wasn't news. She'd already been sure.

But to have things officially confirmed with fact— that was new to their process.

"The home on Calypso is owned by Maya Ambrose, though I had to dig deeper to find that. The public record wasn't available, which can happen when someone appeals to the courts with valid reason to have it not be so."

So there'd be record of the court order, right? But, also...

"She bought a house?"

"More like someone else did, but put it in her name, and is making payments on it through the shell company, I'm guessing to build Maya's credit."

"She intended to use that name indefinitely?"

"It sounds like it."

"She must have been really scared of something..."

"Or purposely hiding something from someone..."

"Like the fact that she was pregnant? And then, after the birth, the fact that she was raising a child?"

"We don't know that yet."

"But it's a logical theory."

"Yes."

She took a second bite of her bagel. And a third. Wanting all of the sustenance she could get.

"Where are we going now?"

"I got together with Winchester last night, the financial expert from Sierra's Web…"

She nodded, somewhat impatiently.

"The credit card we found in Maya Ambrose's name was paid for out of yet another shell company, and that company also made payments to an obstetrician here in Vegas. His office opens in about fifteen minutes."

Haley dropped her bagel.

She'd likely have spilled her coffee too, had she been holding it.

She tried to shut down emotion, but just couldn't. "Kelsey was seeing an obstetrician?"

"It appears that way."

Which meant that there was a baby.

Or, at least, that there had been.

She was an aunt.

"Hold on, Hale." Paul's voice was kind again. Too kind.

"What?"

"There's no birth registered in this state or any surrounding states, for Maya, either."

Dread rushed in. "You're telling me she aborted the baby?"

"There's no record of any payments to an abortion clinic."

Her mind clicked. She was a nurse. Knew some things. "How many times did she visit the obstetrician?"

"Six, according to payment records."

"Assuming she didn't start going until at least four weeks into her pregnancy, the baby would have been viable by then."

"And she might have given it up for adoption," he pointed out. Rightly so. She'd gone there first. But...

"If she was planning to do that, why go to all the trouble of permanently changing her identity?" The more likely scenario—that the baby had been taken from her—didn't bear speaking aloud at that point.

When he didn't answer, she knew that he'd already been down the same path. And reached the same conclusion. Noah's warning about wrong hands was suddenly loud and clear.

Crushing.

Unless...he obviously thought there'd still been time for Haley to save the baby or he wouldn't have risked his life coming to her. She told Paul so, and though he said nothing, didn't feed her hope, he didn't point out any other, opposing explanation, either.

He'd reached the same conclusion.

Anguish, elation, fear, excitement, gratitude, sorrow all warred inside her, and still she maintained.

She was an aunt.

Had been told her niece or nephew was in danger. Noah Willoughby, a twenty-one year old on the brink of his future had likely died trying to get the message to her.

Which meant she had to stay strong and continue fighting whatever stood in their way.

Mostly, it meant that she wasn't going to rest until that baby was found and secure.

Chapter 14

Dr. Zane Andrews was nice enough when Paul first asked to speak with him. In his white coat and gray dress pants, the doctor offered a polite smile at Haley as Paul introduced her as the sister of one of Andrews's clients.

"You do know that I can't give out patient information to anyone, including family members, unless said patient is a minor or under conservatorship and unable to make pertinent decisions on their own..."

Clearly, he didn't think he had any clients with a sister unknown to him that fell under either of those categories.

Based on the waiting room, the minimal reception area and the couple of doors they'd passed along the hallway, Andrews's practice was on the small side.

"I'm Maya Ambrose's sister," Haley said. "You might or might not have heard, but she died in a car accident last month..."

Paul had coached her on how he'd like to see the meeting transpire. She'd played it exactly as he'd laid it out for her.

Andrews's reaction did not. The man stiffened, his smile still there, but not accompanied by any sense of congeniality on the rest of his facial features. Including eyes that no longer met Paul's gaze head-on. He looked at Paul, and at Haley, but his gaze didn't seem to land.

"I'm very sorry to hear that, but this doesn't fall into any category that allows me to speak to you about any of my patients."

"But you do confirm that she was your patient?" Haley asked. "I'm the executor of her estate and if there's an heir we don't know about…"

Zing. She landed exactly as he'd hoped.

"I am not aware, offhand, of having a patient by that name. Did you check birth records? If indeed your sister gave birth, there'd be a public record…"

"We checked, and no there wasn't," Paul spoke up. He didn't like the vibe he was getting from Dr. Andrews. "But there's evidence of Maya having paid you for services," he said, having to go with plan B and push harder. The doctor's gaze sharpened as the smile fell from his face. His glance between Haley and Paul didn't bode well.

"I've been going over all her bills," Haley jumped in. "As executor and all…"

As an attempt to save the interview, the effort was good. Unfortunately, Paul was pretty sure that there was nothing to save. So didn't try.

"Look, we know she was a patient here, we have the dates she paid for visits and we know that the baby she was carrying had to be at least seven months along the last time she paid your bill with said credit card. All we're asking for is some information about the baby's birth, and, if it's something you can legally share, what happened to it."

"I can't help you with any of that."

"Did you deliver Maya's baby?"

The man opened his mouth to speak, shoved a hand into the pocket of his jacket, jingled whatever was in there. "I've told you, I'm not aware, offhand, of having a patient by that name."

Andrews knew something. Obviously he knew Maya. But more than that, he had information they needed. Paul would bet his life on it.

But the betting wasn't going to net him much. The man was nervous. Someone with more power than Paul or Haley had gotten to him.

He couldn't prove it. But the doctor's rehearsed responses had landed with a big thump in the middle of Paul's mental puzzle table.

He pulled out his credentials. "I'm a licensed officer of the law," he said. "Licensed in multiple states. I'm not here to give you any trouble. I just need some information."

Because the other option was to give up and go home and that wasn't going to happen.

"And I'm telling you, I don't have the information you're seeking. I've answered your questions and now, if you don't leave, I'm calling my lawyer, and the police."

Paul stared the doctor down. Or attempted to. The other man didn't budge. He knew Paul didn't have a warrant to be on the premises.

He and Haley were wasting time they didn't have to waste.

Without another word, Paul turned toward Haley, and with a quick glance and a hand at her back, ushered her to the door.

He did not thank the doctor for his time.

Haley wanted to go to the police. When she suggested as much on the way back to their vehicle, Paul shook his head.

Until they had evidence of a crime, they couldn't compel an investigation. And while they'd compiled a lot of circumstantial evidence, Paul told Haley that to turn things over to the police at this point was premature. With everything just being conjecture, the police might or might not prioritize the case. When Noah's autopsy was done, he was sure they'd want to know not only what Paul had discovered, but also focus on finding a murderer. Not search for a baby who might or might not exist.

"You're not sure who you can trust, are you?" she asked as they sped away from Dr. Andrews's office on their way to the first of many stops he had planned—assuming one didn't turn up evidence that made the hunt no longer necessary—all tied to Maya's credit card charges.

"I don't want the police interfering with my investigation," he told her. And then added, "Because while I trust the department as a whole, I'm not sure who might or might not be on someone else's payroll as well."

Immediately, thoughts of the officer who'd stopped them that first night on their way into town came to mind.

"Because you think Gladstone is involved somehow."

"I know he *was* involved. And that there's no evidence, other than his word, that he no longer is."

Glancing at him, sitting there with him, listening to him, having been practically glued to his side for almost three full days, Haley had a rush of memory of what it had felt like to be in love with Paul Wright.

It had felt so right.

And yes, it had gone horribly wrong.

"What?" he asked, as she continued to watch him. She turned away then, keeping her own eye on the traffic around them, aware that they couldn't relax, even for a second.

"I was just…realizing that I know so little about you. About your current life."

"You know where I live. And what I do for a living. And I do it pretty much all the time."

"I don't know if there's anyone special in your life."

She'd told herself the night before, many times, that she was not going to say those words, or any even close to being like them.

And there they were—hanging like the bang of a shotgun.

Leaving a deafening silence in their wake.

Paul drove. The premapped route already in his memory bank. Next stop, an upscale hair and day spa, Delights, Maya's card had frequented.

Ten miles away. Chosen, not for proximity to the first stop—Dr. Andrews—but because of the number of times the credit had been used there.

His mind was not staying completely on route.

Haley wanted to know about his sex life. His life

with women, yeah, his romantic involvements, but that boiled down to sex, didn't it?

The unwelcome words bumbled in and out of his work thoughts, disrupting vital focus.

And they weren't really even right. Or fair. She wanted to know about the state of his heart. His love life.

Did she know how treacherous such a conversation could be for them?

How could she not know?

Of course, she knew.

And if he could tell her all about the loving relationship he was in, tell her how happy he was with a wonderful woman who completed him, then the sexual tension building between them—the elephant on the table that she had to be aware of—would deflate without them ever having to deal with it. Or even mention that it had existed for a minute or two.

He wasn't going to lie to her.

Ignoring that elephant wasn't going to help, either.

"I'm recently separated from the woman I've been living with for the past year," he told her, and then immediately regretted the words.

Her silence settled over him as a balm. Rescuing him from a mistake that could cost them much. And the dark car he'd thought was following them turned off. Into the parking lot of a grocery store.

"Did you love her?"

He wanted to glance her way. To read her face and know...

What?

What did he want to know?

"I thought I did."

Another silence. Again, he hoped they were done.

Most of him hoped. The one small part who wanted to know if she was in a relationship, who wanted to know if she'd ever had as serious a long-term relationship as she'd had with him, poked at him weakly from within, as he made an internal announcement that he hoped she was in a relationship. That she was committed and happy, and knowing the joy they hadn't been able to find together.

Mostly he wanted to not think of her in those terms.

"I'm sorry."

Did she have to sound so damned sincere?

Like she truly cared about the state of his heart.

He shrugged. "I was pretty much over her before she moved out," he said, trying for a nonchalance he wasn't totally feeling. He hadn't been in love with Sarah, but he'd wanted their relationship to work.

"She left you?"

The temptation to glance her way almost won out at the incredulous tone of her voice.

Almost. He was stronger than any of his baser desires.

"She said I wasn't giving her what she needed, which I'm sure was true. And…she was having an affair, had been for at least half of the time she'd been living with me."

The irony of that one should give her some satisfaction.

He turned, turned again and then circled around a block. The red sedan who'd been with them for a couple of miles did not follow.

"Did you confront her?"

Not a question he'd anticipated. Like she'd confronted him, did she mean?

"No. I asked her once if she was seeing someone. She said no."

"So then…"

This wasn't going away. Like a dog with a meat bone, Haley was chewing the subject for all she was worth. Might be time to take away the treat.

Her fondness for conversation about his love life, and his seeming inability to shut it down, could not be healthy for their futures.

"She left because I wasn't giving her what she needed," he repeated.

"But you did what you do and found out the truth…"

"I hired someone else to do so." And he couldn't have her pitying him. "I did it for my peace of mind, not because I was mourning for her. I wasn't in love with her. I wanted to be. I thought I could be. I wasn't. She was right to leave."

He'd pulled into the parking lot behind Delights, unfastened his seat belt, pushed the start button to shut down the engine. Haley hadn't moved.

"That peace of mind…you get it…that someone might need that."

He couldn't look at her. Couldn't get that close. But… "Yeah."

"I was wrong to accuse you, Paul. I was young and emotionally inept and I have regretted that night ever since."

But she still needed the truth.

He gave it to her. "I wanted you to believe that there was someone else. We were dying a slow death and I just wanted it over."

"Was there someone else?"

He had a distinct impression then that Haley wasn't trying to salvage, or even rehash, their past. Peace of mind was all she was after.

"No." With that, he opened his door and got out, heading into the salon with or without her. He had a job to get done. Sooner rather than later would be best on every level, for all concerned.

One word.

No. Frozen, and yet...overwhelmed with emotional impact, she sat there in the stopped car, just...feeling.

Pain. Relief. Tears that couldn't fall. A love that had failed.

A man who'd been faithful.

Her entire body resonated with it all, as dimensions in her life changed again.

Paul hadn't cheated on her.

Over the years...she'd wondered...so many times.

It didn't change the fighting. The problems that had led them to the point where she'd accused and he'd walked out.

But...

He'd left the vehicle. Was striding for the door.

He wasn't walking out on her again. Period.

Out of the SUV, she chased after him. "When we part this time, we say goodbye and walk away at the same time," was all she said when she caught up with him.

He gave her a look—one that melted her bones and sent frissons of desire through her—and opened the door.

She stepped inside the spa with him, needing to be with him, and needing the current episode in her life to come to an end, too.

And as it turned out, the intense start of the day was only the beginning.

They learned things. Kelsey, going as Maya, had been a regular customer at Delights until five months before her death. There'd been much more recent charges from the establishment on her card, though, which Paul had quickly pointed out, only to be told that she'd been on the recurring monthly product purchase plan and the merchandise was mailed automatically from their supplier.

Without a warrant, they'd been loath to share the address they had file for her, even with Maya's sister, executor and beneficiary. A stylist named Coletta had been called up, though, and when asked if Maya had ever mentioned anything about having a baby, Coletta shook her head, mentioning that Maya had talked about her fiancé almost nonstop, though. She'd said she was truly in love for the first time in her life.

Information that grabbed at Haley's heart—and that got them no closer to finding out what happened with Kelsey's pregnancy.

From a gym she'd attended—again until about five months before her death—they'd heard the same story about Maya being head over heels happy in love, but no one knew what the man did for a living, other than that he seemed to do a lot of work-related travel. He was gone a lot, but when he was in town he spent every minute with her. Never at the gym, though. They always knew the guy was in town when Maya missed her workouts...

They visited restaurants, a grocery store and a furniture store, all within six miles of the Calypso house. It was as though Haley was living through glimpses of her little sister's life, and yet not finding her. The truth they sought remained elusive, even as she grew closer to the sibling she'd lost.

The last stop was a clothing store called Madonna's. According to Paul, Kelsey had only used her charge card there once, which was why it was last on the list.

But as soon as they pulled up to the exclusive boutique just after five that evening, Haley's heart started to pound. The mannequins in the window were all... pregnant.

Her chest tight, she knew such a myriad of sensations she couldn't find herself for those seconds.

"I can't believe it," she cried when she could. "It's a maternity shop!"

Kelsey had spent several hundred dollars at a maternity shop.

The place was closing for the day, but when Haley introduced herself to the manager, and Paul showed his credentials, she agreed to speak to them.

Thinking they were about to find the truth, Haley entered the quiet shop, shaking from the inside out.

Only to find that while, yes, Kelsey had purchased enough clothes to get her through all stages of a pregnancy, she'd only been there the one time. The manager showed Haley a teddy bear Kelsey had purchased, and Haley bought an identical one for herself. Even if she looked emotional and drama driven, she couldn't help it. At the moment, she needed something to hug.

Most particularly as she heard that Kelsey had been gushing with love, the manager related, going on and on about how excited Kelsey and the baby's father were. Kelsey had shown off her engagement ring, easily two carats, but the manager didn't remember her ever mentioning the man's name, or what he did for a living.

It was like Kelsey had fallen in love with—and somehow become impregnated by—a mirage.

As soon as Haley and Paul were back in the SUV she asked, "So what…did she end up pregnant by whoever paid her expenses through the shell company and then when he abandoned her, or refused to take responsibility for the baby, she made up the rest?

"Could be the house, the credit card bills were payoffs," she added. "His guilt money."

Frowning, Paul started the vehicle, pulled out into traffic.

And she couldn't pretend to herself anymore. She hoped that Kelsey had been in love. That the father had given her a huge engagement ring and that he adored Kelsey and had wanted to marry her.

But if that was the case…where was the man? Why hadn't he come forward?

Even if he didn't know that Maya had been Kelsey, surely he'd have made himself known in Maya's life, somehow.

Wait…

"What if the father is mourning the death of his beloved fiancé, and is home raising their child?" she asked. "What if he doesn't know that Maya was Kelsey and has a family and a whole other life?"

"Noah had known."

Uh huh. And he'd known the baby was in wrong hands. Had likely been killed for knowing, or spreading what he knew.

"The police knew or you wouldn't have been contacted about her death."

Right. She couldn't just keep clutching at straws that looked like she wanted them to look.

"And there was no birth certificate with Maya's name on it, either."

Yeah.

"What if you were on the correct path in Pahrump?" she asked then, her heart seeming to clog her throat, as panic filled her anew. She'd known…some part of her had known… "What if she was working at Sister's Ranch, or some other brothel, had gotten pregnant, and was somehow forced to give up the baby?" The brothel had to protect the client at all costs, right?

"I never took the possibility off the table. Whether the father found out and this is all done at his hands, or the brothel had a part in it…it's always been there."

Could Kelsey have signed something before she started working there, agreeing that if there was ever a contraceptive fail and she ended up pregnant, she'd give the child up for adoption?

"Gladstone is still a consideration as well. He could have found her, forced himself on her again, and then become desperate to hide the evidence."

And there was another, horrible possibility. One she'd refused to consider. But was she going to hide her head in the sand and risk losing a chance to find the baby?

"I'm going to be an aunt," she said, hardly processing. Allowing herself to really believe. Before she traveled any further on the road her thoughts were taking.

The love she felt for the child she'd never met was there to show her the way. It had been growing within her since the moment she'd read Noah's note.

"Are you also seriously considering a human trafficking angle?" She had to ask, had to look truth in the eye, this time around, not make assumptions and run with them, as she had with Paul's supposed infidelity.

She'd been unable to save her marriage, but there was still a chance to save the baby...

"I believe that it's possible that Kelsey was persuaded to sell the baby, either willingly...or not. And that, in the end, she balked at doing so."

Paul's tone was strained, understandably so as he broached the deplorable subject with his ex-wife about her deceased sister, but he seemed distracted, too.

They'd turned onto a road that led from the Calypso part of town back toward the Strip, and bypassed city traffic. He'd wanted to get into a room and on his computer. Was taking them to another resort—saying that the casino floors made it easier for them to blend in, as the places were swarming with guests who weren't staying at the hotel as well as the ones who were and wherever there was a casino, security would be tighter. They were heading to a place just off Strip. Not out of the vicinity, though. No more places set on their own out in the desert.

The firm set of his lips froze whatever words had been on her tongue. She knew not to make obvious a glance in her side mirror. Just sat quietly, facing forward. Waiting for him to find his opportunity to lose whoever he might suspect was following them.

He turned several times, taking them to a lesser used mountain road at the edge of town. And sat back, as though more comfortable. Which automatically lessened her stress as well.

The sun low in the sky, the peacefulness, the magnificent views of rock and hill that had endured for thousands of years, all brought her a measure of calm.

Paul glanced her way. Unsmiling.

"What?" she asked.

Shaking his head, he said, "Just wrapping my mind around the fact that this is really happening. Kelsey. A baby. Me and you."

As if it was just hitting him?

Or he was finally getting down to the heart of it?

Another bend in the road appeared as they rounded one turn and she thought about how life was that way… taking you around one obstacle, to another unknown.

Remembering their conversation early in the day… the fact that Paul wasn't currently in a relationship, she was about to tell him that she wasn't either, but a roar came up from behind them.

All thoughts flew out of her brain as a force hit the SUV from behind, impelling her forward as their vehicle swerved, and the roar sped off ahead of them. As they finished rounding the curve, she saw the mountain wall they were headed toward and screamed. Paul pulled the wheel with both hands. The SUV swung back, making her dizzy. They skidded on the road, jerked to a hard stop and missed the mountain by inches.

Trembling, gulping for air, her gaze sought Paul. Only Paul.

"You okay?" His voice came to her, pulled her from the cloud of panic, sounding…fairly normal.

"Yeah." She found the wherewithal to speak. And then, "You?"

"Yeah."

He didn't sound okay, though. As he pulled back onto the road, while she thanked God they hadn't crashed or been crashed into by another unsuspecting vehicle coming around the turn, he swore a streak. Turned into town at the first opportunity, and pulled into the parking lot of a grocery store. Getting out, phone already to his ear, he called and reported the incident, rattling off license plate information she hadn't even thought to seek out during the near miss.

And then, hanging up, he strode to the back of the SUV. She met him there, more to be with him than to survey the damage.

"He was good," he said. "Just bumped me enough to make me swerve on the turn."

"He was trying to run us into the mountain." She got the picture. Had already seen it up close and personal.

Paul's shrug surprised her. "He was driving a souped-up pickup with the wheels jacked. More like a mountain joyride than a hit man."

"You think it was an accident."

He shrugged. "It's definitely possible. He came up too fast, came around that last corner and couldn't stop." While his words built a case for believing their near death had not been deliberate, his frown said otherwise. It could have been directed at the scraped bumper on his brand-new vehicle.

He didn't say they'd just been deliberately run off the road.

And didn't say they hadn't.

"He could have hit us a hell of a lot harder," he said, still seeming to be studying the bumper. "If it had been a hit, we should be dead."

Fear shot through her. "Unless he underestimated you. He wanted it to look like a single car accident," she said. "If he hit you too hard, police would search for the second vehicle involved in the crash."

"If he hit us harder, I wouldn't have been able to report the vehicle to the police. They'd be looking for a needle in a haystack."

"So your gut really is telling you it's an accident." She wasn't buying it, but she'd been wrong before.

He shrugged. Wouldn't commit.

As though he might be sparing her any more worry.

She didn't want him to spare her.

What she wanted was for him to wrap those strong muscled arms around her and hold on.

Just until she got her nerve back.

Chapter 15

She had to go. Walking through the casino of the mid-town hotel he'd chosen at random—because random was harder to find—Paul couldn't see far enough, fast enough. Behind every column, along every slot machine aisle, someone could be lurking.

Ready to take Haley. Not overtly, not there, but the ways to quietly take someone out were many. He knew most of them.

He hadn't asked for adjoining rooms. Didn't want her that far away.

She had to go. To get out of Vegas. So that he could get the job done. Find the baby that evidence pointed toward. And get home.

Back to the life that made sense.

That didn't hold the constant threat of being derailed.

As Haley was threatening to derail him.

Danger of the life-threatening kind he could handle

without a blip. But the kind of soul-taking, mind-blinding effect that he and Haley had on each other...

She'd almost died on his watch.

He'd never recover if that happened. Life as he knew it would be over.

She was one of a kind. Not a kind he could live with, but a kind that made the world a better place.

The room wasn't el shaped. Two queen beds, a decent-sized bath off to the right just inside the door. A built-in desk just down from the dresser. And a round table with a couple of chairs by the window. On the fourteenth floor, they had a view of the city.

He set up his computer at the table—leaving her with nowhere to go, but at the desk, his screen would be visible to the room. He couldn't work that way.

Headphones on, he got to it the second he'd dropped his bag and plugged in. Giving himself time to focus, find his calm, to take back a measure of control, before he let her know that he was putting her on a plane back to Santa Barbara first thing in the morning.

He opened his top ten people search sites, typed in both Kelsey and Maya's information and looked for anything that came up in both places. He opened the searches up nationally, went with first and last names and started other searches with only first names. He searched Thomas Gladstone as well, looking for any names associated with him that might also show up on Kelsey's searches. While those ran, he went to the legal databases to which he had access and did the same with those.

And even typed in the account number for the shell company that paid for Kelsey's apartment, the house on Calypso, Maya's credit card and obstetrician.

When all of the searches were up and running, he pulled off his headphones and turned in his chair.

Haley, just coming out of the bathroom, had changed to the shorts and T-shirt he'd seen her in the first morning they'd been in Vegas...had that only been Saturday?

"You have any preferences for dinner?" she asked, apparently deciding that since he'd taken off his headphones he was free game.

He'd meant to be feeling a lot less tense when he faced her again.

For a second or two there, he'd thought he'd succeeded.

He didn't want dinner. He wanted her.

As badly as he wanted as far away from her as he could get.

Before he could deliver his big news—that she'd be leaving—his phone rang. Duane Endives from the Las Vegas Police Department.

He watched Haley as he listened, turned away from her and inhaled her soft rose scent. Stared at the window and saw her reflection. Turned to the wall and saw her shadow.

She was everywhere, consuming him again.

And as the news coming over the phone grew more intense, so did his need to have Haley out of town. He stood as he hung up.

"You have to go," he said. "Tonight." Pulled up flights on his phone. "We're calling a cab to take you to the airport. I'll ride along, and stay with you until you're on the plane." He'd buy two tickets and go through security if he couldn't get bodyguard clearance in time to accompany her officially.

"What was that call about?"

Had she heard him? She needed to get her flowery zippered bathroom bag off the counter by the sink in there, put some shoes on and close things up.

Flight times popped up. "I can get you on at eight," Paul said, as though she hadn't spoken. That gives us time to get you something to eat and arrive at the airport in time to board." He didn't want them hanging around at the gate. If someone was looking for flights to Santa Barbara... He should send her home through Utah. Or Arizona. He knew these things.

Just had to do his job in reverse—get someone lost, not found.

"I'm assuming, based on what I heard of the conversation, that that was Detective Endives on the phone. What did he say?" she repeated, standing there, still barefoot, her gaze intent on him.

"The truck was abandoned a couple of miles farther out of town from our skirmish. It was stolen earlier this afternoon from a used car dealership downtown. There were no viable prints."

"So it could have been kids out for a joyride."

Yes, but it hadn't been. The chances of him and Haley just happening to be the ones out of millions of people in Las Vegas to be in the path of joyriders were too slim to be conceivable.

Added to that the method of operation...stealing a vehicle, one that couldn't be traced, abandoning it as soon as possible after the hit, no prints...it was all yelling at him with the truth. Someone wanted Haley out of the picture.

Someone they had no way to trace.

Added to which, the police still had nothing they

could issue warrants on. Not in Paul's search. They'd search for the car thief.

And good luck to them with that.

"Noah's autopsy isn't back yet," he added.

When it came back suspicious, there'd be a murder investigation that would definitely include aspects of what he was tracking, but the detectives wouldn't be looking for a baby.

Although, with the maternity clothes and obstetrician bills, Endives was very interested in Paul's work.

"And now it's time for you to go."

"No it's not. We haven't found the baby yet."

"I will find the baby, Haley. I give you my word. I will find the baby, but having you here is a hindrance to my doing so."

"I've helped a ton. I've gotten you information more rapidly than you might have coaxed it out yourself in the interviews. You said so yourself."

He had said so, yes, but that was then.

Before he'd known for certain that someone was serious about ending her life.

He should never have brought her along. If she'd stayed in California, no one would have suspected she knew things they didn't want her to know.

He'd let her cloud his judgment from the first phone call.

The past repeating itself.

He shook his head. Typed for flight times from Vegas to Salt Lake and then to Santa Barbara. Preferably one that didn't require a plane change.

"I'm not leaving, Paul. I'm a grown woman. Under my own recognizance, and whether I'm with you or not, I'm not leaving."

She'd come closer. One glance and he prepared for battle. He knew that look in her eye.

Knew it well.

"You're in danger, Haley. Real danger. You could have died this afternoon. Knowing that...you being here is a distraction I can't afford. I can't do my job." He didn't know how to make it any clearer to her.

"I'll be in danger wherever I go. And I'm helping here. You have no idea, when you find the baby, what you're going to be facing. You might need me to care for him or her while you take care of whoever took the baby to begin with. Or you might need my official position as Kelsey's executor and beneficiary, or as a blood relative, to legally get the baby out of danger."

All of which was true, but... "You can be on a flight back to Vegas to handle legalities within an hour," he told her.

Taking another step closer, she said, "I'm not going."

He didn't back up. Or back down. "If you don't, I quit."

She didn't even blink. "You aren't going to quit, Paul. I know you better than that. No way you'd turn your back on a child in danger."

Or on her, whether she knew it or not. Not when her life was being threatened.

Afterward, when the job was done and he knew she was safe, he wasn't going to be able to get away fast enough.

With another step forward, she lifted her chin. And his penis got hard. Which was about the most inappropriate, out of place, uncalled for reaction he could have had.

And exactly the kind of thing Haley brought out in

him. Inappropriate reactions. Over-the-top, intense reactions.

"You won't quit, but if you don't agree to continue
to include me, to let me help, you're fired."

He didn't need her money. Didn't even want it.

"I can look for whoever I want," he said. "I don't need
your permission."

"But without my official stance in Kelsey's life, you
won't get as far. At least not as quickly."

She licked her lips, her eyes blazing. Locked on his.
And...different.

Something there...more mature...but as gut rocking
as anything he'd ever seen in the woman's eyes. And
certainly hadn't found in any gaze but hers...

"And... I'm still going to be looking. So if you're not
with me, I'll be in even more danger."

He was so tempted to call her bluff on that one.

"You got some kind of death wish?" He asked, instead. Not quite pleading with her to back down, but
close.

"Of course I don't." She stepped closer, even when
there was no more space between them. She just seemed
to keep on coming. "But where safer would I be than
right here with you? Who better to protect me?" she
asked softly. And continued burning him at the stake
with, "Today...out on the mountain...all I wanted, all
I needed, was your arms around me..."

His lips captured hers before she could say another
word. Annihilate him any further. And he kept them
there. Moving them slightly to fit more securely. To
prevent any more words from escaping.

He had to shut her up.

To...

Haley's mouth opened anyway. Her tongue moved.
Against his.

He heard a groan. Sounded like hunger.

His? Hers?

She stumbled. He caught her with both arms. Holding her securely against him.

And he was lost.

Paul. Yes.

His taste in her mouth.

His musky all over scent.

"Mmmm..." His gravelly groan.

Paul.

His arms around her, his body under her hands...
no...no...cloth in between. The shirt had to be gone.

"Gone." She spoke her need. Pulled at the garment.

And it was gone.

Then there was more. Skin, muscles. Warmth. Raspy hair. Nipples that became tight little beads when she brushed them.

The belly button she'd once filled with strawberry syrup and it had been gross and they'd had to shower it off.

Water running over his penis...

Her mouth still attached to his, she reached lower.

Grabbed at the fly of his shorts. Found the zipper. Yanked it down. Reached inside. And took hold.

Fingers fumbled at the waist of her shorts. The fabric loosened, and a shot of cold air hit hot skin as her bottoms fell to her feet.

He pushed, she stepped backward at the same time and they fell together to the bed behind her. Her on bottom. Him on top.

Her legs open.

Him sliding in.

Moving.

Moving.

Moving.

And…oh God…oh God…

Tumultuous shivers took over her entire being. Rocking her. Hitting the pleasure button so exquisitely she could do nothing but ride with it. Wave after explosive wave…

Feeling him shudder, and then pulse inside her.

No one moved. Neither of them spoke.

They just lay together and breathed. Tumultuously, at first, and then, slowly, steadying to an even rhythm. One rhythm. As though they were taking one breath.

Awareness came slowly. Haley resisted. And then felt Paul's fingers under her T-shirt, finding her bra-less breasts, going for the nipples, lightly teasing them in a way that got her juices flowing again with a sharp stream straight to her groin.

He kissed her, softly, and she rolled with him, lying on top of him, touching every part of him as though learning his body for the first time. Not thinking. Not storing or noting, just touching. Enjoying. Feeling.

So much feeling.

His warm skin beneath her palms, the bulk of his muscles.

And the velvety softness that he'd pulled out of her, but that was growing hard again already. She moved on him, sliding her body against him, licking his nipples, and when he rolled them over again, lifting her up to place her head on the pillow, she opened her body to his exploration. Letting him do whatever he wanted.

Feeling what he did.

He entered her again. More than once.

Pulled the band out of her hair and let it cascade all around her.

Had her flat on her back. And had her sitting on him.

They gave and they took.

And eventually they fell asleep. Naked. Uncovered. Without ever having spoken a word.

Chapter 16

Jolting awake, Paul glanced at the digital alarm clock on the nightstand. Nine o'clock. Wide-open curtains showed him dark sky glowing with city lights.

He hadn't been out for long.

And he had work to do.

Carefully extricating himself, he pulled the covers up over Haley—first and foremost so he didn't see her, but also to keep her comfortable—and headed quietly into the bathroom where he used a washcloth to clean himself off.

As he avoided any eye contact with himself in the mirror, the information waiting on his computer called to him.

A good sign.

A very good sign.

He'd purged the past that had been lurking inside him,

and the man he knew himself to be—the one who lived to work—had been set free.

As though to prove his point, as soon as he sat down, once again fully dressed, pieces of the puzzle started to tumble into place. His brain had been freed to think and he was able to spot similarities, find names, follow through on various databases, pull out key pieces and then find them in similar places across other searches.

And when his gaze started to blur from reading, he made a list of all public establishments within three miles of the Calypso house and searched for them on social media, scouring photos, comments, anything that might lead him to Maya with her companion.

He didn't find the baby.

Or even the baby daddy.

But at two in the morning, shut inside the bathroom with the water running so as not to disturb Haley, he called Duane Endives. There was evidence of a known hit man who'd been parked outside a coffee shop just down the street from the Calypso house, as seen from a Google photo, and also caught on a social media post. The man had shown up on a Gladstone people search as a known associate.

And he lived in Pahrump.

With that, and the pages of circumstantial evidence Paul had already emailed over, Endives could get a warrant for the man's finances. In the morning, when the judge was in his chambers. While a hit man's arrest was paramount to Paul, it wouldn't be something a judge would want to be called out of bed for.

Most particularly if a Gladstone was involved. He'd want a chance to be fully awake and aware before he signed something like that.

It might or might not be the guy who almost killed them that afternoon. Could be or wouldn't be the man who'd kidnapped Haley the day before. There was a chance the guy had killed Kelsey. And perhaps Noah, too. That all remained to be seen.

Very soon, though, the hired gun's finances would open up to him. They were going to know who'd hired him, and then everything would fall into place. Because once they found the payer, they'd have evidence for a warrant on that person's finances. And that would show them whether or not there were any other murder-for-hire types on the payroll.

Feeling more like himself than he had since before Sarah's departure, he lay down on the unmade bed, intending just to rest his eyes for a few, and woke up to the rustling of covers in the bed beside him. Lying still, he listened as Haley grabbed her bag and made her way quietly to the bathroom, closing the door with barely a sound.

The room's darkness relayed that dawn hadn't yet arrived, but a quick glance at the clock told him three hours had passed since he'd lain down.

And then he heard the click of the lock on the bathroom door.

An afterthought?

One for which he was thankful.

Relaxing, he focused on the relief, trying to ignore a sense of sadness that came with it, but eventually, allowed that, too. Just as he had the night he and Haley had agreed to divorce.

It would come anyway, he'd learned, and would hit harder if it had to fight its way through.

The sense of déjà vu could have been amusing, had

it not been so acute. How relief and sadness could play equally on the same instrument at the same time, he didn't know, but when Haley was in his life, the dichotomous tunes blew with equal strength.

As though it were yesterday, feelings from eight years before played him.

He'd let her believe there was another woman because he'd known that that was the only way she'd ever be able to let him go. Just as he'd known that if she didn't let go of him, he'd never leave her. Yet they'd both been miserable together.

Not all the time.

There'd been incredibly right moments, hours, days. The happiest he'd ever known. Funny how after so many years, he could remember them more clearly than he'd been able to when he'd been living them. And yet, he knew the recollections were accurate.

The night before was proof positive of them.

But the great times hadn't all been about sex. He and Haley had been so happy together on vacation. They'd been content just to be with each other. Had joyfully engaged in activities that either one of them suggested. Had never fought.

But at home, when real life and responsibility took hold...

He shook his head.

He'd never been happier than he had been with her. But he'd never been angrier, either.

Or more disappointed.

And neither had she.

They'd discussed the situation calmly, and at length, the night of their second anniversary, sharing the bottle of wine she'd bought for the celebratory dinner that had been ruined by the fight that had ensued due to his tardiness.

And that lock on the bathroom door—it was just like that calm discussion had been. Using conscious thought and taking action to prevent them from hurting each other any further.

Where that left them in terms of the day ahead, he didn't know.

Hoped it meant she'd be heading to the airport.

But he didn't hold his breath on that, either.

She had to talk to him. To make her feelings known. Or risk the past.

That could most definitely not happen. She'd barely survived the first time. Getting over Paul...even eight years later it was a work in progress.

"Just toast, please," she told the waitress who approached their table in the crowded café, one of many eateries with casino views on the hotel's ground floor.

"You need more than that," Paul interrupted, before she could add on the coffee.

"I'm not really hungry," she told him, and smiled at the older woman standing at the edge of their booth as though she had all day to wait around.

"Bring us two King of Hearts breakfasts and two coffees," he told the woman and while Haley bristled, she chose to hold her tongue.

He couldn't force-feed her. She'd eat what she wanted, leave the rest or watch him eat it. There were bigger issues before them.

In new knee-length red shorts and a red, white and black peasant top, she'd come out of the bathroom of their room prepared to have it out with him. He'd been dressed in jeans and a white short-sleeved pullover and at the door, waiting to go down to breakfast. They hadn't been alone since. Not in the hall, not in the elevator, and most definitely not in the café.

Almost as though he was avoiding any personal conversation. They hadn't eaten inside a restaurant since they'd embarked on their strange and tumultuous journey. Nor had they left their bags in their room as they had that morning.

Something was definitely up.

"There've been some developments in the case," he said, as soon as the waitress had filled their cups with coffee and left them sitting across from each other in the booth for two.

Giving herself a mental shake, and a reminder that the only thing that really mattered was the reason she and Paul were together—the baby—Haley leaned forward. With so many excited conversations going on around them, not to mention the heightened energy level that generally bounced around casino atmospheres, she had to move closer to him to be certain she heard everything.

Without meeting her gaze directly, he gave her a quick rundown of the work he'd done after she fell asleep the night before.

Which explained why she'd awoken with them in separate beds. He'd been up working, not just moving to get away from her.

"I found a suspected hit man, guy who goes by the name of Blue Colonial, watching the Calypso street home. Guy's from Pahrump, and has ties to Gladstone," he said, telling her about his middle-of-the-night call to Duane Endives. And then added, "I had a call back from the detective while you were showering. He got the warrant for Colonial's financials, and they have officers watching Colonial until an arrest can be made."

Which explained the bags still in the room and the restaurant meal. He wasn't as worried for their safety.

That piece of information registered, and was good, but it didn't stem the thread of alarm shooting through her. The tightening in her chest. It was going to end, one way or another. And what if the baby was already gone?

Or…would she have held a new family member by nightfall?

When excited butterflies attacked her midregion, she pushed the baby-in-her-arms thought aside. One thing at a time. She couldn't afford to borrow trouble—or joy, either, as they'd take focus she needed in the moment.

Focus she might need to stay alive.

The joy, or the sorrow, those were hers to live as they came to her. If they came to her.

"Gladstone really is behind all this?" she asked him, afraid all over again. She hadn't detected a single hope of humanitarian capability within the man. Not for her sister, certainly.

So, not for her baby?

The shrug Paul gave as an answer didn't surprise her.

The sudden, sensual memory provoked by the movement of his shoulder did. Her way of dealing with the fear, she supposed. The heightened emotion. Channel to something that brought pleasure.

That's what sex between her and Paul had been the night before.

And she couldn't leave it lying there between them.

Most particularly not with the day ahead looking to finally be productive, but emotionally taxing, too.

They had to kill it off.

Before it destroyed either one of them.

"About last night…" She looked him straight in the eye. And was surprised to see him looking right back at her. And nodding.

"It was so us, wasn't it?" he said, not with a smile, or with affection.

But with the bone-deep sadness that had been the backbone of the last months of their marriage.

"The sex was always good between us," she admitted.

"And helped us ignore everything that wasn't."

He was right. Completely right.

And with that, the tension toward him eased inside her. When it came to them, she and Paul were on the same side.

"So, we're agreed that it was a one-off?" she asked, still holding his gaze.

"One-hundred-percent."

Her heart hurting, she blinked back tears, but she smiled, too.

"I think, maybe, we just turned a major corner," she said aloud.

"I'd like to think so, too." He slid his hand across the table, palm up. "Friends?" he asked.

"Friends." She placed her hand on top of his, and when his fingers closed around it, she held his, too.

And didn't feel as alone anymore.

As soon as breakfast was done, Paul was back upstairs at his computer. He'd sent photos to Haley and she was going through them on her phone—various things he'd picked up from social media, people searches and search engines the night before that he hadn't yet looked at. Paul himself was busy scouring through the financial records of a man he'd never met. One who was not a nice guy, based on the things he purchased—and the people who paid him.

Gladstone wasn't the only name on the list that Paul recognized.

Colonial had been paid by another name well-known to Paul. A family known to have Mafia ties without anything ever having been proven to the point of prosecution.

Within half an hour of getting the records, he'd put another call in to Endives, who was picking Gladstone up for questioning.

Haley, who'd been sitting quietly in the chair opposite him, scrolling, with a frown marring her beautiful forehead, and her perennial ponytail bobbing slightly as her head did, looked over as he hung up the phone.

"You're thinking it's Gladstone."

He wasn't going to lie to her. Had hoped for a better scenario. "The facts are pointing in that direction," he told her. Knowing what was coming next.

Wishing he didn't have to break her heart another time. "And there's no sign of a baby in the Gladstone family." He did it quickly, but then added a ray of hope he'd told himself he wouldn't dole out. "But we haven't seen their finances, yet. Something might turn up."

She nodded. He went back to work.

And five minutes later exclaimed, "Holy crap."

"What?The table bumped against him with the force

of her ejection from her chair and she was beside him, looking over his shoulder.

And he pointed.

Her gaze turned to the screen; she seemed to be studying. He waited.

She leaned in closer, so close he could smell the unique scent that was only her, and had to restrain himself from wrapping his arms around her.

In comfort.

Not desire.

With a need to protect, not her body, but her heart. To give her strength.

If she hadn't stood at that moment, he might have given in to the drive to take on her burdens personally.

"The shell company that paid for the Calypso house, for Kelsey's apartment for…" Her voice broke and she stared at him, her gaze too wide, distant and filled with horror. "That company paid Blue Colonial."

The hit man.

Backing up, she shook her head, over and over. Bumped into the bed, but didn't sit. She sidestepped to the end of it. Kept taking backward steps, as though if she could distance herself, or somehow undo the walking that had brought her that point, she could spare herself what was to come.

"The man who was supporting Kelsey, the one she was so in love with, who put a two-carat diamond on her finger and was going to marry her, hired a hit man to kill her?"

"Her death has been ruled an accident." The words burst out of him. As though he could still somehow spare her.

"And the baby…" Tears filled her eyes.

Her guess was probably right.

"Once we get access to Gladstone's financials, we'll have a better chance to connect the shell company to him," he was saying when she interrupted him.

"No way Kelsey would have knowingly been involved with Gladstone," she said, her tone harsh. "I know my sister. She would not have lived with the man, even for all the money in the world. I'd believe that he somehow got to her, forced sex on her again, her ending up pregnant and him wanting her dead, but not that she'd have lived in a home he was paying for..."

He'd known that, of course. What she would and would not allow herself to accept. Was about to try somehow to prepare her to accept the unacceptable when his phone rang another time.

Picking it up to silence it, he saw Endives's name. And kept his eyes trained on Haley, trying to hold her up with the strength of his gaze as he answered.

Listened.

And, dropping his phone to the table, stood, went to Haley, and was there to catch her as he said, "With the shell company as evidence, they picked up Colonial for questioning. He admits to being paid to keep an eye on Kelsey but swears he didn't hurt her, or Noah. He doesn't know who hired him. Said he got a note in the mail, was told to call a burner phone with his bank account number. A deposit was made to it and he was told who to watch, told to leave the video on an SD card in a tin box in the base of a hollow tree just outside Pahrump, which he did, and a large payment was made to his account. He has airtight alibis for the night Noah died, for Monday morning at Sister's and for yesterday..."

The worst was yet to come.

"He swears it wasn't Gladstone, Haley. Said that Gladstone had asked him two or three years ago, just in theory, how it would work to 'off her,' his words, but that nothing came of it. Said he was surprised to see it was the same woman he was watching. Two different names. Gladstone knew her as Kelsey, his new hire referred to her as Maya Ambrose. He also confirmed that she was pregnant. After he made the video, and deposited it, he never heard from the person again. That was four months ago."

Her eyes lit up and he quickly continued. "The person who hired him was from Pahrump. Came up in the conversation to do with leaving the SD card with the video recording in the tree."

It only took a second for reality to dawn. Her entire system seemed to shut down. Her expression dropped, her shoulders fell. And the light in her eyes went dim.

"Sister's Ranch," she said.

Back to the attorney. To Pahrump. Back to where Haley had been abducted.

"Right now, it's pointing that way." Was the only way pieces were fitting together. "Endives already has a warrant to get the financial records for the shell company, but since it's registered to a PO box, that might take a bit."

"The surveillance tape," Haley blurted, holding his gaze. He didn't look away, though he'd have liked to have done so. The moisture in her eyes, the need...they yanked things out of him that he didn't have to give. "If the guy's a professional...even if he isn't...he'd have made a copy."

He nodded, not surprised that she'd jumped on that.

Haley was a smart woman. And her ability to focus, even in the midst of turmoil, was part of what had made him fall in love with her.

"They've got a photo of a man going in and out of the house," he said.

"And?"

"It's not Gladstone. They don't know who it is yet, but it's not Gladstone. Endives's team is working on ID'ing him, but in the meantime, he's sending the footage here. In case you know who he is."

With one last check that she was still with him, standing on her own and ready to continue the fight, he moved back to his computer. Called up the footage.

Opened it. Didn't recognize the guy. Not from any of the photos and searches he'd done over the past three days. Haley's gaze was pinned on him. He could feel it.

"Come look," he invited.

She did. Falling down into the chair he'd vacated to watch the video several times. Whether to try to get something from the man, or to watch her pregnant sister open the door to him, he couldn't be sure.

But he could make a damn good guess. She was focused on Kelsey, absorbing everything she could out of the few seconds of tape. Taking it into her heart, where it would remain for the rest of her life.

Because that was Haley.

With Kelsey.

Loving and loyal.

Unconditionally.

Even after death.

And it hit him.

He'd never fully trusted Haley because he'd never

felt that she'd loved him as deeply, as eternally, as she'd loved her family.

And it got worse.

He really was jealous of his ex-wife's little sister—and had been all along.

Chapter 17

She couldn't get up. Couldn't quit staring at the screen, at the last glimpse she'd ever have of her baby sister. The smile on Kelsey's face as she answered the door… the way her cheeks and body had filled out with pregnancy… Kelsey truly glowed.

And was more beautiful than Haley had ever seen her.

To think that a man had played her, pretended to love her, to bring her such bliss, only to have her end up dead with no evidence she'd ever had a child…and, in the end, to have her friend, Noah, her only voice…

That did it. That got her standing.

And holding on to Paul's arm, too.

Because she knew where they were headed now. And needed time, needed someone, needed him, her friend, to help her get through it.

"An evil man, with money, and the ability to convince

my sister he loved her, fathered a child with her." Her voice cracked. "He pretended to fall in love with her so that he could either convince her to give up the baby, or, at the very least, be present when the baby came so that he could get rid of the evidence," she said. "Either by selling the baby, having it adopted…or…worse," she said aloud, finding it odd how calm she sounded.

The rampage going on inside her was about to topple her.

Except that, for Kelsey, for the baby, she would not let it. Period.

The fiend would not win.

"The obstetrician, he knows what happened to that baby. And he was afraid. That's why he wouldn't talk to us. Same with the lawyer in Pahrump," she continued as awful vignettes played out in her mind.

And then she focused on Paul. Saw him there, solid, right in front of her, saw her hand on his arm, and read the look in his gaze. Burning fire.

But not at her—not because of her. It was that drive, the thing deep within him that made him engage with everything he had when went on a job, or tackled classes, or anything else he put his mind to…that was what had first drawn her to him.

And there it was, still burning.

Bringing tears to her eyes, and a sob up from her chest that made it hard to breathe and impossible to speak.

Because they were probably too late.

It was possible they'd always been too late—that Noah hadn't known who had the baby, or why, just that something wrong had happened.

Maybe, like with their marriage, they'd been on a collision course before they'd begun.

"I'm not giving up." Paul was clear on that point.

Decision made. Though, there'd been none to make. He wasn't walking away. He'd die, first.

Pulling the other chair over for Haley to sit beside him, he sat in front of his computer and went to work. He had a face. "Finding people who don't want to be found is what I'm best at," he said aloud as his fingers flew on the keyboard.

"Even if we find him, if the baby's still alive, and he's the father, we have no legal grounds to do anything to save it from him…"

It wasn't like her to be negative…unless she was hurting so badly she couldn't handle the pain.

As she'd been the night of their second anniversary.

The knowledge came to him as though it wasn't new, as though it had always been lurking, waiting for him to find it.

"If he's a bad guy, there will be evidence," he told her, reading, scanning and typing some more. "And when I find it, you can use it to petition the court to have his parental rights severed."

She nodded, looking unconvinced. But she was looking. Intently. At everything in front of him. Joining in the search.

Helping him.

"There are a lot of ifs here, Hale," he said, as he typed again. "I can't promise a happy ending. But I can promise that I won't stop until we find that child. One way or another."

Dead or alive. He wouldn't say it aloud.

Things could end badly. They both knew that. But at least this time they'd be fighting the evil together.

On the same team.

With the same goal.

As friends instead of enemies.

After an hour of scouring the internet, of multiple phone calls with Endives, who confirmed that police facial recognition software had come up blank with a name to go with the face seen on the video, Paul announced that the quickest way to find out the identity of Kelsey's mystery man was to head back to Pahrump.

To question people in the small town until he got answers.

Even if they were just signs of nervousness as they swore they'd never seen the man before.

Haley saw the way he looked at her as he made his pronouncement. Saw the worry in his gaze, and said, "I'm coming with you."

He didn't argue.

And she didn't push her luck by asking any questions as he told her to close up her bag and prepare to check out.

By one o'clock that Tuesday afternoon, they'd talked to a dozen people in Pahrump, at the town's biggest box store, the most crowded diner, when they went in for lunch, and gas stations both in town and by the highway. No one knew the guy in the still photo Paul had on his phone.

It wasn't the greatest likeness. Grainy at best.

But someone had to know the guy.

"Unless he doesn't travel in the same circles as common folk," Haley said as they climbed back in the SUV. He had a process for getting in and out, aware, at every turn, that whoever had kidnapped her, and had almost run them off the road, was still at large. The same guy, or two random acts, no one knew.

Endives hoped to know though, as soon as financials came through from the shell company. If someone had used it to pay one dirty-job professional under the table, chances were good he'd used it, or a similar one, to pay another.

Each time they parked, Paul would get out while she stayed low, and she didn't show her head until he'd tapped twice on her door and then opened it.

They repeated the process for getting back in, minus the two taps.

While Haley thought the whole process a bit of overkill, she wasn't in an argue-with-him mood that day.

She'd been nervous, crossing the desert to Pahrump, not that she'd have admitted that to him, but he'd had a backup plan there, too. He'd checked in with Sierra's Web every ten minutes during the sixty-minute drive. Had he failed to do so, they'd have immediately notified the Nevada State Police. And Endives.

Paul's pull was impressive.

Gained not by being born to a rich father, but by earning it through hard work...

What they didn't do was contact police in the area. They'd yet to hear anything from them regarding Haley's abduction report, Endives hadn't been able to find any official record of it, which could just be slow paperwork processing due to the weekend, but Paul wasn't taking any chances.

Depending on how much money Kelsey's lover had had—and all signs pointed to it being a lot—he could have friends in the highest places.

Oh, God, Kels, what did you get yourself into? Did you know?

"She didn't come to me for help," Haley announced as Paul pulled away from the diner. "It's killing me that she didn't come to me. I could have…"

Paul's frown was odd. Personal somehow. "Maybe she needed to stand on her own two feet, Hale. Maybe it was time."

Well, yes, but…

Maybe he was right.

"You used to tell me that I enable them," she remembered. It had been the largest source of argument between them. And brought her defenses up every time.

"I was wrong to say that. I've realized something not very nice about myself," he said, as though conversationally, as he took a side street on their way to the largest local gym.

"What's that?" She couldn't imagine much, at the moment, that wasn't nice about him. Even when he'd fought with her, he'd been decent about it. It was like there'd been unwritten rules between them. No name calling. No bringing up irrelevant stuff and throwing it in each other's faces…

Who did that?

Who made rules of engagement for fighting during their marriage and then stuck to them? Had they brought the battles to themselves by building the ground for them?

Paul hadn't answered, typical for him, and she looked over at him, about to ask him if they'd made their battles a forgone conclusion with all the rules they'd set. Now that they were friends they could talk without getting defensive, but before she could speak, she saw him looking in his side-view mirrors as he slowed and pulled over to the curb.

Glancing out her window, she saw a woman running after them. She was kind of ragged looking, maybe a user, based on the sores on her face, but didn't seem threatening.

Pulling his gun, but keeping it low, Paul told her to duck.

She did so immediately. Heard her window roll down. And heard a woman's breathless voice say, "Look, I'm sorry. I tried to catch you back at the diner. I saw the picture on your phone through the window. I hang out there sometimes. For food, you know. Anyway, I don't want to get anyone in any trouble, but I was thinking… maybe you're here because of what happened and Mr. Downy—he was good to me. Always made sure I had a place to sleep, and food. He offered to, you know, help me out more, but I do what I do, you know? I like my freedom and all…"

Haley sat up. "Mr. Downy?"

"Well that picture doesn't look like him, you know?" The woman, still breathless, gave them a mostly tooth-less smile. Bent down with her hands to her knees, breathing hard, and stood up again. She kept her distance, though.

And was well-spoken.

A woman who'd gotten too old to work at one of the brothels and hadn't had any other life to go to? Or one who'd had her life stolen by addiction?

Would Kelsey have ended up the same?

"It's just… I hang out late at night sometimes…down at the corner by the turnoff to Sugarloaf—where the ritzy people live—and he'd always stop, give me money for a motel room for the night…"

Gut sick, heart hurting, Haley wondered two things instantaneously…what the woman was doing hanging out on a corner late at night, and had this Mr. Downy spent time in the motel room with her as payment for his generosity?

Had he picked up Kelsey, too?

"You know this man?" Paul held his phone out to her, the photo they'd been showing around town on-screen again.

The woman nodded, her stringy blond hair falling into her eyes. "Maybe I do," she said. "The hair…it doesn't look like Mr. Downy, but one night, when he stopped, he had hair like that. I thought he'd been at some costume party or something…"

Haley's heart pounding hard enough for her to feel each beat, she reminded herself to breathe. Were they finally getting to the end?

She wanted it so badly, and dreaded it, too.

"You know where I can find him?" Paul's voice was calm beside her, bringing a vestige of normality.

"Well that's just it. Mr. Downy's dead!"

"Dead?" Haley blurted, eyes wide as she looked at Paul.

"A month or so ago. It was all over the news," the woman said. "His horse threw him…"

Pulling out a wad of money, Paul leaned over to hand it out Haley's window. "Thank you for your time," he said, let go as soon as the woman's hand snatched it from him and sped off before Haley's window was finished rolling back up.

He'd seen the white car pull out behind him at the diner. Had watched it pass him by as he'd pulled over to the curb.

And then it had been back, right behind him while the woman had been telling them that Downy was dead.

"Stay down," he told Haley, relieved when she did as he'd ordered without question. He didn't like it, him ordering, her doing, but he'd do what it took to keep her alive. Swerving, he cut across two lanes, made an illegal left turn and then a quick right and another left. The car was still behind him.

"We're being followed," he told her. "Call Endives. He's speed dial two at the moment. Give him this license plate." He rattled off the number. And then did it a second time as soon as Haley had the detective on the phone.

"Now hold on," he said next, and did a U-turn in the middle of a road just as a light turned red. The white car screeched to a halt. It had either been that or get T-boned by traffic coming from the crossroad.

"I lost him, but stay down for another minute or two," he said then, adrenaline pumping as he watched all around him for signs of anyone else on his tail.

Ten minutes later, he pulled back into the busy parking lot of the big box store and took stock.

"I need to get you out of town." He said what was first and foremost on his mind. He hated to leave while the trail was hot, but losing Haley wasn't an option.

"Like hell," she said, but he'd been prepared for the fight.

"We don't have time for this, Hale. You have to go."

"We've had reason to believe that I'm the one they're after," she said. "Which means that me being with you might be drawing them out. And that's the quickest way to find out who they are, right? By drawing them out? You just got a license plate." She was talking fast.

"Besides, I feel safer with you. I know your skills and I know you'll do everything you can to protect me."

"But what if I can't?" His tone wasn't kind. Or even a decent pitch. "I'm good. I'm not perfect," he said.

"We're in danger, Paul. Both of us. I brought it on us, through Kelsey. If something happens to me, at least I'll go out doing what I need to do."

He couldn't argue with that. Wasn't even sure he wanted to.

And didn't have the chance, as Endives phoned back with an ID on the white car. After obtaining permission, Paul put the call on speaker phone.

The white car also had been stolen from a used car lot. At ten that morning.

After they'd been in town, showing the picture around. Paul and the detective both theorized that the driver of the truck from the day before and the driver of the car that afternoon, who had clearly been after them, were one and the same. Which meant their near demise at the face of the mountain hadn't been the result of a random joyride gone bad.

Paul told Endives about the woman on the street, about her Mr. Downy. Hated that he didn't even have a first name for the guy yet. It wasn't how he did business.

But he didn't often have someone trailing him. Most times it was the opposite. And generally, when his life was in jeopardy, the danger was in front of him, usually in the form of a rifle barrel, right where he could see it.

And disarm whoever had been stupid enough to pull it on him.

"What's bothering me now is that you're still being pursued. If Downy's dead, who's paying this guy to go after you?" Endives's voice came over the car's audio system.

"My guess on the fly is Thomas Gladstone," Paul said, used to working in tandem with others, which usually meant law enforcement in some fashion. "We shook him up the other night. And I don't think it's a rape charge he's most worried about. Especially now with the victim gone. It's his father that scares him. He doesn't want us digging up any trouble that's going to come back to dear old dad. Like his association with a hit man, for instance."

"You two need to come back to Vegas, or go home to California." Detective Duane Endives sounded loud and clear, and Paul saw Haley shake her head even before he spoke.

"No way we're leaving without finding out what happened to that baby," he said. "There's no official record of the newborn's existence, and only circumstantial evidence that the infant was even born alive, so you can't do it. You all have car thefts to investigate, and I'm guessing three deaths as well…"

Endives couldn't force him to leave. He was licensed and working a job.

"Then watch your backs," the man said. "I don't want to see either of you coming back in a body bag."

The words weren't issued with any levity at all.

And Paul felt their fierceness as he pulled out of the lot, looking for a place to lay low long enough to get on his computer.

"We're only eight miles away from the California border," Haley said before he'd even told her what he was thinking. "There are casino resorts between here and there. I read about them this morning when I was looking at Pahrump information."

There'd been billboards for them coming up the highway as well.

With a nod he told her to buckle up.

And headed west.

Chapter 18

Living with the knowledge that someone out to get her could be watching her every move wasn't easy. Doing it and maintaining mental faculties so that she could help in the search for the baby seemed impossible during the first minute or two they were back on the road. Poised to take cover, or to brace herself for a wreck designed to kill them, she strove to take back control of her thoughts.

Which meant not focusing on the danger.

With traffic zooming in front, behind and both sides of them, the task seemed insurmountable. But she kept at it. Trying to tamp down the fear by thinking about the facts. Conversations. Computer visuals that she'd seen that morning. The woman on the street.

And something Paul had said just before the woman had run up to them. She'd been hearing his words from the past—about her enabling her sister—had been seeing the truth in them after having spent a few days in Kelsey's life, seeing what her sister had been doing and how hard she'd been fighting for control of her own happiness, her own life.

"You said you'd discovered something about yourself that you weren't happy with," she said aloud. She'd asked what it was, but the woman had run up and...

"What did you discover?" she asked again. The topic held her interest long enough to get her out of fear's immediate clutches.

With his thick blond hair ruffled, the blue eyes focused, Paul gave her a quick glance, before returning his attention to the road in front of them. And the mirrors that gave him views all around them.

She was watching, too.

They had to watch.

She just didn't have to let the fear debilitate her.

"That I was jealous of your little sister. That's why I was always on you about jumping into immediate action every time she called. Not because you were enabling her, but because I wanted you to jump like that for me. Instead, I'd be pushed aside for her. I got to the point where I dreaded your phone ringing anytime we were together."

Shocked, she stared at him. Remembered the mirror hanging from the side of her door. Checked it out. Seriously.

Saw the cars. And...wow.

The great Paul Wright had been jealous? She'd secretly feared, subconsciously even, in the beginning, that she'd never have what it took to hold someone like him long term. That maybe no woman had what it took to keep happy a man who had everything.

And he'd been jealous? Feeling like he wasn't as important to her as Kelsey had been?

Yet…when she'd called, once again tending to Kelsey, needing his help, he'd dropped everything to be there for her.

"You were right," she said, what she'd finally acknowledged to herself sometime over the past day or two. "I was enabling her. Maybe if I'd let her flounder, wallow in her emotional distress, a little more, she'd have found her own backbone sooner. Maybe none of this would have happened…"

"Don't." His tone firm in a way she couldn't remember ever hearing before. "Maybe Kels should have stood on her own two feet more, but she was who she was, Hale. A person whose emotions were intense and whose brain interpreted them first before seeing logic. And you…with your patience and loyalty and unconditional love…you helped her see the logic. And maybe…taught her how to see if for herself. Maybe that's what really happened here. Kelsey had learned, from and through you, how to handle the emotional burst without falling apart. Maybe you'd shown her, through the years, that pausing long enough to be able to think, rather than always just reacting, was the way to be happy…"

Her gaze firmly locked on the mirror outside her window, Haley blinked back the tears his words brought to her eyes.

"Maybe it was some of both," she said softly.

Glad to put another painful part of their past to rest.

"Grab your bag—we need to go." Paul pushed his head into the adjoining door to Haley's room long enough to speak, and then pulled it back out again.

Loaded up his shaving bag, packed his computer and waited.

They hadn't been in their rooms half an hour.

"What's going on?" Haley appeared a few seconds later, her bag in hand. Her hair in its ponytail, the nearly makeup-free face, the shorts and sandals…did nothing to tone down the natural beauty she'd seen as a curse, feeling she'd never measure up to her glamorous sister and mother. She'd never seen how she'd always shone so much brighter to him.

"We'll leave the reservation open," he told her, heading out the door, first, to check the hall, and then holding it for her to exit. "I just found something we need to check out. I'll tell you about it in the SUV." Where he could be more certain he wouldn't be overheard.

Gladstone's minion—if he only had one of them—would have to lay low at least for an hour or two after ditching the white car, but depending on how much money was at stake, how much Gladstone was doling out, there was no telling what the guy would do to get the job done.

That was the thing about money. It sustained life. Provided a lot of good.

And a whole lot of bad, too.

They made it to the SUV without mishap and Paul pulled away as quickly as he could. He'd seen no evidence that anyone was following them, but he wasn't taking any chance of being caught unaware, either.

"I'm hoping that time is on our side," he said as he sped away, their destination already typed into the GPS system on his phone. "The guy knows I saw him. He knows we're onto him. I'm sure the car has already been ditched. And if he's at all the professional we think him to be, he's going to take a minute to reassess and find a different mode of operation or risk getting caught—which means he doesn't get paid."

And there was the little issue of jail time, too, if it could be proven that he'd taken murder-for-hire payment. Or even, assault-for-hire payment.

He was tending toward the murder part, however. "With Kelsey's death, officially ruled accidental, Noah's death, which looked accidental or at least self-inflicted, and now Charles Downy's death being ruled accidental, I think we have something bigger on our hands than we knew." He told her the stark truth. She had the right to get herself out at any time.

"You don't think the deaths are accidental."

"Charles Downy was a horseman his entire life. The chances of him being thrown at the edge of a mountain he's been riding for forty years don't seem all that likely to me."

"His first name was Charles." She was watching her mirror. And ahead, too.

"Yeah. And there was no evidence of any criminal record. He was forty-five, born to money, but not the kind that gets you recognized everywhere you go. His family money came from ranching, two generations ago, and then simply being good businessmen, managing their money, investing. He was philanthropic..."

"Did he have kids?"

"No."

"And a wife?"

He took a deep pause. Reminding himself that Haley wanted him to do what he did to the best of ability. "That's who we're going to see, Haley. They were high school sweethearts—he was a senior her freshman year.

She doesn't know we're coming. I'm hoping we can just drive onto the property and knock on the door. And that she'll agree to speak to us."

"And the plan if she does?" She didn't miss a beat. And, if possible, his affection for her grew.

And maybe, the thought intruded, just maybe, when the job was done, they really could be friends. He'd like to know that she was in his life. Would like to be in contact now and then, without any chance of bringing in the bad stuff that went along with their being in love.

They couldn't have a healthy love, but…perhaps…a healthy friendship?

She turned to look at him. Waiting for an answer. The plan.

"I'm doing it straight up," he told her. "Other than an explanation for your presence. You work for me, by the way," he said. "And I don't intend to mention the baby. No need to hurt her more than necessary until we know what we're dealing with. I need to find out what she knows, and based on the little I could find on social media—a writeup from a charity ball they attended—I suspect that she doesn't know her husband was having an affair. Something isn't adding up here—a man who's kept his nose clean all his life is suddenly having an affair, housing a pregnant woman, hiring someone to keep an eye on her, and then they both end up dead?"

"But it has to be him who hired the lawyer to warn Gladstone off when Kelsey found out he was using her credit cards, right? He wanted to keep Gladstone away from Kels."

"Maybe because Gladstone is a big Vegas name. Could be he didn't want the notoriety."

"And he could have been protecting Kels." Her tone

was soft, reminding him that, no matter what, Haley was going to see the best in her sister. And for her.

He turned because it was time. Hadn't seen anyone on their trail.

"Did you find any evidence that Downy had ever been to Sister's?" she asked then.

"No, but that's what the ranch is known for, what makes it as successful as it is. Men can go there with confidence that their visit will be completely anonymous."

"What does make sense is that the man met Kels, fell in love, and then they both got in over their heads," she offered.

"Except that doesn't explain Noah's urgent messages. Or the fact that a rich kid would risk his life to deliver them."

"We're back to Sister's aren't we? If Charles Downy met my sister there…and they really did fall in love. And he was trying to live a double life…the whole thing could put Sister's in a really bad position…" Her voice faded, as though she was thinking it all through as she spoke.

But he was right with her, and moving forward, too. "It makes sense," he said. "If Kels worked there, she had any number of wealthy clients. And would have had to sign confidentiality agreements. The two of them, thinking they were going to have a life together…could put the reputation of the ranch at stake. If one of the young women got pregnant, and word got out, if someone feared that Kelsey had blackmailed Downy, for instance, all of the other wealthy clients would have to think twice about just how secure the ranch was to them. If one woman did it, so could another and…"

"Which would also explain someone coming after me when we visited. He was probably sent after me when you started showing Kelsey's picture around…"

"And if they find out we're speaking with Downy's wife, we're putting her in danger, too," he said. "But for all we know, she's already on their list. They don't know what he'd have told her. Maybe nothing. Maybe this will be a horrible shock to her, and your sympathy will be greatly appreciated. I'm counting on you to comfort her, to clean up my mess, so to speak, if what I have to say breaks her heart."

Haley's nod was stiff. "She has to be warned," she said.

"And maybe she'll allow us to look through her husband's records so that I can find anything that points us in the direction of the baby."

"Like what?"

"I have no idea. If that baby was sold, or adopted, someone has to know about it. Maybe there's a payment to whoever that someone is in Downy's things. Something his wife wouldn't recognize. She'd think it was a business deal. But if I can get access to his accounts, I can follow up on every payment he made, find out where the money went and why."

He'd also be able to confirm whether or not any of Downy's accounts made payments to Sister's Ranch at about the time Kelsey would have become pregnant. Something Haley would figure out.

He turned. Found the address. And was able to pull up a long drive that circled near a double front door.

Pieces were falling into place.

He might not have it all right, yet. But they were getting there.

Finally.

* * *

"I can't…" Shaking her head, the dark tumble of curls falling over her shoulders and shadowing her face, Sandra Downy fell to the silk-threaded gray-and-maroon couch in the small welcoming room off to the right of the marble foyer inside the front door. Tears filled her eyes as, hands shaking, she reached for a tissue from the gray-and-maroon glass holder on the table beside her. "You're telling me that Charles had an affair?" She got the words out, but her voice cracked.

As had the expression on her beautiful, though fragile appearing, face as Paul had broken the news to her. He'd shown her the photo on his phone first, asked if the man depicted there was her husband. She'd answered immediately. Saying the shirt he was wearing was hanging upstairs in his closet, still. And Paul had told her how he'd come to have the photo. That her husband had been seen going in and out of a house in Vegas that had been paid for by one of his companies.

"We believe he may have been having an affair…" Paul said, taking a seat in the chair perpendicular to the distraught woman as Haley sat down beside her. Not too close as to be cloying, but there if she was needed. Paul had been right about her ability to bring comfort to emotional moments.

For once she was thankful for her lifetime of practice.

And not just so they could get the information they needed to find the baby. Seeing the suffering on a stranger's face, Haley wanted to help the woman in any way she could.

"We don't think it was habitual activity," she said softly, much like trying to reassure a parent that while a child's diagnosis wasn't good, it wasn't necessarily terminal, either. You couldn't take away what was, but maybe you could direct inner vision to whatever brightness was there. "It doesn't appear that Charles was a womanizer. As a matter of fact, it looks like this one time was it." Haley didn't know that he'd stayed in the motel room with the street woman. He could have just given the woman the money for the room. After all, she'd said that he was kind.

Sniffing, her lips trembling, Sandra nodded. Blinked a few times as a fresh pool of tears formed in her eyes. "I just…it's just… I thought losing him was the hardest thing I'd ever have to go through, and now this…"

"We have reason to believe that your husband, and… the woman…didn't die by accident," Paul told her. But as she raised a shocked face, her chin dropping as her mouth hung open, he quickly added, "This is just conjecture at this point. But there's been some other activity, provable offenses, that seem tied to both your husband and the woman and I've been hired to help find the truth."

All true. And not giving any more than he had to. Paul was good.

Damned impressive, actually.

And kind, too.

Which impressed her a whole lot more.

"I was hoping…you'd be able to help me out," Paul said in a coaxing, but respectful tone. "If you could answer some questions…"

Sandra sat up straight. Wiped her eyes. "I'll do what I can. If my husband was murdered, if there's even a chance of that, I'll do whatever it takes to find out who did it."

Haley felt for the woman as though the emotions were her own—partially because they were also her own. She wanted to tell Sandra that she understood, that she knew how it felt to find out not only that your newly deceased loved one had been living a double life about which you knew nothing, but also that murder was likely involved. She wanted to tell her about the baby.

For the moment, she just took Sandra's hand. Gave it a squeeze. And when Sandra's fingers curled around hers, Haley held on, too.

Paul started with simple questions regarding Charles's routines. His habits. His interests. He asked how and when Charles had taken up horseback riding, how many horses he had. None of it seemed to shed any light on the situation they were investigating, but Haley trusted him to know what he was doing.

Sandra seemed to as well, as the woman answered all of his questions quietly. And kindly. She shuddered once. Teared up a time or two. But she didn't break.

Something else Haley could relate to.

The interview was excruciating, and yet, in some way, it seemed almost…healing…too. Helping someone else through the painhad dissipated her own sting a small bit.

"That's all then," Paul said almost a half hour later, standing. And for the first time since they'd entered the house, Haley faltered. That was it?

They hadn't learned anything.

Not that would help them in any way. He hadn't even asked for the thing he'd said they were coming to find.

The financials. The only way they were going to know who Downy had been paying. The only way they had half a hope of finding out how Downy and Kelsey had met.

Or why she'd felt compelled to change her name to Maya.

How could he just walk out of there?

Why would he do that?

Wasn't he as serious about helping Kelsey as she'd thought?

"Oh…just one more thing," Paul said just as Haley and Sandra were rising. "Would you mind if I had a look at your husband's credit card accounts?" he asked. "My specialty is putting seemingly innocuous things together to find missing pieces. Any charges he might have made, in the vicinity of other facts we've already collected, could be all it takes for us to get to the truth."

"Sure." Sandra shrugged. Shook her head and said, "I have no problem with you having access to whatever you need." She named her late husband's most commonly used passwords. "As I said, whatever it takes…"

Haley's momentary lack of faith kind of stung her for a second. She trusted Paul with her life. With her sister's memory and with her sister's baby's life.

But she'd doubted his ability to do what he'd said he was going to do with the interview?

Sandra offered a cup of tea to Haley, while Paul had his time at Charles's desk and on his computer, and, wanting to be of whatever comfort she could to the woman, Haley looked to Paul, saw his nod, and accepted.

Her job might be to keep Sandra occupied, but she

found herself pulled toward the emotionally damaged woman, wanting to be with her in their shared suffering.

Wanting to know more about the man Kelsey had fallen in love with.

And to know if the man could have sold his own child.

Or worse.

Chapter 19

The need to accomplish things quickly was all in a day's work to Paul. Knowing how to get where he needed to be, helped. And still, his fingers fumbled a time or two on the keyboard as he thought about Haley off in the house where he could neither see nor hear her.

What if whoever had been following them knew where they were?

What if he'd just left both Sandra and Haley off on their own where they'd be easy prey?

As far as he knew, there was no one else in the house.

Sandra had opened the door to them herself.

And she'd mentioned putting on the pot for the tea she'd offered Haley.

Clearly, she'd have help keeping up the five-thou-sand-square-foot home that, according to tax records, she and Charles had been in for more than twenty years. But that didn't have to mean live-in staff.

Spurred by an urgency that, though perhaps not valid, wasn't letting go of him, Paul did the job Haley was paying him to do. He got into the files, sent them to his private cloud, got lucky to find a folder of tax documents in which the man filed all of his electronic statements, and, for good measure, sent over the folder of pictures, too.

He glanced through them as they were sending, and lost himself in them for a moment. They were almost exclusively Charles and Sandra. In various forms of dress from elegant to sweats, with all different backdrops. Dating as recently as six weeks before—a head shot with a red background—and as far back as digital pictures went, from what he could tell.

For the job, assuming he had time to go through them all, the photos could be a gold mine. A chronicle of all the places Charles had been where he could have met someone, or someone could have seen him. Like the lawyer, Grainger.

Or Kelsey Carmichael.

Second only to the photos of him and his wife were ones with him and his horses. He had a stable of them. Quarter horses.

And from some of the stunts he glimpsed, the man could have been a circus act, standing on the back of a horse presumably in motion based on the raised right hoof and mixed placement of the other hooves in the photo.

Most definitely not a man one would peg for falling off a horse at a cliff's edge.

Unless the horse was spooked, ran for the cliff, stopped suddenly upon reaching it and sent his rider flying off him.

It could happen.

Paul could picture it.

And in the Nevada mountains, a spooked horse wasn't all that hard to imagine. In May, it could easily have been a rattlesnake.

Question was…did the snake slither there on its own? Or had it been helped?

More to the point, was the horse spooked naturally? Or had Charles Downy's penchant for horseback riding given rise to his killer's plan to end his life? Had someone known Charles would be out riding and purposely caused his horse to unsaddle him at the edge of a cliff?

Just as that same person had caused a one-person fiery crash that left little but tissue evidence of Kelsey's existence?

And made a dry-and-sober addict appear to have fallen back into old ways with a fatal overdose?

Whoever was behind the deaths—and he was fairly certain it was the Gladstones, maybe even father and son together—had the money to pay a professional who knew how to do much more than shoot a gun. They were dealing with a killer who had patience. And creativity.

Someone who, like himself, knew how to dig deep on his subjects, find a weakness. A person who could then make their deaths look completely natural.

Someone who, even at that moment, could be on the grounds, with a plan in place for Haley to have an accident…

Paul was up and out of his chair before he could finish the thought.

Sandra had a lovely garden of trailing bougainvillea and rambling Lantana, the boldness of the colors giving the area a vibrancy that reached inside Haley, as though to tell her that all would be well. Beauty could survive even in a world where bad things happened, and in a dark time. With their cups of tea in hand, the women walked on engraved cement stepping stones to a gate that led to a beautifully landscaped diving pool with built-in kitchen, grill, fireplace and changing house.

Haley had never yearned for riches as her mother and sister had, didn't need to live in a mansion. But she could see how wonderful it would be to have a haven such as the one the Downys had built to escape to when times got tough.

Understanding exactly why Sandra had brought them out to that place, she sat in a fully padded wrought iron high-backed rocker chair on one side of the little floral-painted glass and wrought iron table where Sandra set down the tray of cookies she'd taken along.

The whole time they'd been together, the woman had been talking about the things she and Charles had done as a couple. To the home. In their travels. And the classes they took.

Most recently a series of cooking seminars after which they'd take turns making dinner.

By all appearances their marriage had been a match made in heaven.

So where did Kelsey fit in?

Had her sister known about Sandra?

Had she ever met her?

"And with the baby coming…"

Wait. What now? Haley stared.

"Baby?" she asked, managing, she thought, to sound normal through the ringing in her ears.

"We tried for twenty years to get pregnant," Sandra

was saying, her lips quivering a bit again. "There was no apparent reason why we couldn't conceive—it just didn't happen. And then...ten months ago, it happened."

Ten months? About the same time Kelsey would have conceived?

Shock didn't begin to describe the sensation covering her in a thick bubble of frozen time. What was she hearing? What did it mean?

"I was forty years old," Sandra said, her smile soft and Madonna-like. "And so worried that I wouldn't be able to carry the baby to term."

They'd hired Kelsey to carry their baby.

Oh, God. The baby her sister had been carrying hadn't been her own.

But it all made sense. The house. The guy watching her. A wealthy couple could do that—afford to pay someone to keep an eye on their surrogate.

Thoughts rushed. Haley had to work hard not to cry.

There was no member of her family—no part of Kelsey still needing Haley.

And...

"But the doctor said I was healthy and showed no signs of an inability to go full-term. She said she'd watch me closely, but that we should be fine. I was still worried, though, and so checked myself into a spa for the first three months, doing nothing but eating healthy and taking care of myself, no stress... Charles said he wanted me to go...he called every day..."

Her chin was trembling at that point, and Haley did the math.

With horror.

"That's when he had the affair," she guessed. Jumping into another place.

Back to having a baby in wrong hands.

And hurting this woman who'd seemingly had everything and then lost so much. She wished to God that she and Paul hadn't told the woman about the affair. That she hadn't had to suffer so…

With tears falling down her cheeks again, Sandra nodded.

But then sniffed, sat back, dried her eyes. "But I have my little Jason," she said. "He's the spitting image of his father. If you look at their baby pictures side by side, you'd swear it was the same child."

"Jason?" Haley asked, looking around them. Other than the tall gate that had been closed when they'd approached the pool, nothing that she'd seen of the house, which was admittedly little, had given evidence of a baby around.

Sandra nodded. "He's with his nanny up at the clubhouse this afternoon. Once a week the neighborhood nannies do a baby-and-me playtime and then sit and visit while the little ones nap. It gives us mommies time to ourselves at home…" She stopped abruptly as the tears came again. "I'd planned to take a hot bath," she said.

And instead, she'd answered her door to two strangers who were about to break her heart. And tear her life apart even more than it already had been.

Wishing she could take away Sandra's pain, wishing she could do anything to help, she was spared the chance as the woman's cell rang. Sandra spoke as gently to her caller as she had to Haley and Paul. Trying not to eavesdrop, Haley stood, took a bit of a walk around the pool. And a peek in the cracked-open door of the pool house.

There was definite sign of baby in there. From the

infant-sized thick foam life vest hanging on a rack, to the baby float. And there…not far from the door, on the sidewalk, just to the side of the little changing area, was a pacifier.

Bending, Haley picked it up. Started to tear up, as she noticed how tiny it was. And thought about the vulnerable lips that would hold it close.

The tiny human being who only knew how to suckle and fill a diaper.

Shoving the pacifier into the tip of the pocket of her shorts, to give to Sandra when she made it back around the pool, she worked on gathering her composure. The visit had been far harder on her than she'd expected.

But she wasn't going to let it get in the way of finding the answers they sought. If anything, the hour she'd spent with Sandra Downy had strengthened her resolve.

Kelsey had been at least seven months pregnant. There had to have been a birth.

And she had to face the fact that chances were good that Kelsey's little one wasn't in nearly as nice a place as Charles Downy's home.

She just hoped to God the baby was still alive.

And that they found the infant in time.

Hearing a noise at the gate, she blinked away tears, and turned around to see Paul coming into the pool area.

The strange look on his face was hard to decipher, but she figured he'd found something. That he had news for her that would most likely have to be shared in private. And that it was extremely important.

So she wasn't surprised when, as soon as Sandra ended her call, he thanked her for her time and excused them—giving the woman one of his business cards with instructions to call him, anytime day or night, if she remembered anything, or felt like something wasn't right.

And he advised her to get some security around her house, too.

Just until the police had more answers.

Haley would have liked to have hugged Sandra good-bye, to have made an overture to see her again, but Paul's energy gave her an urgency far more compelling than her own need to give or receive comfort.

Telling herself she'd call the woman—at the very least Sandra should know, at some point, that her son had a half sibling.

If indeed it turned out that he did.

That the baby was still alive.

And then, as she and Paul climbed into the SUV and he started the engine, she could think of nothing but what he had to tell her.

And frowned at his "Nothing yet" report.

Nothing?

But the way he'd come barreling into the pool area, the tight expression, the focus as his gaze sought her out…

"I just moved everything to my cloud," he said. "I didn't know how much time I'd have."

Which made perfect sense. But…

She stared at him…trying to figure out what she was missing.

"If you must know, I got it in my head that you and Sandra were sitting ducks in danger, on the property all alone, and made a mad dash to rescue you."

Oh.

Ohhhhh.

She nodded. Turned her attention back to the road.

Smiled.

And was glad he was her very special friend.

He might not have vetted anything solid yet from their visit to the Downy home, but Haley had. As she told him what she'd found out from Sandra—the baby on the way, a long-awaited one, at the time that Kelsey turned up pregnant with his child—the idea that Downy had been responsible for Kelsey's death grew...but the theory that Gladstone had had them both taken out still made more sense. If Downy had had Kelsey killed, who'd killed Charles Downy? And why.

Endives called before he got very far down that path.

"A little twist here," the detective's voice boomed loudly over the car's audio system. "I thought you'd want to know. According to death records, Charles Downy died a couple of days before Kelsey Carmichael."

Downy went first?

Could that mean...

A quick glance at Haley showed him a frown, an expression filled with question, just as Endives asked, "Is it possible the Carmichael woman took out her lover and then killed herself?"

More possible than Endives knew, considering what Haley had just told him about the legitimate Downy heir.

If you could see Kelsey Carmichael as a killer.

Or Maya Ambrose as one.

No one really knew what had happened to Kelsey over the past year and a half. Or how it could have changed her. Maybe even starting as far back as the rape three years before.

But with Haley sitting there, he said, "No way that I can see. I knew her for years. Kelsey was a character, but not a killer. She was far too sensitive to take a life. And too optimistic to take her own. She'd have called her sister, first."

"Unless she was in some kind of trouble she didn't want her sister to know about."

He shook his head emphatically on that one. And then, realizing the detective couldn't see him, said, "The young woman spent her whole life bringing her screwups and hurt feelings to her sister. Trust me— if Kelsey thought she was in deep trouble she'd have called Haley."

And just like that he had one answer. Something Haley had known all along. And had tried to tell him. Kelsey hadn't called because she'd thought she'd finally found that which she'd spent her life searching for. Her ship had come in.

Had it not, had she feared for her life, been hurt or betrayed, most particularly betrayed, she'd have, at the very least, called Haley with the histrionics of it all.

Which left the question…who'd take Downy out first, and then Kelsey?

And the obvious answer was the same. Gladstone. It would have been harder to get to Kels if Downy were still around, watching over her, hiring people to watch over her. And if she'd been killed, Downy had the resources to move hell to find out what had happened to her. But with Downy out of the way, Kelsey's death would have been much easier to carry off. A simple phone call to get her in her car would have been all it would have taken…and who'd miss her when she was gone?

Or look into her death?

Haley had accepted what she'd been told—that Kelsey had died in a fiery crash—until Noah had left his cryptic messages.

Ending his call with Endives, he headed the SUV back toward the casinos closest to the California border.

"I need time to go through Downy's files," he told

Haley, taking a second and third glance her way as he drove.

She was watching her mirror, though not being obvious about it. He was watching all of his. Could be that the days of living in danger, getting close to truths, but finding no solid answers to the questions she'd hired him to find, was wearing on her.

Could be, but he didn't think so.

"You okay?" he asked after giving her a few minutes just to sit and chill. To be with herself, she used to call it. Haley needed time to think her thoughts.

He'd known that eight years before, he just hadn't really understood.

It was her way of holding on to herself in the midst of storm. A talent Kelsey and Gloria had not had. So one that would understandably be vitally important to the woman who'd pretty much raised them. Funny to think of it that way, a daughter raising her mother as well as her younger sibling, but in many ways that's how it had been...

She hadn't answered.

"What's up?"

He knew not to push. But asked anyway.

If there was something to do with the case on her mind—and how could it be anything else—he had to know about it.

"I just...feel this tension building in me, you know? Like I'm about to do something I'd never in a million years choose to do, but I won't be able to stop myself."

"Kind of like tearing through a house with my hand resting under my shirt on my gun only to find you strolling casually around a pool while our hostess was on the phone?" The question might have come off better with a smile.

He didn't have one to go with it.

"Kind of," she said, glancing in his direction as he glanced in hers. Almost as though they'd both known they needed the connect. The look only lasted a second. They both had other things upon which to focus. But he'd felt it.

Like, in the beginning of knowing her, he'd felt every single look she'd given him.

"Remind you of anything?" he asked, still talking about actions that were more reaction than conscious choice.

"Yeah. Two years of marriage," she told him, the droll note in her voice bringing his smile to life.

"Me, too."

"I like it much better when things aren't so intense." Which they always were when the two of them were together for too long. The current situation, with their lives in danger and on the hunt for a baby, was understandably charged.

But the emotional reactions…ones he didn't normally experience on a job…were a mirror of what had been in their home during normal daily life, and on a regular basis, during the two years they'd lived together.

"Me, too," he admitted. Knowing they'd just kiboshed any hope of them ever being more than friends.

Chapter 20

They checked into yet another hotel, using a Sierra's Web credit card, at Hudson Warner's urging. Paul had called Hud shortly after he'd hung up from Endives, to report in. In addition to offering any file help Paul might need, Hudson had expressed real concern about their safety, agreeing with Paul's plan to remain checked in at the resort they'd spent half an hour in, while going elsewhere, but insisted that, for added safety, he not check in as himself. Hudson had called, rented the room and put Paul and Haley down as occupants.

Paul hadn't needed the reminder to be careful.

He appreciated the firm having his back, however. Choosing to work through Sierra's Web, as opposed to going it on his own, had been the best career choice he'd ever made.

Not far from town, in a busy area, with scattered casino resorts, they had just one room with two queen beds and a sitting/work area. Hud had offered a suite. Paul wanted Haley closer than that. Just until they knew who was after them.

Used to moving around on the fly when he was working, it wasn't the first time he'd checked into two different rooms in one day. But he'd never done it in the same city before.

"What can I do to help?" Haley asked, as he set up at the desk.

Suggesting that she lock herself in the bathroom where he'd know she was safe and yet not a distraction to him wasn't going to fly.

But...he could use her help.

"Two files are top priority," he told her. "The file of bank and credit card statements and the one filled with all of the deleted items I recovered. There were pictures in the recovered items. Why don't you start there? It'll be easier for you to view them on your phone."

And she might recognize a depiction of something Kelsey had mentioned in a phone conversation. A memory banked away that a photo could set free.

The rest would be on him. The conglomeration of all the little seemingly insignificant pieces rattling around in his brain was what gave him his answers.

It didn't take him long to confirm Sandra's account of a pregnancy. Counting back the months, he easily found payments made to an obstetrician in town. Until they abruptly stopped. At about the same time payments to a fancy named health spa in California started.

Had the spa had an obstetrician on staff? Obviously she wouldn't have been seeing the woman in Pahrump, but she'd have had to have been getting prenatal care somewhere.

"Didn't you say that Sandra said doctors would need to watch her pregnancy closely?" he asked.

Haley's gaze a little blank as she looked away from her phone to him, she nodded. She was curled up on the couch, her feet tucked under her, and for a second there, he wanted nothing more than to join her.

"I'm not finding any record of obstetrician bills past two months." He was scrolling. Searching. Covering all known accounts.

Had even found electronic statements for the shell company that had paid for Kelsey's apartment and house.

And the man for hire who'd watched her place.

Had the guy been hired as protection for Kelsey? To spy on her? Both?

Maybe Downy hadn't trusted his beautiful pregnant mistress.

Leaving the various account windows open, he searched the spa, looking for obstetrician services as part of their offerings.

"Damn." He said aloud as he began to read.

"What?" Haley's eyes wide now, her cheeks pinched with tension, she stared at him.

"The spa…it's not a health spa, in terms of eating and exercising and getting plenty of rest. It's a mental health facility." Every nerve in his body tensed for action, he sat forward. Typed more.

"Oh my God," Haley exclaimed at almost the same time. "This picture. Look." She came over to stand beside him, holding out her phone.

He glanced. Saw Kelsey, an obviously pregnant Kelsey in jeans and a white formfitting shirt, proudly displaying her baby bump, while standing in front of an Italian restaurant in Vegas that had been there fifty years and was well-known to the elite.

He got that the moment had to be difficult for Haley—seeing her baby sister pregnant. Certain evidence of what they'd already known.

But he was onto something. Not sure where it was taking him, but going with his instincts, he typed into the search bar.

"I saw this picture earlier today, Paul," Haley was saying, scrolling up and down on her phone. "Sandra showed it to me. Out by the pool…"

The confused, almost frightened tone in her voice got his attention. He turned toward her. "What?" he asked.

"It was the exact same picture, but the head was hers, not Kelsey's. The face, the brown hair instead of blond…but otherwise…the restaurant, the clothes, even the hands on the belly are exactly the same…"

She'd seen the picture for a moment. Once. "Are you sure?"

"Positive because the diamond she had on today was different from the one in the picture. See this one? It's a single stone. The one she was wearing today, on the ring finger of her left hand, was a big stone surrounded by smaller ones. They glistened in the sun. I actually wondered if Charles had bought her a new ring, with more diamonds, to celebrate the birth of their son."

Paul's gut clenched, his adrenaline pumping. He typed. Fast. Scrolled.

Showed her the bill from the ER. Dated after the last obstetrician bill had been paid, and said, "She lost the baby." It was a guess that made Haley gasp. "Look, she's been at the spa several times over the years. Maybe every time they tried, they failed to conceive. Either way, Sandra Downy likely has a history of mental health issues."

Could be chemical dependency, depression, something more, but…

"She didn't lose the baby," Haley said, letting go of him to reach to her pocket. "Look," she said. "I found this today, out by the changing house. I meant to give it back to Sandra, but you came out looking like you'd seen a ghost and…"

Haley fell to the couch and she was the one who turned white to the point of ghostlike. "Oh my God, Paul. She's got Kelsey's baby. It makes sense. It all makes a really sick kind of sense. She finally gets pregnant after twenty years of trying, then loses her baby, then finds out that while she's at the spa recovering her emotional health, her husband impregnated someone else…"

Her rambles were stilted, somewhat shrill, but made sickening sense, too. He stared at the pacifier.

"Jason." Haley said. "She called him Jason. Said he was at the park with the nanny…"

Her voice trailed off as her gaze glued to him, filled with horror. "She's got Kelsey's baby, Paul…"

And he knew.

Every single piece fell into place. All of the evidence he'd been compiling. Even points from the interview that afternoon. Those deleted files…they'd all been deleted since the last back-up two months before…she'd been getting rid of evidence.

Sandra Downy might have always had an evil streak. Or she might have found the pregnant photo of Kelsey on her husband's computer and been pushed beyond her limits. Either way, the woman was a murderer.

And he had no time to prove it.

Because the murderer had Kelsey's baby.

Kelsey had a son! Dizzy with fear, with elation and despair, Haley sat on the couch and stared at the wall. A dark spot on it. Dirt? A shadow? She didn't know. Couldn't figure it out.

A little boy.

Had her baby sister held him? Nursed him?

Would Kelsey have done either and not called her? Sent a million videos and pictures?

Where had she had the child? Why wasn't there record of her giving birth?

Where was he? At Sandra's as she'd said? Being cared for by a nanny?

With Paul on the phone she could only wait, while her body screamed with tension. Standing, scratching arms that both suddenly itched, she paced. Heard him swearing about legalities. About a child's life in danger.

That child's life. It was Jason.

Had her sister named him?

Growing up, and beyond, too, Kelsey had always said if she had a boy she was going to name him Colton. She'd loved the name, taken from a book she'd read when she was about twelve.

Haley's head hurt. She rubbed her temple. The back of her neck. The pain didn't subside.

Maybe she was hungry. Should keep her strength up. Reaching into the minibar for chocolate candy, she unwrapped it and took a bite. Nearly choking.

Threw the rest in the trash.

Tried to listen to Paul's half of the conversations he was having. Heard bits and pieces. Couldn't stay focused.

And couldn't stay in that room much longer, either. It was still light out. Seemed impossible after all that had happened.

Standing at the window, looking out at the mountains towering in the distance, at a couple of casinos, at cars buzzing down all the busy roads she could see, she struggled to understand how all those people out there could just be going on with life as normal.

As though anything would ever be normal again.

Jason.

If he was Kelsey's, and his father was dead, then... who would get the child?

Did Sandra have legal rights to him?

Had she kidnapped him?

Had Kelsey agreed to give him up?

Did Charles Downy have other family?

Were she and Gloria the baby's closest living biological relatives?

If no one could prove that Kelsey had been killed, that Charles Downy had; if no one could ever tie the attempts on her and Pauls' life, or Noah's death, to Sandra...would she just be able to go on with life as though none of it had ever happened?

Raising Jason?

Oh God.

Sick to her stomach, she wished she hadn't taken that bite of candy.

Went to the bathroom.

And almost lost her lunch.

All the conclusion jumping in the world, no matter how accurate the conclusion, wasn't going to get anything done.

Law enforcement couldn't just go into someone's home and remove their child because someone had found minimal obstetrician but large spa bills and had a horrifying theory.

They needed proof.

Proof of miscarriage.

Proof of Sandra Carmichael hiring hit men. Or at least one hit man.

Proof that Jason wasn't her biological child.

In the meantime, that baby was in her custody. If she chose to pack up and leave the country, chances were no one was going to be able to legally stop her.

She hadn't been arrested.

Wasn't even a current suspect officially, as there were no open murder investigations.

There were only circumstances. Theories.

Accidents.

And a couple of car thefts...

And then there was Paul. And Sierra's Web.

The second Haley came out of the bathroom, he told her to grab her bag.

"Downy was an only child," he said, as she gathered her things together. "His parents are both gone. His will's been probated, and everything other than a monthly stipend to Sandra, was left to his son, Jason. In the event something happens to Jason, the bulk of it goes to children's charities, with a smaller amount left to Sandra."

Everything rested on that baby. Revolved around him.

"The good news here is that Sandra only gets the money as long as Jason is alive and well."

At least he thought it was good news. Haley hadn't looked at him.

Her bag was closed, though. She was ready to go. Without asking where they were going.

Her trust in him hit him hard. Like the sky opening up and giving him the answers to life's mysteries.

Shaking his head, he held the door for her. Knowing he had to get the job done and be on his way—away from her—before he lost his mind entirely.

"Dorian, the Sierra's Web medical expert partner, has arranged for an overnight DNA test," he said as they headed down the empty hall toward the elevator. "We're dropping off the pacifier you found at a lab in town, and they'll need to do cheek swabs on you, as well, to see if there is a familial match between you and Sandra's baby, which will then point to Kelsey as the baby's mother." He told her the encouraging news first.

And reached out to catch her with an arm around her back as she stumbled. "They're doing that overnight?"

Dorian had definitely pulled strings. Called in favors. He owed her one.

He owed a lot of people.

And he'd pay his debt. Just as soon as he was back in real life.

His life.

With Haley living safely miles and miles away.

Chapter 21

Eating fruit and junk food in a parked vehicle in the dark was a new thing. When Paul had told Haley that they'd be spending the night—awaiting the DNA proof that would compel questioning of Sandra Downy, at the very least—outside the Downy residence, at first she'd thought he was kidding. Exaggerating the fact that they'd be staying right there in town, close to Jason, until they could get him away from the woman who'd allegedly killed, or hired the killings of, three people.

He hadn't been kidding.

Nor had he tried to leave her at the hotel, or some other safe place while he sat watch.

The police couldn't do anything to Sandra without proof, but Paul could make certain that he knew where she was until they had reason to question her.

The night, the quiet darkness, stretched before them,

but she was strangely content. There were lights on in the house. Paul had taken a tour of the place and was satisfied that Sandra was inside. He hadn't seen a baby, but if the woman was there, the child wouldn't be far away.

Not with all that money attached.

"It's possible that she's a mom who adores her husband's baby as her own," she said aloud, wishing that, for Jason's sake, his story would have a happy ending. "Women who adopt children love them just as much as women who bear them."

Or so she was told. She wouldn't know, either way.

But she wanted to know...

"Have you considered the fact that this might end with you being a mother?" Paul's question washed softly over her. She didn't look his way, wasn't finding it easy to take her gaze off the Downy driveway, even long enough to blink, but she felt his presence all over her.

Knowing her.

"How could I not have considered it?" she asked. They'd talked about kids. Had both wanted them. Sometime in the future.

When their parents' highly volatile divorce wasn't so new. And Haley and Paul were settled in their careers. Didn't matter that with Paul's inheritance neither of them would ever have to work. They'd both needed to contribute their individual skills to the world in which they'd lived.

Now she was trying her absolute hardest not to think of little Jason as any more than a baby in danger. One who almost certainly had her biology in his veins. One she'd hoped to have in her life in some fashion.

"I'm ready to be a mother." The words came boldly

out of her. The darkness, Paul…sitting in a vehicle all night long to protect that small life…made it impossible for her to hide anymore.

Or made the truth feel safer. Right.

"I'm thirty-one years old," she continued when he said nothing, okay to just be talking to herself. "I want a family of my own. I'd always thought I'd do it the traditional way…fall in love, get married, then have kids raised in a two parent home, but…this is okay, too. If it happens. I know it'll be hard sometimes. I know my whole life will be turned upside down. I'm not at all prepared. I have nothing I'll need. The house isn't babyproofed. I don't even have a single diaper, but I don't care…"

Silence met her words. She listened to them again, in her mind. Heard their truth all the way to her core.

"I'm going to be exhausted," she said, with a bubble of elation. And then, sobered. "I will be if I get him," she said. "Middle of the night feedings, and all. But it's not like I'm green when it comes to caring for kids. I know their developmental stages, their biological stages and their emotional stages. I know how to deal with fear, with tantrums, with tears, in the worst of times…"

"You'll make a great mom, Hale. I always knew that about you." The tone of his voice, a lurking sadness, had her turning to him. She could see the glint of his eyes, part of his face in the moonlight. He'd purposely parked them away from streetlights, in the shadow of a small free library, nestled between six-foot-high flowering bushes.

With a perfect view of the Downy long drive across the road and down the way, and the still lit house in the distance beyond.

"Just make sure that if you get a chance to raise him, you let him know that he's valuable because of who he is as a human being, not because of the money attached to him."

She wanted the statement to be strange, coming from him. The way it spoke to her heart, she recognized it. "I never ever wanted you for your money, Paul. I swear to God, I didn't."

His shrug seemed easygoing enough. Slouched down in the seat, an apple in his hand, he didn't appear as though he had a care in the world.

But she knew differently. She'd never met another man who lived his passion to the fullest. Who cared more about…anything.

"Your dad thinks money is what matters most." She said something she'd always thought, but knew would only cause an argument if she voiced it. "And I think that's why he always made you feel like your money was what made you who you were. Because to him, that made you the most valuable thing on earth."

"It wasn't just my dad that held that belief. The way you sister and mother used to talk… putting money first on their list for attributes of a potential husband… When I heard Gloria say that even if she was in love with a man, if he didn't have money, she wouldn't marry him because after the newness wore off, the love would fade to complacency and eventually boredom…"

She shook her head. "I don't think she really believes that," she told him, relieved to move the conversation away from them. Thankful for the lightening in her chest, the ease of the contraction on her breathing. "She never talks about how she grew up, and I suspect it's because she was so badly hurt that she's afraid to trust love. But she's always loved us girls. There's never been any doubt about that."

Gloria had spent her teen years in foster care with a wealthy family. That's all she'd ever shared of her past.

"The way I felt about you… I didn't like how at risk that put me."

His words hurt. Their truth hurt. And the way they resonated within her hurt, too.

Felt. Past tense.

They'd had something great. And had ravaged it, beat at it, tested it, until it broke.

And so instead of having kids of their own, being at home in the house they'd built together, arms entwined in the bed they'd chosen, with their offspring dreaming peacefully down the hall, they were sitting upright in a lookout vehicle, with a console and bag of food between them, guarding a baby they'd never even seen.

"I never spent a dime of the money you deposited for me as part of our divorce settlement."

She'd never wanted his money. It didn't change the present. But if these days together could put the past to rest, they'd both be happier.

"Growing up with my father, the way he'd trade up women every six months…the one thing that mattered most to me in a relationship, even more than love, was faithfulness."

A jolt pierced her heart. Left it oozing sadness. She hadn't known that about him.

Should have.

Maybe if she'd listened better.

"We were so young," she mused aloud. "The way I fell for you, it was all so intense. I had no idea how to deal with it all. It wasn't like my mother was any kind of relationship role model."

Just as his father hadn't been. And then the older misfits had eloped just weeks after meeting at Paul and Haley's wedding and had filed for divorce just six months later. Definitely not an example to their kids of how to have a happy or healthy relationship.

She'd loved Paul with all her heart. Maybe he'd loved her that much, too.

And still…peace was better than the constant tension that had filled their marriage. The unfulfilled expectations and hurt feelings. If she'd known, before they married, that he'd want her to stop tending to her sister, she never would have married him.

Ironic that there they were, eight years later, tending to Kelsey together.

Haley never had been one to appreciate life's ironies.

Chapter 22

Two in the morning and Paul was still wide awake. He'd told Haley to take a nap, tried to tell her she'd need her rest, but, though she'd grown quiet, letting silence settle over them for more than an hour, she hadn't given up on her surveillance of the house in their sights.

And didn't seem fazed by the possibility of having her life turned completely upside down by the unexpected advent of a child, becoming a full-time parent, when it meant that her world would never be even remotely the same again.

He loved that about her. The way she took things on, and stood up to whatever challenges they brought.

Except their marriage.

It was the only thing he'd ever heard of that had beaten her.

He felt responsible for that. Hated that he'd done that to her.

That they'd done it to each other.

Trying to figure out a way to tell her so that didn't lead to more pain, or conversation neither of them would want, while also weighing the advisability of breaking the peaceful silence that had fallen, Paul lost all thought of apologizing for anything when he saw the red glow on Sandra Downy's driveway.

Brake lights.

Someone was backing a car down to the street.

He'd known it. She was going to run. Probably already had a flight booked out of the country, not that he had any legal means of finding that out.

"She's coming." Haley's tension was palpable.

He couldn't let it affect him. "I know." Starting the SUV, he put it in Drive, ready to follow the ballsy woman wherever she thought she was going. No way was he going to let her take Haley's baby, her family, out of the country.

He watched as she headed in the direction opposite of them, was giving her another half mile before he set out, when suddenly he saw brake lights again, and the expensive sedan backed up. The car swerved, corrected, swerved again as it sped backward more quickly than it had been going forward. It was like she was gunning the thing.

"She's going to crash into us," Haley yelled.

"No, she's not." She wouldn't risk slowing herself down with a car that couldn't drive. Or hurting herself, either. He wished he could be certain she wouldn't injure the baby who was very likely strapped in the car with her.

It was because of the baby that he remained where he was. He could outdrive the woman. He'd had no doubt about that even before he'd seen her swerving all over the road.

But he wasn't going to risk a crash that could hurt Jason.

Still, he had no idea what Sandra Downy was up to. He knew what she was capable of, though. And when she was almost abreast of them, he knew her plan. He'd seen her window go down.

"Duck!" He hollered, reaching out to slam Haley's head to her knees.

Saw her hair splayed across her thigh, reached for his pistol and heard a shot blast as pain tore into his shoulder.

Two more shots rang from outside the car, landing with thuds. With her nose smashed into her knees, Haley could hardly breathe, had never been more frightened, had no idea if Paul was okay and didn't know how to help.

"Get me a shirt or something." His voice sounded strange, but she didn't have time to think as the SUV jerked and he pulled out into the street. Falling forward, she hit her shoulder on the dash, but barely cared as she dove over the seat for a bag.

She wasn't sure, but she thought she'd seen a dark spot on Paul's shirt. If he'd been hit...

"Detective Endives..." The voice came over audio and for a second she thought she was hallucinating. Wondered if she was caught in some bizarre nightmare. Wondered if it was possible for her heart to pound so hard it would just stop.

"She's on the move." Paul gave street names. Directions. "I didn't see the infant, but there's a good chance he's in there. I saw the top of the car seat. Back right."

Haley lunged for the zipper of her bag, swore when she couldn't get it unzipped. Scraped her finger along the edge. Started to cry, and jerked harder, shoving her hand inside the bag as she got it open. Her fingers met material, she grabbed, pulled and turned around in her seat, T-shirt in hand, and pressed it to the spot on Paul's shoulder, just beneath the collarbone. Shivering when she felt the wetness there.

She wanted to tell him he'd been hit, but he was talking. Giving more directions. And she realized he was the one who'd asked for the shirt. He knew he'd been hit.

Endives patched someone local into the call.

Paul drove like a bat out of hell. Swerving. Squealing tires. Turning corners. Giving directions.

Blood oozed.

"We've got her," a voice said just as a police car pulled up behind the expensive sedan, another one quickly moving in beside it. They weren't going to force Sandra to crash. Not with the baby inside. But they weren't going to let her get away, either.

"She's armed," Haley screamed.

Paul had already told them so. He'd told them he'd been hit. The police finally had cause to make an arrest.

Five minutes down the road, Sandra's car slowed. Pulled to a stop.

And Endives told Paul to get to the hospital.

Light in his face. Paul hated light in his face. Which was why he slept with the curtains closed. Maybe if he just kept his eyes closed instead...

The light didn't go away, and though he wasn't ready

to come up out of the restful place he'd been, Paul opened one eye.

Saw his computer set up on the desk.

And all vestiges of sleep evaporated.

Where was Haley?

He was ready to move, but aware of the soreness in his shoulder and upper body—bruising from the bullet that had grazed him, not pain from the wound itself. He hadn't even needed stitches.

He'd lost a lot of blood, though. Had been a bit sluggish. Hadn't argued a bit when he'd been told that they'd be heading to the hotel via police car as the department was impounding his SUV as evidence until they could get the bullets out of the leather.

He'd made it upstairs on his own power. With Haley watching his every move, as though he was suddenly going to tumble over at her feet.

As though she'd have been able to hold him up if he'd started to go down.

More likely he'd have taken her down with him.

Haley.

Moving only his head, and only slightly, he saw her. Sitting in the corner of the couch, her knees drawn up to her chest, with tears rolling slowly down her cheeks.

Haley, who never cried when people could see her.

God, he loved her.

The thought brought full consciousness and a sudden welcome to the pain inherent in his movement as he bolted out of bed. "What's up?" he asked, standing there in the shorts he'd changed into before bed the night before.

Hours before, really. The clock read ten. He'd been asleep five hours.

Hoped to God she'd slept, too.

She'd showered. The hair slicked back into a pony-tail was wet. And her black shorts and black-and-white tank were new ones he'd seen her buy.

Wiping her eyes, as though she could pretend her tears hadn't fallen, Haley stood, too. "Nothing's wrong," she said. And then amended, "A lot, if you look at the last few days. I'm just…missing Kelsey, worried about Jason—is he okay? Is he Kelsey's?" She shook her head. "How are you? Does it hurt?"

She came toward him, as though she was planning to check his wound herself. Probably wasn't a good idea to have her touching him.

She was a nurse. It would be odd if he refused to have her check under his bandage. He could kind of re-member agreeing with the doctor to accept her follow-up attention before he'd been released the night before.

"I'm assuming no one has called," he said, steeling himself while the soft, gentle fingers pulled at the tape securing his gauze in place.

"Does it hurt?"

"Not much."

Knowing that his time with Haley was coming to an end that day…that hurt more.

But not as much as staying with her would do.

"You must be going over the edge sitting here wait-ing to hear if Jason is Kelsey's…"

She nodded. "I imagine he's with child services…" She'd asked about a possible baby in the Downy car when a Pahrump detective met them at the hospital the night before. She had been told that there was indeed a baby boy with Sandra, and that he would most likely be put with child services at least until morning.

"This looks good," she said, quickly applied salve and rebandaged his shoulder. "You'll probably only need this another day or so."

And then they were standing there, her chest to his shoulder, looking at each other. Saying so much, and nothing at all.

"It's going to be okay." It wasn't enough. And all he had.

"I know." She gave him a sad smile. And jumped half a foot back when his phone rang.

Dorian. Watching Haley's worried expression, holding her gaze, he picked up. Listened. And hung up.

"It's a match," he said.

"We're biological family?" Her eyes wide, mouth hanging open, she stood there staring.

"Yep." He smiled. Expected her to do so.

Instead, she burst into tears.

He had no choice but to hold her through them.

As it turned out, an officer who'd been on duty the night before had kept the infant with her at the station, rather than calling in social services at four in the morning. By the time Paul had rented a vehicle and they made it down to the station, a judge had already been contacted regarding his temporary placement. He'd been told that there was an aunt, a pediatric nurse, who wanted the baby.

So they sat at the station, in a cozy little room, with cups of coffee, and waited some more.

Paul got on the phone and bought a new car to take them back to California, but she was going to tell him to go on without her. She wanted to stay in Vegas for a day or two. To see if she could get any of Maya's things out of the house that had been vacant since Kelsey's death.

And he had a vacation to get to.

They'd been there less than ten minutes when Detective Olson, the man they'd met at the hospital the night before, joined them. Fortyish, he had a nice smile.

But he wasn't smiling as he joined them, taking a seat at the table. "I just thought you'd want to know what Sandra's been telling us," he said, hands folding on the scarred Formica. "She admits that she lost her baby, had a hard time with it and went away to be helped, and that while she was gone her husband had an affair. She claims that Maya had agreed to give them the baby, but that when she gave birth, she changed her mind. So Sandra thought she'd lost Jason. And then when she'd lost Charles...she says she fell apart completely. Said it was a complete shock to her when authorities showed up at her door with the baby, saying that Maya had been killed in a car accident after dropping the baby at the sitters..."

Haley shook her head. "She doesn't know Maya is Kelsey," she said. "If Kels had really been giving up her baby, she'd have had no reason to use the assumed name. They'd been hiding their affair and the baby from Sandra. Then she found the picture on her husband's computer, hired Blue Colonial to follow her husband to Maya, and then hired someone else to take care of all of them."

Olson shrugged. "More than likely. We still have a lot of questions and will get to the truth. She told us that the baby was delivered at home, in the house on Calypso. Named a midwife. And said the birth certificate names her and Charles as the parents. We've yet to find evidence of any birth certificate for him, something that the judge will work out when he places the child, but we did confirm with the midwife that the baby was born, in the bathtub, some new birthing plan, at the house as stated by Sandra. Midwife says that Kelsey and Charles were both there, and when she left, mother and baby were doing fine. She was shocked to hear, just two days later, when she called to check on them, that Maya had been killed."

Two days later? Jason was less than six weeks old? Haley's lips trembled again, as she held back what seemed to be years' worth of suppressed emotion.

"Who answered the phone?" Paul asked. On task.

"She said a woman."

Paul nodded. "Sandra."

"Most likely. Phone records should show us that."

Olsen had a few more details to share. A conversation with Jason's nanny who confirmed pretty much what Sandra had told Haley the day before, that she'd been caring for him, that she took him to the clubhouse in the afternoon and while he napped visited with other nannies. That he was a good baby. And that Sandra had been good to him.

Haley was thankful for that. Eternally grateful that Sandra had slowed her car the night before when she'd been surrounded, rather than try to run and risk an almost certain accident with Jason in the car.

But she would never be okay with the woman having masterminded her sister's and Charles's deaths. And poor Noah's.

Never. Not ever.

Another knock on the door brought a female officer to the room. Haley never saw her face. All she could see was the blue wrapped bundle in her arms. The puffy little cheeks, and eyes peacefully shut. He had pursed lips. And a wide little nose.

"Oh my God…" Her smile so wide it hurt her face, she blinked back another surge of tears. "I can't believe it…" There should be panic. Maybe it would ascend.

In that moment, all she knew was pure joy.

"The judge ruled that the aunt gets the baby…"

She heard the words. Knew there'd be legalities. Probably more time in Vegas while they got sorted out.

None of it mattered.

She reached for the sleeping infant. Moving him gently from the officer's arms to her own. Moved him with an ease of having held hundreds of babies over the years.

But for the first time, she held one of her own.

And she was never going to be the same.

With the body snuggled up against her, she absorbed his warmth, knew a homecoming she'd never imagined and tore her gaze away to find Paul. To share the moment with him.

He'd left the room.

Without a goodbye.

He'd left the room when the representative from the car dealership stood in the doorway, waving paperwork for him to sign and a key. He'd gone to finish his car transaction.

And when it was done, when he had the keys to his new white SUV, he just kept on leaving. His bag was there; he picked it up, thought to put it in the vehicle rather than leave it in the hall for someone to trip over— and then he'd just gotten in and driven away.

Haley had already declined his invitation for a ride back to California. She'd made it very clear that she wanted some time in Vegas at the Calypso house, and she hadn't asked him to share that time with her.

He made it to the border, across the border. Through one town, and then another. Figured Haley would take the rental back to Vegas, or get another one. Maybe drive it back to California. With Jason being hers, that meant that everything the baby inherited would be at her disposal. Could be a car in the deal, for all he knew.

The house was probably Sandra's. She was going to need every asset she had to pay for lawyers. Haley wouldn't want anything in it, anyway. There was no reason for any part of Sandra Downy's life to touch Jason ever again.

Paul wasn't quite done, though.

He not only wanted Olson's final answers, confirming that Sandra had hired someone else to kill Kelsey, Charles and Noah, to confirm that she'd been behind grabbing Haley on the street and warning her to leave, but also to find out why Maya Ambrose had been created. And whether or not Kelsey had ever worked at Sister's Ranch. Exiting the highway, he re-entered on the other side.

He wanted to know how Haley's first feeding went with Jason. If she was going to change the baby's name to Colton when a birth certificate was made for him. If he'd have the last name Carmichael.

He wanted to tell Haley he loved her. That he'd never felt anything like it for any other woman, and that if he left her again, he'd never feel that way again.

He wanted to tell Haley that he didn't want to die

without having known where they could go in life if they were together.

He wanted to tell her that he was fine to take bullets for her, but he was scared to death to make a mockery of their love a second time.

But by the time he made it back to Pahrump, to the police station, she'd already left.

Haley was just coming out of the courthouse across the street from the police station, holding her new son close to her chest, while an aide carried a donated car seat out to the vehicle she'd rented to take them to Vegas, when she saw Paul standing on the sidewalk. His shoulders hunched, his head down, he just stood in front of the police station, as though lost.

His shoulder. The bullet. Something was wrong.

With Jason held close, she asked the aide to wait and hurried over. "Paul?"

He jerked upright. Wiped a hand over his face. But not before she'd seen the moisture there.

"Paul?"

"I thought I was too late."

"Too late for what?" Heart pounding, she didn't dare hope. She'd had her miracle of a lifetime. Was holding him close to her heart.

"Thing is, I'm going to argue with you," he told her. "And you're going to argue with me, too."

She opened her mouth to argue his point, but closed it again.

"I want to find out why Kels changed her name. And whether or not she was associated with Sister's Ranch."

The words were stilted. Almost rehearsed sounding.

"I know the answers to both," she told him. "I had a

message on my cell from Noah's partner. I called him just before I went into the judge's chambers. He's going to meet me for dinner tonight, at a little place Kelsey loved not far from the Calypso house. It turns out that Noah had a key to the place, which his partner, Liam, now has, and is going to give to me. She changed her name because of Gladstone. She didn't want him to be able to find her. And she never even went to Pahrump. She met Charles at a function she was attending with Noah. Charles was planning to leave Sandra, by the way. He was just waiting until she was a bit healthier to file for divorce. And Kelsey fully supported the decision. They also chose the name Jason together. Which is why it was in his will. There was also a codicil which has now been found, leaving half of everything to Kelsey.

"And…" she continued, "Gladstone was actually behind grabbing me on the street. He'd hired a guy to warn me off so I didn't drag up things that got his dad all riled up again. So, the creep's been arrested, after all. And they were able to trace a phone call to a second hit man, a more expensive professional, and to follow both of their GPS' to the same drop off point for the cash. Sandra tried to make a deal by confessing to hiring the guy, but said she'd only hired him to warn off Charles and Maya and Noah, not kill them. The guy she'd hired, though, had saved a recording of the actual conversation where she was hiring him to kill them so Sandra's likely going away for good, too."

Instead of being glad to have it all done, to have a clean slate, Paul seemed a little crestfallen. And…then he didn't.

Chin raised, shoulders firm, he stood before her, with the aide holding the car seat just off to their left, and said,

"Thing is, Hale, there are shadow sides to everything. The theory of opposites."

She wanted to hope. Didn't dare. "Okay." Could Jason feel her trembling? Would he wake up in time for Paul to see how incredibly blue his eyes were? Paul's eyes were blue. Haley, Kelsey and Gloria all had brown eyes.

"When you have intense good feeling, for example, the shadow side is intense not so good parts."

If he was going where she prayed he was, she hoped he got there soon. There was only so much a woman could take, even one as strong as her, without falling apart a little bit.

"Emotions are messy."

"Yeah."

"Life is messy."

"I won't argue that one with you."

People passed by. Didn't seem to notice that the world was spinning in circles. That the sun and moon were shining brilliantly together in the cloudy sky. They just kept walking.

"Messy isn't to be feared."

She wasn't as sure about that, but she was listening…

"What's to be feared is a stale life. And that's what you have without emotion. A stale life."

Her dreams were coming true. It hit her with a flash of light so bright she couldn't see.

And then she could.

"Are you going to ask me to marry you again, Paul? Because if you are, I wish you'd just do it rather than taking me on this roller-coaster ride of…"

He bent and kissed her. Fully. Deeply. On the lips. In the lips. With a baby in her arms, an aide watching and people who were walking stopping to watch, too.

When he lifted his mouth, she whispered, "The answer is yes."

She'd wanted to keep their business to themselves, but delighted applause broke out. She had to get the car seat and let the aide get back to work.

"Will you take him, please?" she asked, very aware of what she was forcing upon Paul as she gently held out the baby to him. "Jason, meet your new daddy," she said, waiting for Paul to blanch.

To step back.

Instead, he stepped forward. Took the baby as though he'd been holding infants all his life.

"I've got so much to teach you," he said, looking down at the still sleeping bundle. Looked up at Haley and said, "And so much to learn."

"Well learn this," she told him, looping her free arm through his as they smiled at the people around them, and she took the car seat from the aide with her free hand. "And never doubt it again. Family, in all of its guises, and imperfections, with all of its headaches, is the most valuable thing on earth. And for keeps."

Just like she'd kept Kelsey. And Gloria. Like they'd keep Edward, too. Like she'd kept Paul in her heart for eight lonely years. And he'd kept her. There were definitely going to be challenges ahead.

But they'd met the biggest one of all.

And conquered it together.

* * * * *

#2231 AGENT COLTON'S SECRET INVESTIGATION

The Coltons of New York

by Dana Nussio

Desperate to redeem her career by capturing the Black Widow killer, cynical FBI agent Deirdre Colton seeks help from principled rancher Micah Perry who's among the murderer's collateral victims. First she must stop whoever is threatening the widower's life and that of his toddler son.

#2232 CAMERON MOUNTAIN RESCUE

Cameron Glen

by Beth Cornelison

When rescue volunteers Brody Cameron and Anya Patel are trapped by a landslide, they discover not only a mutual attraction, but also evidence of a serial killer's lair. When they become the focus of the killer's wrath, they must join forces to save their lives and find their happily-ever-after.

#2233 ON THE RUN WITH HIS BODYGUARD

Sierra's Web

by Tara Taylor Quinn

Posing as a married couple on an RV vacation, bodyguard McKenna Meredith and wrongfully accused fraudster Joe Hamilton face danger and death from multiple unknown sources. As their perilous road trip continues, they learn to see past their obvious differences—but with their lives on the line, it may not matter.

#2234 COLDERO RIDGE COWBOY

Fuego, New Mexico

by Amber Leigh Williams

Because of a tragic accident, Eveline Eaton's modeling career is at an end and she must return home to the town she escaped from over a decade ago. It's hard to heal, however, when she begins to sense that something or someone is stalking her—and the only person who believes her is Fuego's silent cowboy, Wolfe Coldero.

Get 4 FREE REWARDS!

We'll send you 2 FREE Books plus 2 FREE Mystery Gifts.

FREE Value Over $20

Both the **Harlequin Intrigue®** and **Harlequin® Romantic Suspense** series feature compelling novels filled with heart-racing action-packed romance that will keep you on the edge of your seat.

HARLEQUIN
PLUS

Try the best multimedia subscription service for romance readers like you!

Read, Watch and Play.

Experience the easiest way to get the romance content you crave.

Start your **FREE TRIAL** at
<u>www.harlequinplus.com/freetrial</u>.